Endure

Josef Peeters

Edited by:

Sarah Farrugia
HEARTT Writing & Editing
cosmo12@bigpond.com

Book cover design by: Rocking Book Covers
https://www.rockingbookcovers.com

ISBN-13: 978-0-6450288-3-6

DEDICATION

To the fearless, tireless, selfless heroes of our time;
the health care workers. Their stoic resolve and unfailing
endurance during the globe's darkest hours of the 21st century is a
debt that can never be repaid. We owe them so very, very much.
They have my deepest respect and gratitude and I dedicate this
book to them.

OTHER BOOKS BY THE AUTHOR

Fiction:
Dumped (psych drama)
Daintree Denizens (thriller)
Mt. Moulamein (sci-fi)
Transience (magic realism)
Black Heart (psych. thriller)
Series (horror):
Eat What You Kill (Book 1)
B.A.M. (Book 2)
Eye for an Eye (Book 3)
The Guardians (Book 4) Out soon

Non-Fiction:
Wood Whisperer Volume 1
Wood Whisperer Volume 2
Wood Whisperer Volume 3
Giving Up (Short, autobiographical)

Visit Josef's web page for all purchase links and detailed book descriptions;
http://lakesidecaravanpark.wixsite.com/josef

ACKNOWLEDGMENTS

My editor, Sarah Farrugia deserves a mention for her outstanding efforts to produce something of worth out of the rough drafts I send her. I must also give a shout out to my book cover designer, Adrijus, who deserves a medal for putting up with my outlandish requests and tight deadlines to come up with incredible covers.

Nietzsche wrote: "And if thou gaze long enough into an abyss, the abyss will also gaze back into thee."

FALLING

Circumspection may have been at the root of the quote that flashed into the mind of Adam Harrow as he fell into the yawning chasm beneath him. Sliding, may be a more appropriate description for the young man's exit from the stark reality above. On his backside, swiftly, down the landslide he'd caused. The journey took very little time, yet it felt like an eternity when all he saw was the encompassing darkness around him after the brilliant sunshine and barren landscape above.

The hole through which he'd fallen closed behind him it seemed, for the light disappeared the moment he descended. Adam was not to know that he had stumbled across an old opal-mining shaft which extended some distance at an angle that followed an old seam. Many degrees cooler than the blistering atmosphere above, Adam had no option but to accept his ignominious plummet into the great unknown for the time being.

The angle was too steep to prevent his descent with nothing solid nearby to grasp. He saw nothing. Only the images he created in his panicking mind and the quote he'd learned many years ago. He knew it should not be taken literally. He knew it referred to a metaphorical abyss rather than an actual bottomless pit - like looking deep within one's self to discover that what lurks there may well be something...unpleasant.

The bottom arrived soon enough with Adam landing painfully on his backside, jarring him through to his teeth. He tasted the blood where he'd bitten his tongue. Adam cursed his carelessness silently.

He frowned at the irony of his descent. It had taken him a lifetime to finally climb up and away from his previous abode. He had been topside for just a fraction of time! His 'escape' into the real world was all he had ever dreamed about since the age of consciousness - away from the lessons, the truths, the never-ending tales of woe and despair delivered by an ever-aging guardian.

He looked about him in vain. The invasive darkness was impenetrable. Adam tasted the ancient dust he'd disturbed with whichever microbial nasties that might be lurking therein.

Acknowledging a wave of panic as a result of that thought, from his trouser pocket, he whipped out the device. Flicking the switch with practised ease, he listened for the familiar clicks denoting the possibility of a lethal atmosphere. He did not need to see the dial to know that he was relatively safe. The clicks did not have the frequency or volume to indicate significant toxicity. Adam relaxed considerably and returned the instrument to his pocket.

It would have been too cruel for him to have eluded death for so long only to succumb on his first venture on the outside. All that effort of keeping himself alive for twenty-five years gone to waste after only seven days of reaching freedom? That would have been a harsh twist of fate.

Unable to stand immediately with his heavy backpack, Adam twisted around painfully to steady himself on his hands and knees. Bringing his legs under him, he eventually gained his feet, rubbing his sore backside vigorously. He was pleased he hadn't landed directly on his coccyx or worse. If he had broken a leg or injured himself internally, it would have been a very slow, undignified end.

He struggled off the straps of his backpack and placed the heavy load on the ground in front of him. He searched one of the side pockets until he found the small, manually rechargeable lantern. He wound the handle a few times just to top up the charge. When it flared, Adam groaned with the realisation that his exit would not be possible from the hole through which he had fallen. When he thought about it logically, he understood how lucky he had been. An enormous boulder had lodged into the hole through which he'd passed only seconds ago. Had it not caught above him, he would have been crushed.

He shone the lantern about him. There was little to see but dust and dirt. The dust was slowly settling but the earth was everywhere. He was surrounded by sedimentary layers of geological history which he felt certain Donny would have been able to explain in great, boring detail. Donny had felt the need to impart all of his knowledge upon young Adam as he grew. Day-in, day-out, year after excruciating year.

Adam did not make out the exit from his spot in the dry earth immediately. The area in which he stood was tunnel-like. A long section of about twenty metres extended before him, then seemed to end. With the dust still managing to obscure the deviation in the tunnel's direction, the young man saw only a dirt wall at the end. Where he stood, the tunnel was around a metre wide and perhaps double that in height because Adam was able to stand comfortably. At one hundred and seventy-five centimetres, he was neither tall nor short.

A small twinkle from the wall of the shaft caught his attention. On closer inspection, he saw a pale mineral with minute specks of colour glinting in the light. Potch, if his memory served him correctly. Usually greyish to white, sometimes black, upon which opal is formed. Donny had shown him pictures in an historic document on semi-precious minerals. Adam's retention of information handed down to him by Donny enabled him to feel confident about his observations. If he played out the logical sequence of deductions from that assessment, he correctly assumed that he had blundered into an old opal-mining shaft.

Adam understood that he may have passed many other levels on his descent to the bottom. He wondered how long the miner had worked it and if he survived. He reached for the instrument in his pocket once more to test the area around him. The needle did not waver, nor did the instrument make a clicking sound. Whatever had been detected before had been from above, only minute traces of it would have been brought down with him. It was safe here. He did not require the injection.

The injection was for an extreme event only and he had just the one. A highly experimental solution aimed at mimicking the properties of lead to shield the system through the blood. A Russian scientist had developed it in secret many years after Chernobyl. The pellets he had, were for water purification, patented by the same man and had never been tested in a practical situation. It was purely theoretical. Donny had secured a copy of the Russian's notes, never meant to be shared, from which he produced both items.

Adam would ensure that he was prudent with those rare, live-saving substances. He carried with him the basics for existing in a dangerous world. His backpack contained enough canned and dried food to last him a week or more. Enough bottled and tested water for that same length of time. He had pellets for purifying contaminated groundwater if he came across some...if they worked.

Adam doubted he would come across any water in an abandoned mine. Most likely tainted if he did. Testing, testing,

testing! It had been drummed into him ad nauseam. It only needed one moment of carelessness to spell the end. He did not want the end. He had only just been granted a beginning. He would not waste that minor miracle on foolishness such as forgetting to test something. Adam Johnathon Harrow was made of better stuff than that. Donny would be ashamed if all his hard work was for naught because of something so simple and mundane as forgetfulness.

Peering upward again at the blocked entrance, he hoisted the heavy pack onto his aching back. Adam slowly made his way along the tunnel. He hooked the lightweight lantern to a loop on the strap of his backpack, and with the tunnel lit, he followed its continuation. The tunnel veered right then left again which had given the appearance of a dead-end from where Adam had stood before. The ground was reasonably level. The air was ten times cooler than above, and probably ten times safer.

Although the air was still quite dusty he didn't think he required his breathing apparatus. It seemed to be settling quickly enough as he trundled along the straight section of the tunnel. He threaded his way through the narrowing chicane at the end of that first section to find himself facing another, longer excavation.

He ran the geography through his mind. Coober Pedy, an opal-mining town from days of old. High-quality gems were mined from the many claims crisscrossing a small parcel of land, with many of the miners living permanently underground to escape the debilitating heat above. Adam had seen many of the mullock heaps when he walked around up there. The area was already a sparse and denuded environment before...everything. When Adam walked up there, it was like walking on a barren planet devoid of all living matter.

If only he hadn't...

Adam forced that kind of thinking from his head. Donny warned him that berating yourself for incorrect decisions only led to worse decisions. 'Learn the lesson and move on', he would say. 'Don't get bogged down in the why of it', he repeated often.

Adam accepted that he had done the wrong thing to end up many metres below ground and seemingly trapped. Asking himself why he had foolishly exposed that small section of metal to discover its purpose, would not help him out of his present situation. He'd been trained to deal with most problems he was likely to face.

Twenty-five years of lessons, problem-solving, reading historical documents and ancient books. Tests and exams were his way of life forever. It was all he knew. All of it to prepare him for the day of his release. Only, he'd learned the truth. Donny had lied to him. It hurt more than he could admit. When the truth became known, his planning had begun.

The tunnel continued for many metres without alteration in direction or design. The glinting pockets of potch embedded in the walls appeared sporadically as he moved slowly forward, breaking up the mundanity of the tunnel walls. He passed several thick wooden support structures shoring up sections of the tunnel where the miner had deemed it necessary to prevent cave-ins. The odd niche or two, no deeper than a few metres, told of a slight derivation from the main shaft to explore an opal-seam tail, Adam surmised. He was a little vague on that score, having never been schooled comprehensively in mining techniques.

After a short time, he became weary from the weight of his pack. He needed to rest up and drink. His shoulders were feeling the strain and his backside ached. He hoped he had not sustained a lasting lower back injury or damaged the vertebrae. That would have repercussions lasting many years.

He needed a strong back to carry the essentials for life with him at all times. The nomad requires the home on his back to house all the clean, safe nutrients and liquids to keep him nourished and hydrated throughout his travails.

Once he stopped walking he heard faint, distant sounds. He'd missed any such sounds earlier. His footsteps and the jingling, jangling items hanging from his backpack - torches, emergency flares and glow-sticks, butane lighters and scare-whistles - made quite a racket.

After placing the pack on the ground, Adam moved forward a little with only his lantern in hand. He trod softly with his boots to mitigate drowning out the barely-audible sound emanating from quite a distance within the long tunnel. It was an intermittent, scratchy sound. It reminded him of Donny's old radio set. Once, there was music and information on that radio, then there was only static. What he heard reminded him of that forlorn and desolate sound.

Donny played around with that radio for ages trying to regain a live channel, a station or just anyone with a CB or a Ham Radio set-up to talk to, anything. He witnessed the sadness in Donny on those days. The hopelessness that overcame him at certain times threatened to undo his mentor. Adam even saw tears in his eyes once. Donny was not following his advice at those times; 'Never give in to self-pity and self-absorption', he would often say. 'Stay in the here and now, never the past. Never the past. We can't change what happened. We can only hope to move forward, to prevail and survive - to endure'.

That was Donny's most used term. He repeated that more times than Adam could count. 'Endure at all costs, Adam. Never forget that one axiom from which all else is derived. Never lose hope and don't lose sight of the objective; to live'.

Bloody Donny! The saviour of his life and the bane of his existence at the same time. No hope of surviving if Donny hadn't done all that he did, and no hope of being free if Adam followed the man's rules. A paradox and a perplexing mystery. That was Donny.

The tunnel narrowed considerably now, causing Adam to feel the first signs of claustrophobia. He recognised the symptoms - accelerated heart-beat, shaking and sweating. He wondered if he should turn the light off. Without the ability to see the closeness of the tunnel walls, he might not feel so anxious.

Wrong!

It was far, far worse. Adam almost hyperventilated. He turned the lantern back on and tried to relax, following his regimes. The sound he'd heard was no longer perceptible. Though it had been scratchy and unintelligible, he missed its presence. He couldn't even be sure it was a radio. After all, what would a radio be doing in an old mining tunnel long after the miner was dead or gone? How could it still be operational? Electricity was a thing of the past and no batteries were capable of providing power for years, considering the amount of time Adam estimated the mine had been abandoned.

After one hundred metres, Adam came across a metal hatch-like door in the side wall. It was slightly ajar, mounted within a stainless-steel frame, with another directly opposite. He detected a faint odour in the vicinity, with an edge of musty, mouldy putrefaction about it. The door wouldn't budge when he pressed lightly against it. Adam pushed harder and felt the door opening a fraction more, unused hinges squealing in protest. The sound was magnified many times in the close environment, cutting through the deathly silence.

It was startling and unnerving for him. He didn't know why he was afraid. He was breathing heavily, disregarding everything Donny had taught him. 'Focus, boy! It doesn't matter that you're scared. When you've proven that there is a force aligned against you, then you may be concerned, but never, frightened. Fear can paralyse you, while concern will temper you for the challenge you face'.

He hadn't faced any challenges worthy of fear in his twenty-five years of life other than surviving the rebukes from Donny for failing his exams. *Bloody Donny! He had to stop thinking about Donny.*

Adam smiled as he edged the protesting hatch inwards. The smile soon left his face when the room within was illuminated by his lantern. The odour became more acute inside the room as Adam stepped forward. He assumed he was investigating the miner's bedroom. When he found the miner on the steel cot up against the rear left wall, he finally discovered the source of the foul smell.

The parched skin was drawn tight against the skull in the rictus of death. The semi-preserved body had escaped the ravages of climate or insect infestation. It was almost as if the corpse had been mummified. The bed appeared to be in a shambles of twisted sheets and a stiff blanket overflowing the cot. The body had one rake-thin arm extended over the bed, tilting down from the elbow at an unnatural angle. The miner had suffered a gruesome death in Adam's view.

Peering around the messy bedroom, he saw much evidence of the notion that it was not a swift or easy death. He spied a light fixture in a bracket near a desk. It wasn't functional. After replacing it with his own lantern on the bracket, he searched the loose papers and other materials on the desk. A photo in a frame stood on the rear shelf. Ostensibly the miner with his partner, a very attractive brunette. The photo must have been taken many years before the miner's demise because they appeared to be in their thirties.

"Roland Simpkins. *Professor* Roland Simpkins, if you will." Adam corrected himself when he read aloud from the letterhead he held in his hand. "Subject undergoing...something unrecognisable in your bad handwriting, Professor, worrying...something, signs and showing indications of clinical...de...pression! Depression! Well, well, well. Some pretty fancy qualifications for an opal-miner, mate!

Only, you aren't an opal-miner, are you? Says here you're an anthropologist and human behaviourist, whatever that means. Studying what down here? The behaviour of worms? If you were the only one down here, who were your subjects? Oh, Donny, Donny, Donny, what are we to make of this little conundrum? Answer me that, why don't you?"

A range of differing possibilities and scenarios drifted through his mind. The fact that Roland Simpkins was not a miner puzzled Adam. He wondered if the man had stumbled into the mine in the same manner he had. But that didn't make sense. The dusty report in his hand and others scattered upon the desk denoted other activities afoot at the time the man lived.

The Spartan furnishings and lack of personal effects gave him the impression of a transitory nature to the abode and its inhabitant. One small upright locker contained a uniform of sorts, with an insignia that he couldn't identify. Several lab coats and civilian items completed the wardrobe. Utilitarian footwear resided on the bottom shelf along and a briefcase containing more notes similar to the ones on the desk.

"Veddy interestink," Adam mumbled to himself. "Wat ve haff here, Herr Donny, ist a veddy confusink number of possibilities. None of vitch makes za sense, ya? Vy am I speakink like zis? Hmm? Like Herr Einstein, nicht var? Donny has told me all about the great and magnificent Herr Einstein and I sometimes speak like him, or what I imagine he spoke like, when I am faced with a puzzle.

"So, I am in an opal mine, expecting to find nothing remaining of the miner who should have abandoned the mine at the beginning of it all. Or maybe he took refuge here thinking he could escape the ravages of it. If I was going to find a corpse, always a possibility, I would never have expected it to be a professor of anthropology and human behaviours. Was it after? That would make *some* sense, I suppose. Yes, now that would answer some of my questions if I follow your path of reasoning, Donny," said Adam bemused.

"The good professor was studying human behaviour after it happened. Victims, no doubt. Why down here, though? Certainly safer I would imagine. Safer than in a hospital or other topside environment. Then why is he dead? If it was so much safer down here, he shouldn't be dead, should he, Donny? And, what...oh shit!"

Adam went to his trouser pocket reflexively to retrieve the

instrument. The silence of the reading after he'd turned it on allowed him to exhale in relief, though breathing was not the worst of it.

"Holy flippin' Pando! I forgot to test, Donny. I could have been a bloody goner! I don't even have the injection with me! I left it in the bloody backpack."

Adam retrieved his lantern from the bracket above the desk then sprinted back to where he'd left his pack. Out of breath, he sat next to his pack, shaking his head at the monumental stupidity he displayed that could have cost him his life. His breathing gradually regulated but his mind was in turmoil. So soon after realising freedom and he could have blown it big time...again!

"Okay, Donny, okay. Lesson learned. Test everywhere first! Do not enter a room, a house or anything without testing it first, then test again methodically while inside. You told me over and over and the first thing I do? I forget the golden rule!"

STRANGE

The second chamber, opposite the room he'd visited moments ago, hewn from the surrounding sandstone and limestone geology, proved to be much larger. After testing the chamber before entering and again after he stepped inside, Adam was confident about the level of safety, receiving only a few intermittent clicks.

Several sets of bunk-beds held several corpses in a similar condition to the body in the first room. The same disarray existed in the second chamber. Remnants of desiccated food items remained on side tables and the main table in the centre of the chamber. Stained coffee mugs and curled playing cards on the table suggested a scenario where people had been cooped up in the chamber for a lengthy period.

A theory began to emerge in Adam's mind when he started adding up the clues. He thought he understood why the people had died. It wasn't his initial assumption. It was after the event that they died. He need not worry in that case. He wouldn't be requiring the injection by being exposed to the bodies. He breathed easier, despite the heightened odour of corruption.

He inspected the walls covered in pin-ups of beautiful women in various states of undress. Among them were pictures of wives and loved ones, he assumed. There was only one female among the male corpses. It was easy to identify her cot. It was the only one with the centrefold of a nude male with an engorged phallus, hanging next to it. The lockers near each bunk contained more uniforms with the strange insignia. He'd seen it, or something similar before, but couldn't bring it to the forefront of his mind.

There was little else to keep him searching the room. He felt awkward about investigating their personal belongings. He didn't want to know their names. Whatever happened was sad. At least ten people had died down in the mine - which wasn't a mine, so far. He began to feel anxious, wishing he could be anywhere but where he was. He cursed himself again for touching the bit of metal topside. His damn curiosity! When would he ever learn to just leave things alone?

He closed the metal door after he exited. He had no desire to return to that room again. Could the professor have been studying those unfortunate souls under the conditions of isolation within the abandoned mine? It seemed he had been studying someone and made copious notes about his observations. What was the point of that study? Did the results matter at all given the past state of affairs around the globe? Adam could not think of a more useless exercise. It was immaterial and quite disrespectful as far as Adam was concerned.

Questions arose in his mind. Why didn't they get out when things were looking so bad. They had to have the means of egress from the mine, yet they all died down there. It didn't make sense. Adam had been prepared for bodies and other grisly sights - Donny had made sure of that. He was repeatedly warned about what he should expect once he left. It didn't, however, prepare him for what he found in the abandoned mine. Then, he supposed, it didn't matter where it happened if everywhere was the same. According to his learnings, it should be the same wherever he went.

In the main tunnel once more, he moved forward with his backpack. Sections of the tunnel had been shored up with mortar. Presumably where loose earth may have caused problems for the inhabitants. It was not unusual for miners in Coober Pedy to build extravagant rooms and chambers in their mines. He'd read of a motel that existed entirely underground in one of the old mines.

The next doorway on the left contained a communal bathroom with several toilet stalls and shower cubicles. Adam observed the clever combustible toilets similar to the one Donny installed in their bunker, which incinerated human waste into mere ashes. The remnants of odour coming from the stalls indicated a lack of power or gas to ignite the wastes during the latter stages of the occupation by the group up-tunnel, Professor Roland Simpkins and his subjects.

After testing the room opposite, Adam stumbled upon the jackpot! A kitchen with a fully stocked larder of canned and packaged goods, none of which were contaminated. He couldn't believe his eyes. Packets of pasta, boxes of cereal, cans of baked beans and franks, tinned ham, Spam, and all manner of soups and curries. One product that hadn't stood up to the ravages of time were the containers of UHT milk. The smell had long gone but he saw evidence of the milk having spoilt and exploding its way out of the waxy containers.

Bottled water by the hundreds, stacked in shrink wrap on plastic pallets, lined one rear wall of the walk-in pantry. Adam ran his instrument over everything, top to bottom. Negative readings caused him to smile. If worse came to worst, he would not die of starvation or thirst for a very, very long time. He may be stuck down in an old mine for the foreseeable future but he wasn't going to be hard up for anything.

However, he didn't want to be stuck in a mine for the foreseeable future. He'd only recently emerged from similar accommodation and dreaded the prospect of continuing that way of life, especially alone. Heck, he would even welcome Donny's company in that case. He had to find a way out. He'd taken to talking to himself over the last week and he didn't trust where his mind might go if he kept it up.

One other very important discovery had him salivating. Sealed cans of coffee grounds. Donny had given him coffee once and he'd fallen in love with the smooth, aromatic warmth. They had coffee every morning for a month before it ran out and he'd been missing it ever since. Donny explained that he would once have had fresh coffee served to him in something called a cafe. People would go in to order coffee and breakfast. Something called bacon and eggs, with hash browns and tomato. To hear Donny talk of it in reverent tones made it all the more interesting and tantalising.

He'd seen a packet of powdered eggs in the pantry. He wondered if that was the same thing and if it would taste the same. He saw powdered milk as well, so he knew he had the makings of a fine breakfast in the morning, with a generous helping of coffee. One long banquet table sat in the centre of the room, with salt and pepper shakers and other condiment bottles lining the middle. All were bad, way past their use-by dates. A square box high in one corner of the room puzzled him.

It was tech. Of that, there was no doubt. Old tech. he felt. Not a computer. Donny had taught him about computers and even coding. Once upon a time, laptops were used to communicate with people all over the world according to Donny. Adam wondered how that could be. The big black box with the dusty glass front looked a bit like the screen to Donny's laptop when it was turned off.

There were more light fittings in brackets around the room,

some of them rechargeable. He found none of them to be functional. He'd been taught how to fix simple things like that so Adam was most confident about his abilities to reverse engineer most mech., to find how it worked and get it running again. He could conceivably salvage parts from the other ones he'd seen to get a couple working again.

He caught himself suddenly. He admonished himself severely for thinking like that. Donny would have...well it didn't matter what Donny would have said or done. Adam was on his own and had to stop thinking like he should make the best of the situation. He could not afford to accept his predicament, his entrapment, within the mine - that wasn't a mine.

Although extremely curious about the strange events that brought ten lives to an untimely end, he refused to accept the same fate for himself. He needed to find a way out. Going back to attempt to remove tonnes of rubble and one enormous boulder from the shaft through which he'd fallen, was not an option at the moment. It may well be that he would have to revisit that option at a later date, once he'd exhausted all other avenues.

He could not and must not accept incarceration below ground yet again. Too much of that had gone before. It was the reason Donny had chosen the location for their home, their survival. According to him, the reason for remaining below persisted, although to a lesser extent. The danger remained. 'Life could be extinguished by the silent enemies out there, up there, far too readily and generally, you wouldn't know about it until it was too late.'

"Test and rest," said Adam out loud, repeating 'Donny-isms'.

But Adam could not stay underground any longer. He had to get out before he went mad. Donny had been slowly driving him insane. He..."Enough! Get out of my head, Donny. I'm on my own now, following your instructions to the letter, just like you taught me. What would have been the point of all those lessons if I never got to go topside? Huh? Answer me that, DONNY!" Adam shouted angrily.

He shivered with frustration and guilt. He felt his mind being twisted every which way with thoughts of Donny and his present plight. When he'd made good his escape he thought life would be so very different, easier and calmer. His time of freedom, under brilliant, star-filled night skies had been divine. He'd read about them, seen pictures of them, been taught about them but never seen them. It was a spectacle to behold the first night. He could never have imagined anything more beautiful.

Life aboveground held promises of a future for Adam, one he firmly believed he could not have tolerated belowground, with Donny, for another year or a month, not even a day. It had all been leading up to the day he could depart his home, their home, Donny and he. It was all a lie in the end. Donny had no intention of allowing him to leave. It came as quite a shock when Adam first guessed that Donny was not being honest with him, holding back on certain facts and claims.

He had been raised to trust everything he'd been told by his overbearing guardian. Never once did Adam question Donny's motives or his assertions that he would one day leave the sanctuary below ground to find his own way once topside. Not until the exit day was postponed, year after year, always under the auspices of prevailing conditions topside not being optimal for survival.

Living belowground became a burden Adam could no longer countenance. He was told he'd be able to venture aboveground when he reached the age of eighteen, then nineteen. When he turned twenty-five, he'd had enough. He found a way. He was up there, breathing in the air. He'd been sleeping under the stars and the moon, seen sunshine for the first time. It was exhilarating and frightening at the same time.

Then he came across a set of dunes in such a distinct formation that they seemed unnatural. It was unlike the rest of the landscape, dotted with mullock heaps from old excavations. He walked past most of that to come across a section of fenced ground with many out-of-place dunes. The tall chain-link fence had come down in numerous places over the years, beckoning Adam with easy access.

What seemed most odd to him, was the fact that the dunes only existed within the fenced enclosure, measuring some two or three hectares. Beyond the broken fences, were the natural stunted trees, scrub and rocky, arid soil of central Australia, Coober Pedy, part of what used to be the state of South Australia.

It was the precision-like uniformity of the dunes that aroused his curiosity, leading him to venture within the fence-line to the extreme edge of one long row. A glint of metal caught the morning sun, peering through the mound of sand. The very moment Adam began to brush away some of the sand to uncover the protruding metal, the earth gave way beneath him, sending him sliding down Alice's hole to Wonderland, or Nietzsche's abyss, depending on your literary predilections.

He cursed his curiosity and his impetuousness. Those character flaws may see his demise, trapped below ground for eternity. Adam had to shake off the depressive mood threatening to overtake him. He had to concentrate on the present. Accept and move on. Proceed to the next problem, solve it and reach the next hurdle and so on until he managed to escape. When that moment came, he would have to find some way of ensuring the safety of the edible treasure he'd discovered while allowing him to return from time to time to replenish his stores of food and water.

Such a find must be protected at all costs. It was a veritable life-saving discovery. Adam had only so much food and water with him when he made his way topside. He was unable to carry more than a week or two of the essentials. His frugality of luxuries enabled him to carry more provisions, however, he required at least the basics for outdoor living and safety in the prevailing conditions of the day.

The device in his trouser pocket, was, without doubt, the most important element for his survival in the hostile environment aboveground. The manual charging instrument for the rechargeable batteries the device used being the second vital component. Without those two pieces of low-tech., he could not test the atmosphere of an area, the water or articles he came across during his journey.

The unseen enemy was relentless in its efforts to denude the earth of all life. Survival depended on a strict regime of testing everything before proceeding. Adam had already lapsed carelessly, once, in that regard. It could have cost him his life. Could have caused him months of excruciating agony before he finally succumbed. He had to remember. He had to apply extreme caution to his every endeavour.

He exited the communal dining/kitchen chamber. The tunnel continued in a straight line for many metres. His lantern's reach was limited. He'd searched every nook and cranny within the first three branches leading from the main tunnel without finding any means of escape. Surprisingly, the air within the system did not seem stale or poisonous from age. Some form of circulation must exist for that to occur. A filtration and circulation system that had ceased to function fairly recently, for the air to be breathable, was the best bet.

According to his instrument, the air was safe to breathe, as it had been since his first test with only minor traces detected. He wound his lantern up to full charge once more before leaving the area of the dining chamber. With his backpack sitting as comfortably as possible upon his back, Adam advanced along the narrow tunnel. The scratchy, hissing sound returned as he walked. Intermittent and faint, it was nonetheless real. Adam had seriously considered that he may have imagined it earlier.

WConsidering the state of his mind, he could never be overly confident that he was one hundred per cent in the present. There was always a possibility that he was daydreaming, or remembering, or just plain inventing something to take his thoughts off the constant dangers he faced. For all Adam knew, he could be completely insane and everything he experienced was just an elaborate part of his febrile imagination.

It felt real, so he supposed it was. No way to prove that. Everyone is a slave to their minds to a certain extent. If that mind is seriously flawed, the owner would not be aware of that defect. Adam could only conclude, and desperately hope, that if he was questioning his sanity, he must not be insane. However, if there is no one around to compare yourself to, was it even possible to know the state of his mind?

"Stop it, Adam. That is a looped argument. There is no escape from that or answer. Keep to the present, look forward, not back. Keep your wits about you to take note of everything around you. Concentrate, concentrate, concentrate!"

He was breathing hard as he began to walk faster. There didn't seem to be any end to the long tunnel and he was feeling the telltale signs of claustrophobia once more. He sensed the panic developing in him. A senseless fear driven by the need to be free from the underground prison.

When at last he arrived at another steel door, also slightly ajar, his fear morphed into apprehension. In truth, he had travelled only a few hundred metres and the last chicane had once again given the impression of a dead end. It had only seemed like forever that he had been walking and panicking. He managed to interpret the presence of a steel door in the main tunnel as a sign of an end. One way or the other, he felt he would know if he was able to escape once he stepped through the door...after testing the interior, of course.

Lesson learned. He could not afford to keep making the same mistakes. Sooner or later it would backfire on him and he would pay dearly for his carelessness. The steel door had a revolving latch similar to hatches in submarines or ocean-going vessels. Donny had given him many naval books to study on his own, feeling a comprehensive lesson in aquatic transportation wasn't important enough to warrant the time they had together, better suited to guidance on land-based subjects.

Adam had particularly loved reading about an ancient vessel that struck an iceberg on its maiden voyage. Many fictional versions of that account became immensely popular when they were screened in something called cinemas, according to Donny. Adam hoped he might see one someday on a big screen as described to him. He looked forward to it. Adam had viewed only a few movies replayed on Donny's laptop.

He slowly pushed against the heavy hatch. There was no restriction of movement to the mechanism despite the years of neglect. The layer of dust that showed Adam's handprint was evidence of the time factor involved. No one had touched the hatch in a very, very long time.

He immediately activated his instrument to test the interior before venturing further. He stuck his hand with the device around the frame of the hatch into whatever room lay beyond. Through the small round window in the hatch, he saw the needle of the device give a small flicker but nothing more, and only one or two desultory clicks could be heard. Satisfied that it was safe to enter, he opened the hatch fully and stepped inside.

It was enormous! He couldn't truly make out the ceiling, it was that high. It was the largest area he had ever encountered, other than topside where it was completely open. In the distance, he made out specks of coloured light, blinking in the darkness beyond the reach of his insignificant light.

Immediately to his right stood a field of upright mech. Many rows of identical structures with an array of tiny lights and dials on each. There were probably around a dozen rows with maybe that and more of the structures in each row. As he walked forward in silence, in awe, he noted a name emblazoned on each of the structures. A name he'd learned about from Donny. Something to do with electric transport back in the day; Tesla. He thought he might know what the structures were when that information came to light. He also made a vital connection to the dunes above when he thought about that.

Adam had an excellent memory. Not infallible, by any means, but very good. Good enough to remember pictures of solar farms in the books Donny gave him. Good enough to read about banks of batteries being charged by solar energy to provide clean, limitless power. Good enough to remember that South Australia had been offered assistance at some point by the billionaire CEO of Tesla to provide the state with power.

The dunes he'd stumbled across was a field of solar collectors, buried with sand over time. Not the grid that once supplied a large portion of the electricity required by the state, but enough to power the tech below. He had inadvertently disturbed the sand covering that array. What he surmised about that was that the batteries were now being charged by the uncovered array topside, though how much of the sand had been disturbed remained a mystery. Certainly not the entire field, he thought.

Adam felt very proud of himself for figuring out a piece of the puzzle. His training and education had served him well for the first time in his life. He hoped like crazy that he would find nothing to refute his deductions. With the device in hand, testing every step, Adam walked on again.

The rear wall, when he finally reached it, was covered in a dizzying collection of high-tech, low-tech and just oodles and oodles of mech. Hundreds of low-wattage, stand-by bulbs flickered in a kaleidoscope of colours. Banks of tech were slowly coming to life as the batteries gained enough charge to power them. Adam had no idea what they could be for. To the left of the tech wall, was a pane of opaque material next to a set of large stainless steel doors. Glowing softly next to the doors was a panel with a hand imprint. Next to that was a strange contraption at about head height. The stainless steel platform of the contraption looked a little like a chinstrap from a helmet. Parallel to the platform on the wall was a small lens flickering with a green light.

Adam walked up to the odd object. He intuitively placed his chin on the platform. A thin green line emitted by the small lens fell on Adam's eye when...

"Unauthorised access, unauthorised access..." came the loud recording.

A klaxon blared somewhere nearby, a revolving light fixture shone blue and red emergency colours throughout the chamber. Adam clutched his chest, feeling as though his heart may jump right out of it. He had never before experienced such loud and alarming noise or confusing lights. He raced back the way he'd come, slamming the hatch closed behind him when he finally made it out. Breathless, scared senseless, he slunk to the ground.

The blessed silence returned. The seal on the hatch managed to mute the sounds from within. Only the lights could be seen swirling around through the small porthole in the door, strobing the tunnel before him when he turned his lantern off.

STRANGER

When his over-taxed heart had returned to a semblance of normal, Adam rose from his position on the ground. The tunnel had been dark for some time. He assumed the lighting had ended either because it had a finite time limit, or the power had drained. The length of time the solar receptors above had been exposed and collecting the sun's energy since his foolish meddling did not seem long enough to keep major emergency beacons and sirens going for very long.

The absence of the strobing light gave credence to that assumption. He turned his lantern back on. Steadying his nerves for a return to the weird chamber, Adam slowly cranked open the hatch. Utter silence greeted him; for which he was immensely grateful. If he'd had a choice, despite his desperate curiosity to find out more, he would have avoided returning. Knowing his exit was blocked behind him and wanting nothing more than to be aboveground once more, free, he moved forward, past the ranks of battery soldiers standing sentinel and resolute like the unearthed clay Chinese soldiers he'd read about.

A glance at some of the dials each of the soldiers wore on their chests indicated only a flickering single bar of power in a row of ten different coloured L.E.D. bars. It seemed his assumption was correct. Not enough power to keep the hellacious sound and strobing going. He hoped he would not trigger any further episodes in his explorations. He didn't think his heart could stand it. He was still trembling.

The scratching started again from somewhere near the central bank of tech. A speaker, he thought, similar to the one through which Donny had spoken to him. The sibilant static crackled as it sucked more power from the charging batteries. All the blinking green and red lights seemed to be getting a shade brighter the longer he stood watching them.

"...hell...ans...plea..."

Adam felt fear manipulating his breath as he took in short gasps, hyperventilating. It took some moments before he was able to control it.

The words, or part-words, shocked Adam to the core. More and more it seemed to him as though he had stumbled down Alice's hole into a freaky tech world rather than a tea party with fun characters, loopy as they were. He didn't know what to make of it.

"Hello? Who's there?" He shouted, more to make noise than in expectation of an answer. "Anybody?"

Silence.

He frantically changed the multi-functional lantern to the torch option, shining the beam in all directions, feeling the panic rising inside him once more. He wondered if he may be able to get more lights working. He thought that the lights may even come on automatically if the batteries managed to gain and hold their charge. As long as the alarms didn't start again. He forced his breathing to return to normal. He invoked his mantras as Donny had taught him.

"Concentrating on the present was all that mattered. What had been or what may happen will look after themselves. Focus only on that which you may control'.

Who was he kidding? He didn't even have control over himself. Donny was a liar. Had he always lied? Was everything he had imparted just a massive hoax, a lie?

Adam chided himself. That was unnecessarily cruel, and he was being ungrateful. He probably wouldn't be alive but for Donny. The man may have had his faults but he raised Adam through some mighty tough years growing up. Had Adam faced a recalcitrant teenager such as himself in similar circumstances, he doubted he would have had the patience or kindness to guide the kid through those times.

Donny had been his whole world since he could remember. If he was being truthful with himself, he would admit to missing him sorely. He could surely use his guidance in the present situation. No. It wouldn't have happened if Donny had been with him. Donny would have had the good sense to stop Adam from reaching out to reveal the purpose of the metal corner protruding from the dune. Donny may have liked to explore that corner of metal just as he did but would have taken precautions to ensure his safety.

If Adam had thought like Donny, he would have found a long branch with which to poke at the metal from a safe distance. Standing only a metre back would have saved Adam from falling on his arse down that landslide into the abyss. Adam recalled seeing the long line of panels being revealed by the shifting sands as he was descending. It didn't make any sense to him at the time. He had no idea what to make of it given the glance he was afforded before being swallowed, like Jonah, into the gaping maw.

It only made sense when it was too late. When the world below began making screeching sounds and produced scary lights and even began talking to him. Donny showed him pictures of solar farms in journals and books whenever he found them. Donny always returned from his long journeys with all kinds of new books for Adam to read. He hated Donny for leaving him alone for long periods but loved the new material he brought home.

Donny said it was getting harder and harder to find anything new. He had to travel farther and farther with dwindling resources, like fuel for the old automobile. Adam didn't take that car when he escaped. He had no idea how to drive one, or even turn one on. He heard Donny say something about an ignition once but never fully understood what that meant and didn't pursue the enquiry.

It was scary and exhilarating when he finally made it topside. He wasn't sure what to expect despite having had facts and images drilled into him by the relentless lessons orchestrated by the ever-forceful Donald John Harrow. Adam began calling his father by his given name when he turned sixteen, after another terrible quarrel between the two of them. He forgot what caused it. It didn't matter. There were millions of arguments and fights once he became old enough to begin testing his will, coming into an age where everything just seemed...overwhelming and...wrong!

The changes in his body came on suddenly. One minute he had a hairless body, then it grew everywhere almost overnight. Hair on his chest, on his arms, around his cock and balls! And that was just another whole kettle of fish, that area. Erections all the time, especially in the morning. Dreams! Holy bloody Pando, the dreams. He woke sometimes sweating and panting like a dog, finding his underpants moist and sticky.

Once he found out what caused that moisture and how to produce it intentionally, there was no stopping him. Night and day he flogged that thing until he thought it would drop right off. Donny caught him at it once. He nearly died of embarrassment. As ever, Donny explained what was happening to him in a calm, gentle manner, bearing no signs of disgust or shame. Adam heard how they were natural feelings for any boy growing into adulthood. Donny did tell him that there were times when it was deemed inappropriate, like during his presence. Donny didn't want to witness anything of that nature. 'Best kept private, my boy', Adam heard him say in a surprisingly gentle tone.

So much to learn that Adam didn't think it would ever end. About himself, about his father, the world, his mother, females in general. Donny always said that he shouldn't be expected to explain the female mind. That it was a riddle best left to other females.

His mother? He wished he had known her. He felt such guilt at times that he thought it might squeeze his heart to death. Donny eventually told him that his mother died soon after giving birth to him. While he didn't come right out and blame Adam for his wife's passing, it was evident each time he spoke of it. If Adam felt up to cycling the generator, he watched short films of her with Donny, at a beachside somewhere in Queensland. The disc had been viewed that many times by them both that it started pixelating until they no longer recognised the images.

There were some things he missed terribly about home. He knew nowhere else. Donny had moved them when his wife fell pregnant at the worst possible time. He had been preparing, purchasing a property and a backhoe. He began the excavations on weekend trips, when he was allowed, when the internal borders were open. It took a year to get the bunker built ten metres underground with solid reinforced concrete walls half a metre thick. It cost a fortune his father said.

The signs were there for anyone to see. Donny was, however, one of the only ones to take it seriously. He begged his neighbours and friends to join him, to build an entire underground community. No one listened, and in the end, they ignored him altogether as being a crackpot, like some American doomsday-prepper they'd seen on something called television.

They had to move quickly when Judy fell pregnant. That was the terminology Donny used. That Judy *fell* pregnant. Curious choice of words he thought. How did someone fall into pregnancy? Did his father fall one day and accidentally insert his penis into her vagina? Surely there had to be a little more effort that went into the making of a child than someone tripping into a vagina?

That was before Donny gave him the 'talk'. After he'd been caught doing something pleasurable and probably disgusting to himself. Who'd have thought the creamy stuff he produced by the bucket-load could produce a child? Whack, whack, whack and bam! Just like that, an Adam or a Billy or a Martha comes along. Just so long as you aim it right and the stuff ends up where it's supposed to go instead of into a pair of cotton undies or a hand.

Females. They were a wonderful mystery to him, and every other male on the planet according to Donny. He'd seen pictures of them, of course. Even seen pictures of nude women in a very old magazine that survived the ravages of time and weather in a dilapidated homestead visited by the old man. Donny snickered when he handed Adam the mag telling him to go easy on himself. Adam didn't understand what he meant until the magazine fell open at the centre which unfolded into a magnificent large image of a nude woman showing *everything*.

Adam spent many an evening in the company of Miss November and her cohorts in the other pages. The other information about females came from Donny, the font of all things. The man seemed to know just about everything and made sure that Adam knew it as well. As to the luscious scents of a woman, the luxuriant locks cascading down their silky-smooth backs, the feel of their velvety softness, the heat and moisture of their sex, Adam had only verbal explanations with which to go by.

He came along too late. Too late for girls, too late for parties and drinking, too late for cars, too late for...living. Adam thought he couldn't possibly miss what he'd never known but that wasn't entirely true. He longed to experience the scenes he'd read about and seen in books and magazines. He yearned to be part of the life his father described to him daily.

The ocean? What the heck could that be like? A never-ending body of salted water for as far as the eye could see, from one horizon to the other. Fish? Never seen one. Animals? Nope. A storm? Never. The moon, the stars, the sun? Only on the glorious day when he finally managed to get out. Holy, holy, holy, that was a day. Open space, dirt, and air, wind, starlight and moonlight. The sun! What a magnificent phenomenon. Hot, though. It became incredibly hot, just as Donny said it would in an Australian outback town only seven hundred kilometres from the red centre. He loved it anyway, despite the rough, barren landscape. He couldn't believe the first time he came across a tree. It was a stunted, twisted and gnarled wattle tree, but it was his first tree and Adam thought it was so tall and wonderful that he might burst with excitement.

"Stop! Holy Pando, Adam! You have to stop drifting off with the fairies. Here and now, here and now. Concentrate young man, concentrate. Donny would not be impressed, mate. Use your noggin and think this through. Get some answers and get the heck out. Listen to me! Bloody bonkers! Talking to my..."

"...llo...one..."

"Shit! Not again. Hello? Who's there?"

Nothing but static answered him. A hissing, crackling sound that increased in volume the closer he came to the wall of equipment taking up a large portion of the rear wall. Several lights flickered to life overhead suddenly illuminating much of the dusty gear adorning the multi-tiered shelves before him as he approached the wall of tech.

Monitors, many monitors. Displays and arrays of a medical nature, showing flat-lining heart monitors and the like. A whole heap of medical stuff he couldn't recognise. Printers long past working order, clogged with rotting paper and dust. At some point, moisture had made its way into the tunnel system. On the ground were boxes of copy paper that had formed into solid blocks after being soaked.

t did rain in Coober Pedy sometimes, he admitted. Even the Simpson Desert came alive every so often when inundated with a deluge. Lake Eyre filled occasionally. So, it wasn't so impossible to imagine that water had managed to find its way down into the mine. Not high enough to affect the tech. which was all stacked up on benches and shelves. He could see the watermarks left on the chairs and the legs of the benches. Only a half a metre or less, thought Adam.

"Hello there?" came the high-pitched voice as clear as day, startling Adam once more.

"H-hello?"

"Won't you please answer?"

"I-I just bloody did," said Adam.

"No? Oh well. Sa...t.me...orrow."

"Wait," cried Adam in alarm.

But he didn't know where the voice came from. He needed more light and he needed to examine all the mech. and tech. carefully. It couldn't have been a recording, it seemed live, if not sporadic. He would have to find out where the stranger was and how he might contact this unknown hope. The other priority that required action was to issue a warning to the stranger. Warning them of the inherent danger they faced.

STRANGER STILL

Lights blazed in the canteen as Adam enjoyed his repast. While powdered eggs and baked beans did not constitute a full and nutritious dinner, his curiosity for the taste of eggs overcame practicalities, for once. He had vacated the large chamber several hours ago, determining the need for the batteries to be further charged before he tried to investigate any further.

It was such a shame that he hadn't found the treasure trove of edible food aboveground where he could return to it any time he wished. He could have used it as a base for his explorations. His ultimate goal was to make it to one of the coastlines. He needed to see the ocean. He could not conceive of it in his mind despite numerous pictures and explanations. He secretly suspected Donny of manufacturing the photos somehow, though why he would do so escaped him.

He was hungry and tired after a stress-filled day. He'd wrapped and removed the professor's corpse from the single bedroom chamber to the dormitory containing the nine other bodies. After cleaning the professor's room of dust and dirt, he thought it ready enough to suit his purposes temporarily. His explorations of the weird tech. chamber revealed no exits other than the large stainless steel door. He'd already set off the alarm for that with nothing more than his eye. He didn't think he would be breaching that structure anytime soon. Not without some major investigations of any paperwork on the mech. within.

He was told he had a gift for all things mechanical. Ever since he was little Donny had been supplying him with old mech. to disassemble. When he understood the principles behind the devices, he reassembled them in mostly working order. He'd left most of his tools behind, though, and hadn't found any others. The lights had returned slowly while the batteries regained some charge, as he thought they might. With any luck, some of the other gear in the main chamber would be operable if he worked how to turn any of it on.

It would be dark topside soon. He wondered how long it would take for the batteries to fully drain once the sun was gone. He supposed it depended on if they were fully charged beforehand. It would probably take a few weeks or more to charge the rows upon rows of batteries he'd seen. Sunlight wouldn't be a problem. Nothing but blazing sun in the outback. Almost a desert.

The mine - that wasn't a mine was quite a puzzle. Why would all that power be needed and by whom? Certainly not ten individuals and the amount of tech and mech. he'd observed so far. Something else behind the mysterious door could require a lot of energy perhaps? It was the only thing that made sense to him.

The professor was studying something, something to do with human behaviour according to his credentials and all the papers Adam had read so far. It was dry reading. Boring, actually. He came across a bunch of names on one report, about a hundred. He assumed that they were the subjects of the study. The nine people in the other quarters were possibly supporting crew, seeing as they had uniforms as well. The good professor could not have been expected to monitor all that tech in the main chamber as well as cook and clean, could he? No. He'd be all too hoity-toity to descend to that level. Donny said that most teachers he'd come across were a bunch of intellectual snobs.

That left the question of the subjects. Where the heck were they? How could a bunch of techno-weenies and Uni-nerds end up underground all those years ago? What was the purpose of the study and what happened to everyone? The place was clean of contamination, so that ruled out one possible cause for which Adam was immensely grateful. One aspect of the effects topside had not filtered down below yet. Mind you, there wasn't all that much in the area directly above either. That was the reason old Donny had chosen the place, wasn't it?

Nothing of interest in Coober Pedy bar old, worthless opal mines. No reason for anyone to repeat the actions there that destroyed the coastal areas. Of course, he only had the old man's word for that. Donny had never gone far enough to bring back concrete evidence of what he claimed. Maybe if Donny had seen it first-hand Adam may have been convinced. In the end, he was able to tell when his father was lying; too often.

Could the study have been set up underground for the same reasons that his family ended up there? Did they know? If so, they knew before everyone else. They survived...for a time.

The voice he'd heard through the static haunted him. It had an alluring quality he wasn't able to identify. It didn't seem to be a recording, he was relatively confident about that. Unless the person making the recording was unsure of themselves or very nervous. No, the person would not have said, 'same time tomorrow', if that was the case and if Adam had understood it correctly.

Someone of unknown origins, from some unknown location, was attempting to talk to someone, possibly the professor in the main chamber. The transmission was not yet clear and consistent for any number of reasons. The batteries were not yet charged? An antenna was down? Mechanical failure or technical glitch? Atmospheric interference? So many possibilities that Adam couldn't begin to make a conclusive deduction.

He would spend the entire next day in the chamber, combing through everything, to locate an exit or an understanding of the circumstances behind the professor and his gang being underground in an abandoned opal mine in Coober Pedy.

'Lazy boy! You need to think faster than that if you want to stay alive. Sleep will not get you answers'.

Donny was in his head again. Donny had always been there. He was inescapable. Everywhere he went, everything he did and Donny would be there to rebuke him, encourage him, teach him and mostly annoy the fuck out of him. If he never heard or thought about another Donny-ism again, it would be a blessed relief. Try as he might, he was stuck with the nuisance for however long his life persisted.

'Endure, Adam. Above all else, no matter what you may experience or encounter in your travails; endure at all costs. The survival of possibly an entire species, human beings, Australians, at any rate, rests with you'.

It sounded melodramatic when that statement was delivered by his father, yet it still managed to engender those sentiments in Adam when he was reminded of the conversation. It was a grandiose proclamation and a considerable burden if he took it seriously. Honestly, saving his race? Adam did not detect any falsehood in the man as he spoke those words but found it impossible to accept them regardless.

He had no wish to shoulder such onerous responsibilities, despite it being the sole reason for his survival. Donny predicted much of the future before Adam was born. So confident was he in his appraisal of the prevailing global conditions at the time, that he sold everything he owned to establish an underground bunker in the middle of nowhere, a place so desolate it would never be considered a target, to escape the terrible consequences faced by the capital cities and other townships of Australia.

Adam began to yawn despite the early hour. Even when he was in his room he retired early, exhausted by the unending lessons and mental challenges provided daily. His head was filled with enough useless information to sink a ship. Information that Adam firmly believed he would never require. Mathematics being the worst of it. Sums and equations, formulae, calculus, algebra and on it went. Science, history, history, history.

Donny hammered history into Adam until he felt his eardrums would explode and eyeballs would drop out from sheer boredom. Geography came a close second to being his most detested subject. He was asked to memorise the world map and in particular, the map of Australia until he knew every contour and deviation of the long coastline. The names of the towns and cities meant nothing to him. He saw the sparkle in Donny's eyes as he lectured about life in the cities but failed to capture the same interest in Adam.

He was tired of it. It was all so bloody depressing learning about humankind's innumerable conflicts and hardships brought about by greed or religion. For many reasons, humanity was not worth saving in Adam's opinion. If it all ended with him, it might not be too bad a thing. Mother Earth would be profoundly happy with such an outcome. It had suffered under the tyranny of humanity with its unethical and immoral outlooks, denuding the planet of precious fossil fuels and minerals, raping forests and spoiling oceans with mountains of plastic, for as long as mankind lived.

In the relatively short time of mankind's domination, the planet suffered horribly, unjustly and unconscionably. The population needed to be held accountable and perhaps it was. Many trials and tribulations had befallen mankind over the centuries. Other creatures had enjoyed millions of years as rulers of the planet, never once seeking to destroy the very foundations of their existence. In the blink of an eye, humanity had tested the thresholds, challenged the limits and forsaken all in their path of destruction. Pollution killed the oceans and their inhabitants. Mining and drilling had depleted the planet's fossil fuels, despoiled the environment, and threatened the climate significantly enough to bring about worldwide disasters and famine on a massive scale.

And as bad as all that was, it did not compare with what was to come, at least for Australians. Stuck down on the arse-end of the globe, Australia was to suffer like no other country on Earth. What was discovered by an Australian would eventually lead to its downfall and possibly be the catalyst for humanity's extinction.

Adam yawned again as he concluded that he was probably grossly exaggerating everything as usual. In his musings he allowed opinion to rule over fact, something Donny warned him about ad nauseam. Facts and proof would see the truth emerge, not speculation and innuendo. Suppositions based on cold, hard facts were the only defence in an arsenal of mistruths and fallacies. Some of the latter coming from none other than Donny in the end, leading Adam astray, denying him the truth or access to it.

He sighed as he thought about the sadness he felt. He missed his home terribly even though there was nothing left there for him. Adam had burnt those bridges, destroyed them in a spectacular symbolic explosion. There was no returning to those roots. He'd eliminated any possibility of that and in so doing, left home for good.

The eggs and baked beans remaining on his plate had turned cold and unappetising. He rose to discard the leftovers into a waste disposal unit. He would wait till morning before turning on the device, once the batteries had charged some more. He washed up his dirty cutlery and dish using heated bottled water. Although a faucet existed over the sink, he didn't trust any water coming from it until he'd had the chance to test it first. Something he couldn't be bothered with at present.

Once more he berated himself for being lazy. He'd been told over and over again that the slightest slip could spell the end for him. It would take only a minute of exposure to the toxic elements to render him incapacitated and fighting for his life with little hope of survival. As a matter of fact, a major exposure would be preferential to a minor mishap. Death would come more swiftly.

When Adam finally retrieved his device from his trouser pocket to test the dribble of dirty water coming through the faucet, he was surprised to hear the tell-tale clicks, advising him of unsafe contamination. Not demonstrably high readings but sufficient to cause alarm and caution. He had filters and tablets with him for reducing its capacity to cause harm. Eyeing the pallets of bottled water at his disposal in the canteen area, he didn't think he'd need to resort to the running water any time soon.

He hoped to be well clear of the mine before he reached that stage. He couldn't bear the thought of remaining trapped in the mine for even a short period. He'd determined that only the area, whatever it was, behind the secured door in the main chamber would hold the possibility of providing an exit. He didn't hold out much hope of finding anything else in the areas he had searched already.

The cave-in occurred in a long stretch of tunnel. That long tunnel he'd traversed ended in the main chamber. An entrance/exit may have been situated behind the cave-in, which Adam would only be able to access if he removed all the rubble that came down with him to block it off. He had no idea how far the rubble reached into the other portion of the tunnel. For all he knew, it may have collapsed along its entire length.

Forward of that blockage, where Adam had explored, the tunnel was shored up with concrete and support sections. The main chamber was lined with concrete entirely, giving it a hollow resonance. Deafening when the alarm tripped. Haunting when he heard the scratchy voice.

It was so very odd for him to hear a voice that did not belong to him or Donny. In all of his twenty-five years of life, he only ever heard other voices on the recordings his father had of him and his mother and the few movies they watched on his laptop. He had so few of those. Adam always wished that Donny had provided more of those wonderful movies despite their antiquity.

A trembling through the soles of his shoes interrupted his reveries. He could hear a loud roaring sound coming from the outside tunnel. The earth shook about him, causing him to stumble from the canteen. A billowing cloud of dust and debris was headed his way. He retreated through the hatch, closing it tightly after him. In the small porthole, he witnessed the cloud of dust inundating the area immediately outside the door.

Although his heart raced for the fear he felt, he was unsure what it was he was fearing. Being buried alive was probably top of the list, but the canteen area seemed to be standing up to the assault at present. If the tunnel outside the canteen had caved in, he would lose access to the other sections of the mine, including the main chamber and the possibility of an exit behind the secured doors. That scared him most of all. The air within the canteen would eventually be replaced with carbon dioxide emissions after he'd consumed all the oxygen. He wasn't aware of any air filtration system in place, yet he surmised that there should have been.

If there was a system in place for extracting air from within the mine and replacing it with air from the outside, it may have been the reason no one survived. Depending on the prevailing wind conditions at the time, it would have been easy to assume that Coober Pedy had been exposed at some point. The question remained as to why the good professor and his minions did not exit the area once they were exposed if that was the case. They had to have known about the dangers of exposure to either element. One or the other had to have killed them all.

Adam was only concerned with one of those possibilities for himself. That was why he tested, tested and re-tested as he'd been instructed from the time he could remember. The device he had, possibly the only working one in existence on mainland Australia, had the propensity to save his life, to avoid the lethal consequences awaiting him out there, aboveground, underground, anywhere!

The tremors ceased and the noise abated. The dust cloud continued roiling outside the hatch. He was relatively pleased to see the dust outside the small porthole. It meant that the tunnel remained open. If he saw only static brown through the window, he would have to conclude that the entire tunnel had collapsed.

If it had stopped, had it stopped for long? Was Adam now faced with a timeline to discover a path to freedom? Could the entire facility face collapse very shortly? All because he, Adam Harrow, wiped away a small amount of sand covering some metal he'd found aboveground? Surely something as insignificant as that could not have instigated a cascade of calamities resulting in his final hours?

"Stupid, stupid, stupid! Why would you not take precautions? Donny always said, 'Touch nothing! Move nothing. Explore nothing. Find water, find shelter, find safety and the means of surviving after testing everything twice'. When will I learn? Okay, okay, you were right, Donny. I'm sorry. I'm an idiot. You happy now?"

Adam slunk to the ground, holding his head in his hands. He groaned as the enormity of his dilemma sunk in. He shook his head as he tried to sort through the problems he faced in descending order of priorities. Forgetting about what he may find once he opened the hatch, leaving aside anything more he may discover, should the tunnel be clear up to the main chamber, he concentrated hard on the next basic steps.

e would need to get some rest soon. Of that he was certain. He was exhausted. More from the stress of the day than exertion. Without exploring outside the canteen, he decided that the new cave-in was evidence of possible further destruction. Whatever had caused the initial tumult had not yet come to an end. That may or may not mean the entire structure was in jeopardy.

The main chamber was reinforced with concrete, ergo, possibly the safest place to be for the foreseeable future. Bearing in mind that he may be unable to figure a way of opening the huge stainless steel doors any time soon, Adam groaned anew at the prospect of moving vital stores to the main chamber in the event new tunnel collapses were imminent. He did not want to be caught in the canteen if that happened, and he didn't want to be left without sufficient supplies if the canteen became unavailable.

Tomorrow was shaping up to be an energy and soul-sapping affair provided he didn't get blocked in during his sleep. That thought scared him most of all. He released the hatch slightly to peer into the gloom beyond. Nothing but choking dust. At least he was able to access the tunnel to get out. How long that would last preyed on his mind. So much so, that he decided he would be unable to simply catch some shut-eye. As buggered as he felt, he needed to execute his plan to begin hauling water and other vital provisions up to the main chamber where he would close the hatch and hope for the best.

Adam went quickly to examine the stores of food and water. The only means available for the transport of the goods was a pallet jack standing next to the pallets of water. Essentially just a two-pronged trolley for lifting and moving pallets into position on a smooth surface, it would prove cumbersome and difficult on the rough ground of the tunnel system, if it even fitted. That could only be determined once the dust had settled enough for him to open the hatch and step out.

He checked the bottled water again. They were 600ml bottles of water, packed into shrink-wrap packs of twenty-four. He worked out that each pallet held approximately fifty packs. Assuming a consumption rate of around two litres of water per day, he figured he had enough in one pallet for around 360 days. Adam considered it a waste of time to attempt to transport anything more than one pallet of water. He wouldn't want to remain alive if he went through that lot.

Assuming he was able to transport the pallet through the tunnel, he would require a minimum of two trips. One for the water and another for the food and everything else he deemed necessary, like his portable single-gas burner. He couldn't take any of the appliances in the kitchen area with him, besides a small microwave oven which he may be able to power from the batteries. He only had a dozen gas canisters for his stove. He would have to conserve those for as long as possible. Donny had managed to find the spare canisters at an old petrol station, he said. He'd been saving them for years, for when Adam finally left, he said.

"Bloody liar," shouted Adam.

Much of the canned goods would have to be eaten cold while they were still edible. That was yet to be determined as well. The baked beans were okay. Who knew about the rest which was all way past their use-by dates? Only the dehydrated stuff, like soups, would require added water and heating to reconstitute a meal. He would be sure to take the powdered milk and eggs, and...coffee. If he managed to plug in and power up the microwave, he could have coffee every morning. If not, he would be relegated to only periodic cups using his precious gas supply.

Adam wished he could stop thinking about long term plans. Unfortunately, he wasn't overly optimistic about his chances at locating at an exit. *If* he could get the huge doors open, and *if* an exit existed on the other side, there remained the possibility that he would not be able to get out anyway. The exit could be blocked by tonnes more rubble, or encumbered with advanced security.

Reluctantly, Adam began to make preparations for hauling the gear down the tunnel. He would attempt a pallet of water and his backpack on the first trip. Then he groaned again. He was proving himself to be the moron Donny told him he was. No way was he going to get the pallet through the narrow hatchway. His night just grew longer and more tiring by a magnitude of a hundred.

Adam moved one pallet of water to the side of the hatch. He pulled the pallet jack out from the pallet and through the hatch, barely managing to squeeze it through by tilting it sideways. With a heaving sigh, he started hauling the packs of bottled water through the hatch into the tunnel on the left side of the doorway, with the pallet jack lined up on the right side with the handle facing the way to the main chamber.

Once all the packs were transferred, he struggled with the heavy plastic pallet until that too was through to the tunnel. Once the pallet jack was in place under the pallet, Adam began to move all the water bottles back. When he made it to the main chamber, he would have to repeat the entire process to get everything inside the final chamber. He would be working hard for his supper that night. By four AM he was done in.

The last haul included the professor's light metal cot. Once he closed the hatch to the main chamber, he fully expected not to have to, or be able to, return to the other facilities. If he was correct about that, he prayed that the chamber he was in was reinforced enough to hold up to the collapse taking place above and around the mine. The dust had settled long ago and everything prior to the professor's sleeping quarters was gone. Nothing but rubble remained. If he ever thought he might have a chance to go back and have a crack at getting back out that way, it became an impossibility after the last shakeup.

Adam walked a couple of paces to the unmade cot calling out for him to rest his weary bones for a few minutes. He was fast asleep before he knew it.

STRANGEST

"Hello, is anyone there? Please answer if you're there."

Adam fell from his cot. He'd slept through the day. Inside the large chamber, all the lights were blazing, throwing off a comforting glow. Adam wasn't sure if what he'd heard was from a dream or the same voice he'd heard the day before.

"This is Princess Penelope calling from the M.C.P., anyone? Please answer?"

Adam started to believe he was dreaming upon hearing the royal proclamation loud and clear. No way would a princess be talking to him. Adam was running, stumbling, mumbling and bumbling his way over to the bank of tech. where the voice seemed to be coming from. Everywhere he looked machines and equipment were coming to life, making beeping sounds and chirruping like regular little birds. Not that he'd ever had the good fortune to hear birds live, only recordings. The ranks of soldier's medals had advanced through the lit bars to be about halfway, Adam thought.

When he arrived at the benches, he was at a loss. He didn't know what he was looking at or where he should begin his search for the mysterious voice of...*Princess Penelope*? It was absurd. He had to be hearing things, making it up from a dream. No, it couldn't be that. He'd never read anything about a princess or heard the name, Penelope. It can't have been his imagination making it up, could it?

"Think Adam, think! What would Donny do? Probably tell you off for being a fanciful little twerp, that's what. Princess bloody Penelope, my arse! I..."

"Same time tomorrow then."

"No STOP! Wait. Who?"

Adam peered about the dizzying array of equipment without a single clue as to how to proceed. Lights were blinking, equipment was emitting a low buzzing sound along with clicks and beeps. Somewhere in the nest of tech. was a speaker, he thought, and a microphone. He understood that was how the word was pronounced. Donny spoke into something like it. The speaker in his room transmitted his voice and that was what it sounded like.

Blinking sleep from his eyes, Adam slowly worked the lethargy out of his system. Had to clear his head, think straight. He looked at his watch. It was just after five in the afternoon, around the same time the voice had manifested the day before. Princess Penelope said she would try again at the same time. Someone from... He had to write down what he heard to remember it accurately and attempt to decode its meaning.

"Holy Pando, I need something to write on," said Adam approaching a kind of panic. "Oh, I know. The good professor had some writing materials which I placed...shit! Somewhere. I was going to try and read through some of the reports. Where, where, where... My backpack! Where? There!"

After retrieving the paper and a pencil from the small bunch of items he'd borrowed from the professor's room, he sat with pencil poised. He nodded his head as he recalled the strange words. He read over what he'd written with a look of disbelief.

"Hello if you're there. Please answer. This is...Princess-bloody-Penelope, 'if I got that right', from...N.C.B. or M.C.B. Please answer."

Adam ran over the words a dozen times or more making less and less sense each time.

"Australia doesn't have any bloody princesses! Pretty sure the royal family from jolly old England have been nowhere near this berg for a long, long time and Donny never mentioned a Penelope among the princes and princesses. Vat vood ze gut professor do in zis situation, hmm? Hey, he isn't studying the royal family by any chance? Is that why some princess is trying to reach him?

"That would be one very persistent princess in that case. The good professor and his minions have been dead for yonks. She must be one desperate broad...female!"

Adam was shocked to finally make the connection that it was a female. It had to be a female if she called herself a princess and with a name like Penelope.

"Holy Pando, Donny. A female! Where is she though? That's the big question. Not down here, that's for sure. I thought the professor's study group would be down here for some reason. Not going to get a princess down here, are you professor, no matter how inviting you made it sound? Not with all that happening out there at the time. Hah! M.C.P. The same letters on the lab coats and uniforms, just under the other letters...N.A.S.A."

Adam recalled Donny mentioning those particular letters to him on more than one occasion. It was coming to him slowly. Something to do with... He lost it. He...he needed breakfast is what he needed. He needed some brain food and some of that terrific stuff called coffee. Donny called it the elixir of life, after whiskey. Adam didn't know what the other stuff was, but he knew about coffee and he owned some of that, a lot of that.

Adam was excited, he was exhilarated, though exactly why, he couldn't say. If he thought about it logically he would have had the answer. For the first time in twenty-five years, he heard the voice of another human being that wasn't Donny or a recording. On top of that, it was a female voice. Maybe it belonged to someone looking like Miss November? Wouldn't that be a treat? Adam immediately superimposed the voice onto the centrefold.

"Princess Penelope November! Holy Pando, what a combination."

His fantasies were on overdrive and the reaction to those images caused delicious sensations below. He wondered if he should... No, he had to feed himself and get on with his preparations for the evening ahead. There was so much to do and he was on a possible timeline. His survival depended on finding an exit before the whole shebang fell on him. He eyed the ceiling and walls nervously.

There weren't any support columns, no beams or anything to support the massive roof overhead. He thought he would be relatively safe in the main chamber but that may have been wishful thinking. Just a bloody big cavern with a pair of dirty, great, big, steel doors that he wasn't able to open…yet. He was hoping an exit existed behind those doors and he hoped he could find some means with which to gain entry. He didn't want to fool around with that scanning thingy beside the doors again. He didn't want to know how long and loud the alarms would be with the batteries almost fully charged.

At least he had ample light. Several computer consoles on the benches also attracted his attention. From practising on Donny's laptop, he'd had a basic understanding of the tech., the...software, he heard Donny call it, the brains of the hardware. After a meal, he would attempt to turn them on and explore their secrets. He had the feeling that answers were to be had within the machines. He desperately needed some clarity because he had far too many unanswered questions floating around his head.

When he first fell through the hole to the professor's wonderland, he thought that initial cave-in would be it. He never imagined multiple downfalls. If the whole lot came down...

Well, he couldn't think of that. It wasted time and energy to think of what may or may not happen. His mind continued to regurgitate those thoughts despite his resolve to leave them be. He set about opening a couple of cans of food and brewing some delicious coffee. He did not waste his precious gas supply on heating the canned goods, which he ate straight from the can after making sure to test it all first. As expected, the coffee was as exhilarating as he remembered it. The powdered milk was a bit ordinary, but he could live with it.

After rubbing his body with a bit of soapy water to rid himself of dirt and odours, he dressed in a pair of shorts and a T-shirt. He wore simple sandals on his feet. It was a comfortable temperature within the chamber. He wandered over to the shelves and benches of equipment. Adam chose one swivel chair after dusting it off, in front of what he hoped would be a computer terminal. A dim red L.E.D. light glowed softly on the bottom right-hand of the screen. He pushed it.

After a few seconds, he groaned. A window had opened up asking for a password. He imagined the other consoles, belonging to possibly the other personnel would all probably require codes to access the mainframe. He saw the large unit that he assumed was the hub of the machines at one side of the benches. How many tries at cracking the password did he have? What would happen if he failed? Would it automatically self-destruct? Was that a thing? Was any of the information that sensitive to warrant safety protocols like that?

Adam stared at the screen asking for the password, noticing six dots in the place where the password should be typed. Was it that simple? Donny told him that he did not have to repeat things all the time on his laptop, that it remembered things like passwords and such if the owner allowed it. Did the professor allow his password to be remembered so he wouldn't have to input the code each time? If that were the case, all he had to do was press the 'enter' button to proceed, maybe? Nothing ventured...

The screen turned black!

Then the background image of the symbol emblazoned on the lab coats appeared. The letters, N-A-S-A, and the accompanying letters, M-C-P underneath. A circle of blue with what looked like stars, a split red strikethrough over white letters, and a white, incomplete circle within.

"So, it had to be M.C.P. that you said, Princess? What the heck is that then? This all looks pretty damn official, lady. On the left side of the screen, there was a vertical line of icons, with most of them resembling a yellow folder or a file. He knew about those. Donny taught him to write his essays on the laptop then save them to a file which he should identify with a name and a date.

The files icons on the screen before him had a few identifiers but none that he understood to mean anything. Pleased with himself for having proceeded so far, Adam rose to refill his coffee from the remains in the pot before he settled down to read everything he could. He returned to the comfortable chair with his brew. Then he realised how desperately he needed to go. He hadn't thought about that aspect of being trapped in a single chamber. What was he going to do about going to the toilet?

He urgently required to perform his ablutions after sleeping for twelve hours or more. The ground beneath him was bare earth but he had nothing handy with which to dig a hole, and he assumed the ground to be impacted hard enough to make it a chore at best. He felt himself squirming with the need to release while his mind raced through the possibilities.

He mulled over the thought of filling his opened cans with his solid wastes. He could find a corner behind all the soldiers to urinate but he couldn't do the same with solid matter. If he raced to the bathroom down the tunnel to relieve himself, fate may choose that very moment to release another cave-in. Being stuck forever in the shithouse was not a pleasant prospect. He had several empty cans from his meal. That would...

"Shit! Yeah, that's right Adam, shit. What are you going to do about your arse afterwards? Bloody toilet paper, mate! You forgot to bring any toilet paper, you idiot!"

There was nothing else for it, he would have to dash for the bathroom and hope for the best. Should he take anything with him in case...? No point in that event. Worst case scenario and he was trapped in the dunny, he would just die a slow death. Adam flew through the hatch along the tunnel before he soiled himself. He returned with armfuls of toilet paper a little later. He made several return journeys to ensure he had sufficient. He also managed to find a chemical porta-potty tucked away in a corner of the bathroom, in a storage cupboard below the packs of cleaning supplies and mop buckets.

That required the pallet jack to move. Not because it was overly weighty, but because it was cumbersome. The cassette would have to be removed and emptied when it was full. Adam had some heavy-duty, plastic kitchen rubbish bags which he thought might solve that issue. He also retrieved a few utensils from the kitchen which he would use to dig as big a hole as he was able.

He berated himself once more for seeing to long-term problem-solving. It was in his nature after so many years under the tutelage of his father to be practical in all things. He found it difficult to refrain from doing so. Life trapped in an underground mine, albeit with a host of interesting stuff to play with, did not make for a positive future. He could survive for quite some time with all the provisions he had, but would he want to? If there was no way out, would he be content to live out the rest of his years there?

He'd been taught that life was so precious it should not be wasted, not taken for granted and never treated lightly. After what happened, it was his duty and his privilege to make it, to survive. He would honour his pledge to Donny to make every attempt to do so. He would leave no stone unturned in his efforts to find a way out.

Relieved of his intestinal burdens and having completed the immediate tasks of providing for his future ablutionary concerns, Adam settled in the chair again facing the list of file icons. He decided to simply explore them methodically, beginning with the topmost first. A spreadsheet of names appeared after he selected the file. He then clicked on the first item.

Around a hundred names with gender assignations and other indicators to identify the persons appeared. In the next hour, Adam had an idea of the participants, if that's who they were, of the study being conducted by the good professor. Further investigations revealed a comprehensive dossier on each individual ranging from educational qualifications to sexual preferences. The latter supposedly being a non-optional component of the study.

There was no indication of a Princess Penelope or other royal personage involved. No mention of Penelope in any of the files. He discovered a lot about all sorts of highly qualified professionals but not one hint of background about his mystery voice.

The next folder he opened was labelled 'case notes'. Adam assumed it was where the hand-written notes would be transferred once the good professor had completed them. At least the computer files were legible. Nowhere could he find what the study was about, what the letters, M.C.P. or N.A.S.A. stood for. The latter set of letters tickled a memory that was still hiding beneath the surface of his consciousness.

The emblem supported a theory of space if the white dots within the blue circle could be allocated as stars. The white circle could conceivably be described as an elliptical orbit. He had no idea what the split red slash could mean. Unless it was meant to portray, abstractly, a rocket ship? A memory was breaching the surface as he thought about those possibilities. He decided to let it come of its own accord.

The case notes, reams and reams of them, covered innumerable days and nights of subject behaviours. From the time they got up in the morning, what they wore, with whom they cohabited, what they ate and everything in between with all manner of accompanying number codes. It was as boring to read with full access to all the data as when he could only decipher every second or third word of the professor's bad handwriting.

A bunch of people going about making a life for themselves. Growing food, improving implements and conditions from limited items. Conducting experiments on the soil and rocks dressed in suits. From what Adam could gather, it was all underground, fuelling his suspicions that the study group, whoever remained, was behind the huge metal doors through which access had been denied so far. What was the bloody point?

Did scientists believe, even back then, that life would be forced underground? Not according to Donny, a politician with a ministerial appointment in medicine before the shit hit the fan. No one took him seriously when he shouted out the warnings to his fellow pollies and his constituents. They thought he was nothing more than a crackpot, a doomsday prophet. All too late had they learned the truth of his predictions. All too late had the people of

Australia experienced the events that would alter the course of history and life on the continent.

"Space Agency! Um, no. Space Administration...The National...something...Space Administration. It was an American mob that sent manned missions to the moon. Adam finally remembered."

It was getting late and Adam couldn't read anything more. His eyes were fatigued. He didn't want his natural body clock to become disoriented. He needed to keep with the usual day and night clock despite being trapped in an artificial environment with no delineation between the changing times. It was close to midnight according to his watch. He needed to get some shuteye and begin again in the morning after breakfast.

His first priority would be to find some way of communicating with the voice, her highness, Princess Penelope. It sounded ridiculous even contemplating the notion that a princess existed behind the doors, let alone that he might speak to her. Was it an elaborate joke, a hoax for the unwary? Was he about to make some monumental faux pas? Could he endanger himself somehow by attempting to communicate with the voice? It didn't seem possible. He didn't know how it could be harmful. But he didn't know everything.

"You don't know everything kiddo! Well, Donny, you probably don't know everything either, smartarse! Man, I have to stop talking to you like your still there, listening to every bloody word, breath or sound I make! Couldn't even fart in private! That was funny that time..."

Adam stopped himself from relating the humorous tale. He grew sad. How it ended wasn't a proud moment in his life. He should be paying his father some respect instead of sharing funny anecdotes from their past. It was behaviour that was beneath him, not how he was raised. The Honourable Member would not be amused by his son's misadventures in creating an escape and the way he now treated his mentor and saviour. His flippancy and disregard for everything he'd been taught was uncalled for. He owed his life to the man who did everything to ensure his survival in a world turned upside-down by global events.

Adam admonished himself severely before brushing his teeth and heading for the cot to grab some sleep. He had to be serious about his situation and urgent in his need to find a way out. Donny said that he needed to get to the eastern seaboard as long as it tested safely. Failing that, he needed to find an inland, uncontaminated water source, near some safe land to cultivate the seeds that Donny saved. Preferably in a valley somewhere that might evade prevailing conditions bringing certain death on the breezes.

Unfortunately, there was also the other thing that Donny told him. Something he found impossible to digest at times. His curse and his salvation in one. The reason he would never know the companionship of another human. The reason he must avoid contact at all costs.

FIRST CONTACT

He thought he may have located the switch on the device that might enable him to respond to the voice. He'd spent half the day examining every piece of mech. and tech. near the speaker where he believed the sound emanated. The rest of the day was spent reading, going back through the mountains of reports filed by the professor and his pupils, if that's who they were, or support crew.

He'd answered some of his questions but developed many more. He was unable to access any of the other terminals along the bench. Their passwords were not automatically inputted by the computer as the professor's was. Adam guessed that the professor may not have had a mind for keeping hold of passwords. He reserved his mental processes for important duties it seemed. It may have been that his cohorts required access to his computer to accomplish their tasks or add their reports.

Several folders he had not yet accessed were labelled under nine names, one of whom was female. That correlated with the nine bodies in the dormitory opposite the professor's chamber. Adam was forming a mental picture of the human structure at least. Some of the earliest entries dated to mid-2019, two years before he was born. Before the...

Adam cut off that thought. He didn't want to think about all the information Donny supplied him with immediately following that year. It depressed him, even though he did not live through it. He lived those years vicariously through his father who spoke with raw emotion whenever he mentioned them, sometimes to the point of tears. Especially where Judy Harrow was concerned. Judith Coral Harrow, beloved wife of Donald Harrow and unknown mother to Adam.

He decided that he would start from the earliest notes and reports. He became quite nervous as the time approached for the voice to make contact once again. He formed a million questions in his mind but drew a complete blank as to how to approach them. His social graces were practically nil. He had no idea how to react or communicate with another human besides Donny. He supposed it would be the same process, if, he could manage to make contact. He had only the time it took her to ask once or twice if anyone was there to work out the tech. or mech. involved in answering her. Without a similar speaker device in his room through which he and Donny communicated, Adam would have had no idea how to proceed.

A flat-screen monitor next to the speaker suggested a camera link-up which may or may not be working on either end. He assumed the monitor on his side had a camera mounted in the frame surrounding the screen. Donny's laptop had one similar which Adam played with to view himself. When Miss November became somewhat haggard from overuse, Donny showed him how to scan the image to record it onto the computer forever. Then he told Adam not to mess on the keyboard when he accessed her digital image. It was said with a smirk.

"Hello, anyone there?" came the bored, monotone voice.

"Shit, crap, holy Pando!" stammered Adam, spilling his cup of water. He eventually settled his nerves enough to tap the key which he believed would activate his response.

"Hello?"

A sudden yelp followed by a crash and a thump followed.

"Hello, are you still there?" asked Adam hopefully.

"Is-is this real?" asked a very nervous voice, almost a squeak.

"Is what real?"

"You? Are you real? Am I speaking to someone at...oh."

Adam heard sniffing sounds and other movements he couldn't identify. Then the scratchy sound disappeared altogether.

"Hello, hello?" Adam shouted desperately.

"Sorry, sorry, had to find something and start pedalling again. Takes a moment to get going," said the voice breathlessly.

Silence.

"Are you there?" she asked.

"Yes," he replied.

"Well?"

"What?"

"Are you real?"

"Of course I'm real. What else would I be?"

"Who-who are you, where are you, what are you doing there, how many are there, what happened...?"

Adam waited impatiently for the phalanx of questions to abate.

His head was spinning and he wasn't sure how to respond. He had no idea anyone could speak so fast and ask that many questions in one breath.

"Answer me, please?" asked the voice plaintively.

"Which-which question? Slow down, would you?"

"S-sorry, sorry. Don't go, please. I-I haven't spoken... I, since... So hard..."

"What's happening? What's that sound?"

"Crying. Haven't... Oh, so long. Who, who are you? Can you tell me that? Is, that, that...are you the one?"

"You're not making much sense there. I'm...Adam. Adam Harrow. Are you, are you a real princess?"

"I don't know what you mean. How do you know my name?"

"Why are you breathing so hard?"

"Charging the batteries for this gizmo. It takes a lot of energy. I have to keep going or it will shut off."

"So, real princess?" Adam asked after an awkward pause.

"My name is Princess. Princess Penelope."

"Your parents named you Princess?"

"That's what they called me, yes."

"So it...it's a pet name rather than your real name?"

"I'm not a pet!"

"No, I get that. I said a pet name. Like Donny used to call me Sport all the time, or Sonny, or Tiger."

"Donny?"

"My father."

"You don't call him Daddy?"

"Not since I was a teenager," Adam intimated with a note of impatience.

"Mama called me Princess, that's that."

"Fair enough. Didn't meant to insult you or anything. Where are you, exactly?"

"I wouldn't be able to give you exact coordinates or anything. Listen, I can't keep this going for much longer. Can you help me get away from here, Adam?"

"I don't know. Where are you?"

"Mars."

It took Adam time before he could digest the information. He couldn't be sure there wasn't someplace locally by that name, or even abroad. He didn't want to come straight out and either laugh or call her a liar, having just made contact.

"Can you repeat that, please?" he asked to be sure he had heard right.

"Mars. You know? The planet?" she enquired without pause.

"How is that possible?"

"I was born here. My mama was part of the original group, the M.C.P.."

"What's that?"

"The Mars Colonisation Project. Mummy said it was headed by Professor Simpkins. That's the person she said I should contact. Is he there?"

"Oh-um, yes and, no. I mean, he's dead."

"No! Oh, no, no, no. Have you taken over? Are you in charge? Can you get me out of here?"

"Whoa, slow down there. I can't answer all that at once."

"I can't slow down. I can only keep this going for a short time. Please help me?"

"Look, you can't be where you say you are. There hasn't been any news of Mars missions, let alone manned missions or a colonisation effort! Donny would have known, would have told me. He was in the government, you see. He knew a lot of things. You have to be mistaken."

"Are you calling me a liar-liar-pants-on-fire?"

Liar-liar-pants-on-fire? What? Is she five years old or something?

"Look, no offence but it just doesn't seem possible, that's all. How long have you been there?" he asked for want of something better to say.

"All, all, my...life," she replied breathlessly. "I was born here. The first one and the only one. I guess I'm a Martian."

"Do you mind if I ask how old you are?"

"Why would I mind? I don't really know, though."

"Donny tells me women can be touchy about their age. How come you don't know how old you are?" he asked after thinking for a moment."

"I never kept track. We're underground so I don't get to see the sky at all to keep track of days, and besides, Martian seasons are longer than on Earth anyway. I have to go, I'm running out of breath.

Can I speak to you tomorrow?"

"Just tell me why you have to generate your power? I would have assumed that any colonisation effort would have included a means of generating power utilising methods, like solar, wind or even fuelled?"

"Pow-pow-power went off a long time ago. I remember when we..had...it but...we had...series of quakes here. After that, it all died. Like I'm going to any moment. Bye."

"Wait! Hello? Holy Pando, what have I stumbled into here? Who the heck are you people? Donny? You never said anything about a colonisation attempt. You didn't even say anything about more exploration efforts of Mars before, during or...well, you couldn't tell me about after the hard years, could you?"

Adam returned to his cot where he lay staring at the concrete ceiling far above him. He ruminated on everything the female said. Something about her manner of speech struck him as being quite odd. It didn't fit with the image he had in his head of an educated person, not that he'd experienced much of that, only Donny. He had read many a book written by eminent persons, educated persons trained in their areas of expertise, like psychiatrists and physicists for instance. Books by those kinds of people didn't include such phrases as, 'liar-liar-pants-on-fire', or someone referring to their mother as 'mama'.

Adam rose from his cot to walk over to his stockpile of provisions, selecting a can or two for his planned dinner. He'd managed to find a place to plug in his microwave once he followed the power leads of the mech. on the benches. He poured the contents of the opened cans into a plastic receptacle which he placed in the microwave to heat for a few moments. The delicious aroma soon permeated the space around him. Spaghetti and meatballs it read on the label. The picture looked appetising and the smell was divine as it was heating. The contents didn't appear so glamorous in reality, though.

There were many items he had never heard of or tried before among the stores of food. He opened a bottle of water, his third for the day. He wasn't too concerned. He had plenty. If the day came when he believed he had to start rationing his water, he would end it. It didn't bear contemplating living trapped belowground all that time. He couldn't abide the thought of being unsuccessful in finding a way out.

Adam allowed his mind to drift back over the weird conversation with...Princess Penelope! *How could anyone name their child Princess? And what sort of surname was Penelope in that case?*

The meal was as delicious as the aromas hinted at. He went through the two cans in no time. He washed it down with some peaches in syrup. He'd made sure to test everything first, before and after opening the cans. As surprising and confusing as his conversation had been, he remembered to follow the golden rules of survival.

Adam performed a few stretches and yoga exercises to limber up a little. He wasn't tired yet and he didn't feel like reading anything more that day. He wandered over to the big steel doors. There were no handles on the double doors. He wondered why they were that big anyway. When he bent down to inspect the hard-packed gravel in front of the doors he noticed a tread pattern for the first time. He supposed that might be the reason the doors were that size. To allow passage of a vehicle of some kind, or vehicles, plural.

Looking about the cavernous interior of the chamber, he deduced the need for a heavy mech. to have created the space and possibly whatever lay behind the doors. On the wall immediately to the left of the doors was the scary security...thingy.

"Retinal scanner! That's what it is," he said suddenly when he remembered Donny telling about things like that, especially in government installations. "That's why the alarms went off. My eye didn't work, right? Sure, that makes sense. Wow, what's so secret then? Does the square mesh underneath that thing analyse your voice then? So even if I did the disgusting thing by taking out one of their eyes, it still wouldn't work, would it?"

Adam knew he was stymied by the security setup. He ambled past the enormous opaque window measuring around ten metres in length and three metres high. Next to that, as he walked further left, stood an enormous array of what appeared to be electrical installations. Levers, gauges, blinking standby lights, dials and readouts, none of which meant anything to Adam, except for a row of something looking distinctly like circuit breakers. He knew about that from his room. Donny had to talk him through resetting them every so often when they had an outage. Something as simple as an electrical storm could trip the breakers. Of course, when it all went awry, they had to rely on their own resources, like solar and a diesel generator. Only, Donny ran out of places to top up the diesel in his jerry cans. That left them with only solar.

He supposed they were something similar to the circuit breakers, only ten times as large, all in the 'OFF' position. Peering about, he failed to understand what they would be powering. Everything within the chamber seemed to be running off a similar bank of breakers near the battery soldiers. When he checked on them earlier in the day, they were nearing full capacity. The aftershocks of the cave-in that deposited him in the mine must have uncovered more of the array aboveground.

He could think of only one possibility for the breakers in front of him; that they were intended for whatever resided behind the mysterious doors. He contemplated turning them all on. Either they wouldn't work at all or would unleash some new hellish mayhem. He didn't need any more alarms giving him heart attacks, that was for sure. What if something behind the doors had shorted, causing the breakers to trip? If he turned them back on would he be causing further damage, possibly catastrophic?

What if he only turned one back on? Give him time to find out if it did anything? Methodically, calculating the effects, and possible dangers. If he was correct in that the breakers were intended to connect the power supply for whatever existed behind the doors, he may never know what might be happening. Which also meant it probably couldn't harm him if things went wrong. Before he could change his mind, he leaned forward and hauled one of the large levers, moving it to the 'ON' position.

Without warning, the enormous opaque window cleared, revealing an astounding sight.

BLOODY WEIRD

Adam wasn't quite sure what to make of it. Clearly, he was seeing through to the other side of the glass but logic decreed that what he saw wasn't credible. In ways, it resembled much of the landscape aboveground. However, it was devoid of any life, denuded of trees or grasses, devoid of any animal life, resembling a barrenness, unlike anything he'd seen. The red soil and rocks were redolent of the desert areas near the red centre he'd seen pictures of, minus the big rock, Uluru.

It was essentially, a chamber as large as the one in which he resided without any of the same equipment. Also, the shape was circular compared to his being rectangular. Dotted around the perimeter of the chamber were air-lock structures leading to domiciles, presumably. There were portholes situated on either side of each projection. There were five of them that Adam could count, extending out from the perimeter walls by about three metres.

He could see that they might have been white at some point but that they were almost completely stained red by the soil. A large six-wheeled, all-terrain vehicle, unlike anything he'd seen in his limited experience, was parked in a bay to one side, at the extreme right of his position at the window. The centre of the area was pock-marked with what looked like neat holes, possibly drilled because he couldn't think of an animal capable of performing that feat.

Unlike the chamber on his side of the glass, the one he was staring at had what looked like a natural rock ceiling. Most noticeable on the ground, were the evenly-spaced mounds to the left of his position. Maybe raised garden beds or something like that. Only, it couldn't be that if they were underground with only dim artificial light coming from somewhere he couldn't make out.

There were areas fenced off using temporary steel posts and coloured plastic ribbon. He wondered if it was a mining expedition considering the test holes he seemed to be witnessing. Everything had many layers of red dust covering it, indicating years of neglect. The scene bespoke of desolation and abandonment.

"As it is above, so shall it be below," mused Adam out loud.

"Alright, nothing blew up in here or on that side, so let's see what the rest of them do, shall we?"

He heaved the rest of the levers into the 'ON' position. And suddenly...nothing happened. He didn't know what to expect. Sparks flying? Explosions? At least something. That nothing at all changed was a great anticlimax. One of the levers revealed something monumental when the glass cleared, the rest proved to be duds in Adam's eyes.

He was about to return to his cot when he felt tremors beneath his feet. The ground shook and rumbled. When he made it to the locked hatchway, he peered through the porthole to see the tunnel collapsing. It stopped around fifty metres from his position, leaving that distance clear but effectively blocking off any access to the previous chambers, including the kitchen and toilet. Just as well he'd thought to move that toilet paper and found the porta-potty.

Adam felt very proud of himself for predicting the possibility of a continuing collapse. His only worry then was whether it would persist and affect the main chamber. He wasn't worried about the adjacent chamber because that seemed to be deserted...maybe? He had a theory about that because something didn't add up earlier. He didn't make the connection at the time but he thought of it soon after.

There were several such anomalies he discovered when he ran back over everything in his mind. Some of the things he'd read in the professor's notes, some of the assumptions he'd made, seemed to be coming together. There was still a plethora of unanswered questions. When he peered back through the porthole, he saw nothing but the swirling dust which would no doubt settle in a few hours. When he went back to the large window, he saw only the same as before.

Adam decided he had more research to do that evening. He would begin at the start, the earliest notes and reports. He would browse some of the other folders with vague titles and acronyms. According to the view outside the hatch, his time may well be running short. The main chamber was heavily reinforced with concrete walls and ceiling but nothing stood in the way of Mother Nature. It might be gravity causing the destructive forces, or simply the ground settling itself after so long having been crisscrossed with mine shafts weakening the subsurface.

By the time his eyelids began drooping and head started

nodding slowly downwards, he had learned more than he could have dared. It didn't answer all the questions but he believed he had a grasp on the most pressing ones. Of course, many other problems presented themselves with the new information. He had only one or two folders left to read through on the professor's computer terminal, or his portion of the mainframe, at least. Unless Adam could access the students' terminals, he had almost completed his task covering many years of notes.

He suddenly shook himself awake, forcing his eyes open. He could not afford to miss her transmission. He would have to have a list of questions ready for her and a separate list of information to provide her...if she called again. Something told Adam she definitely would, with possible news of an important nature. She may even try to contact him earlier.

Adam forced himself to attend to his ablutions before he caused any medical problems by holding it in. He washed himself down after stripping naked. He was beginning to smell bad and he didn't like it. Donny had impressed upon him the need to remain perfectly, hygienically clean at all times. His life depended on it, most probably. The old man was never certain of outcomes. Only vague bloody warnings and dire consequences should his son neglect the duties as outlined by him.

He used some of his precious bottled water which he poured into a large steel bowl. He had a squeeze-bottle of liquid disinfectant soap which he applied liberally once he'd moistened his entire body. The lathery smoothness felt good against his bare skin. It had an unfortunate clinical odour about it, but beggars couldn't be choosers. The cool water as he rinsed off the suds helped to reawaken him. After towelling himself dry, he made himself breakfast and coffee. According to his watch, it was ten past three in the morning.

He wandered over to the large viewing window. Nothing had changed besides the lights being brighter. His eye was once more drawn to the regular mounds to the left of the window. Something about them triggered a memory. Something to do with the early days, before he came along...

Graves!

The horrible thought came to him very quickly. He'd seen the pictures of hastily dug gravesites with similar mounds covering entire valleys in parts of the world. Didn't happen so much in

Australia because there were too few people around to perform the burials in the end. The magazines and newspaper pictures depicting those horrific scenes that Donny showed him, made him very sad.

So, death happened on that side of the glass as well, hey? No escaping it, is there? It's bloody everywhere.

His mood grew sombre with a host of depressing and negative thoughts entering his mind. Introspection whilst in the abyss saw him growing uglier of mind and temperament, less patient and increasingly self-pitying. It was a hazardous, spiralling journey of self-immolation, a metaphorical elimination by fire.

When he broke from his incapacitating waking-nightmare, he was sweating from head to toe, shaking uncontrollably, muttering and murmuring incoherently. Donny warned about the dangers of too much introspection while alone. He foresaw the day Adam may take his life rather than face a new day, another challenge. The onerous burden of his responsibilities to himself and the rest of Australia placed squarely on the shoulders of a young man coming of age under very dark circumstances, was perhaps too heavy to manage.

It was the connection he made to the mass graves that brought on the bout of acute melancholia. It triggered such emotional devastation in him that he fought an ever-increasing battle to maintain a modicum of self-control. He'd asked Donny if he was going insane once when he came out of a particularly upsetting incident.

"Hah! Mad as a bloody Hatter, Champ. We all are by now. Wouldn't be bloody human if we didn't feel something about it all. The trick is to understand that and make sure it doesn't overtake you. Work with it not against it and never let it take complete control. That is what separates the erudite from the dim-witted clods, Sport."

His father was nothing if not often snobbishly eloquent in his aphorisms, his Donny-isms. No matter how sincere he was in his speech, he always came over as somewhat pompous and arrogant. His shit never stank if you asked him, and Adam had once. *Result of excellent breeding,* he was fond of announcing to anyone silly enough to be listening. In Adam, he had a captive audience for twenty-five years of spouting such rubbish along with the occasional gems he imparted to his protégé.

Shaking his head sadly, Adam moved away from the window

just before a shadow of movement passed across one of the portholes in the domiciles on the opposite side of the glass. His breakfast waited and he needed the caffeine to remain awake. He removed the bowl of 'scrambled eggs' from the microwave, allowing the steam to dissipate after he removed the plastic lid. He found a can of something called tomato sauce which sounded like it might accompany the eggs nicely.

Donny grew real tomatoes in their small patch under growing lights. Adam had never actually seen it until he escaped but Donny had described everything to him in great detail, including images taken on a digital camera and transferred to the laptop, via a memory stick. Everything he received always passed through the airlock system, or through the drawer slide, after being thoroughly disinfected. It was supposed to protect everyone else from them should the time come. Adam didn't know what that meant, or when the 'time' would come.

The meal was delicious. He would remember to repeat it often. He was over the moon about the different taste sensations he discovered in his stash. Donny made all their meals and eventually, everything tasted bland and boring. It was supposedly because ingredients were getting harder to come by on Donny's foraging trips.

Adam had to prevent himself from frolicking once more into the realms of long-term thinking or venturing back into any form of negativity. His only mission was to get out, to be free, to explore and reach the coast eventually. He needed to discover if life persisted elsewhere.

However, he first needed to escape his current incarceration. It became less and less certain that he would accomplish that task the longer he remained. His options were decreasing every time more of the old mine-that wasn't a mine collapsed. If the main chamber succumbed to the disturbances without his ability to retreat to the other side of the locked doors, he would be doomed to die a horrible death by asphyxiation or get crushed under tonnes of rubble and concrete. He favoured neither result. He was unable to retreat, incapable of moving forward, unaware of an exit. Trapped for the foreseeable future with only himself for company, memories of Miss November and a phantom princess in the ether with whom to converse for an undefined period.

For twenty-five years everything moved at a glacial pace for Adam with nowhere to go and not much else to do besides learning, reading, and the requisite living basics. His life began anew the day he left Donny for good.

He vowed never to return, to complete his assigned tasks, to make good on everything he'd promised. To accomplish that he needed to think positively. He must follow the mantras he adopted early in life. While he detested the fact that Donny had taught him those life lessons, he recognised the wisdom in reiterating those messages to himself daily. It did not pay to dwell on the past, on the mistakes, on the horrors that were. Life lay in the here and now, the road forward and the strength of a man's resolve.

Despite the caffeine hit, his eyelids grew heavy from the fatigue of heavy concentration throughout the night. He was pleased he had done so, learning many facts to help him decide on a path forwards. He faced certain problems resulting from those findings. The biggest one to arrive at approximately five o'clock in the afternoon, or earlier if what he suspected became a reality.

"Hello, Adam? Mr Harrow?"

"Hah! What did I tell you?"

Adam moved over to the benches where he tapped a key on the keyboard to accept the connection.

"Bit early for you isn't it?" he asked casually.

"Oh, I couldn't help myself. You'll never guess what happened..."

"Hmm, the power returned suddenly?"

"How-how could you possibly know that?" she asked quietly, almost awestruck.

"Because *I* turned it on."

"You...you're on Mars? Is this part of a rescue mission? Were our messages received? Oh, this is so exciting I..."

"Whoa, Princess. Slow it down, huh? It isn't a rescue mission. No, I am not on Mars and...neither are you," Adam almost whispered.

"I don't understand," she said after a long period of silence. "I know my mama and ninety-nine others were part of the Mars Colonisation Project. Our clothes and suits all have the initials embroidered on the sleeves!" she stated with a rising, indignant ire.

"Hey, don't shoot the messenger, okay? I stumbled into all of this by accident and you should be thanking me for getting your power back on for you. No more cycling like a crazy person just to talk to someone."

"I'm not a crazy person," she shouted.

"Wow, way to get hooked up on something. I didn't say you were. Look, ratchet down the hostility if you want me to keep speaking to you, otherwise I'm off the air and you can fend for yourself."

The silence became palpable. Clearly, Princess was used to acting like a princess and getting away with it. Faced with a person who was not about to simply bow to her will, she had to mull over her choices to come up with a new plan it seemed.

"Adam? Are you still there?"

"For the moment. If you can keep it dialled down to a reasonable conversation level then I can try to explain what I think I've found out?"

"You're wrong. My mama specifically told me, and others did as well before...well, they told me they were part of the project," she said with her voice breaking slightly.

"That much is true as far as I can tell. There was a joint venture between Australia and the American institution known as N.A.S.A to conduct a colonisation experiment, in the hope of gaining information about long-term problems arising from a small group of highly skilled human beings living close within an alien environment."

"Well, there you go then. You were wrong. I was right," she stated in a precocious manner.

"It never went to Mars, though. It was never meant to go to Mars. It was a project headed by Professor Simpkins with the assistance of the Australian government. They constructed a subterranean living environment to mimic Martian conditions beneath the soil. The 'colonists' were told they would be placed in a habitat equivalent to living in one of the many large caves discovered by unmanned expeditions to the planet over the years."

"No!"

"Donny would have told me if something as major as a colonisation mission to Mars took place. He was high up in the government of the day, he would have known."

"I don't believe you. You're a liar-liar-pants-on-fire!"

"Oh for goodness sake. Am I speaking to a child?" he accused.

"I am not! I am a full-grown woman with titties and hair and everything. I don't like you. You're mean!"

Adam scratched his head in confusion. Something wasn't right. *With titties and hair?*

Adam started to think he may dealing with someone of reduced mental faculties. How could he convince a mentally-challenged person that he was right and that she was a delusional paranoid trapped in childhood? *So much for Miss November!* He thought uncharitably.

He knew about living alone. He knew what loneliness was capable of doing to the mind. He saw the graves. If she had to cope with that much death, on her own for who knew how long, anyone would be stark-raving bonkers. Donny may have been with him all those years but he was never truly...*with*...him, in the proper sense of the word. He often imagined he was losing it, even before he escaped.

"Look...sorry if I offended you. It must be awful to be alone...wherever you are. I know what that feels like, believe me. I'm not calling you a liar, I'm just trying to convince you of the truth. I know I'm on Earth, okay? I've been topside, been breathing the air before I stumbled into this warren of mystery. You know about Mars, right?"

"Of course. Mama taught me everything about the planet we live on," came back the terse reply.

"Your mother, who is...was she? Her name, I mean."

"Sheba. Doctor Sheba Thomas."

"And your father?" asked Adam, recalling the name she quoted from his researches.

"He died."

"Sorry to hear that. It seems like almost everyone passed away from the group of one hundred. Your father's name?"

"Mama said his name was Doctor Brandon Archer. She made me remember his name. Told me never to forget what a fine man he was before he went."

The silence stretched on.

"I'm not sure you will understand this, but I think your name is either Penelope Archer or Penelope Thomas if you keep your mother's name. On Earth, when two people get married and have a child, the person takes on the surname of either parent. I think your mother used the pet name of Princess for you. I read about both of your parents from Professor Simpkins' reports. They sounded like very good people."

"Can I be Penelope Archer then, after my Daddy?"

"You can be whoever you want to be...Princess," Adam replied kindly.

"I know I can't be a princess. My Mama wasn't a queen like in the stories she told me about with castles and dragons..."

"Have you ever been outside your habitat?"

"I couldn't at first because there were no suits small enough. After, when...some became available and I could fit into them, I left to-to...bury them outside using the Rover. Mama taught me how to drive it. Then we ran out of everything, like oxygen for the suits. I can't go out anymore, even to talk to my Mama."

"So, you know the atmosphere on Mars is not suitable for humans, right?"

"Course, dummy!" she spat.

"What if you could breathe the air outside your pod? Would that convince you that you aren't on Mars?"

"I'm not going out without a suit and don't have any oxygen cylinders left. Not going to die just to prove to you I'm right."

"What if I told you I'd seen your compound, that I saw the domiciles arranged around the perimeter of the enormous cavern, that I've seen the graves?"

"That would only mean you have a working monitor. Professor Simpkins used to monitor all the colonists Mama said. She used to speak to him through one so they saw each other."

"Can you see outside one of those portholes?"

"Course."

"Mind taking a look now?"

"What for?"

"I want you to describe what you see."

"Why?"

"Humour me, okay?"

Adam heard some movement and rustling.

"Well?"

"I don't know what you want me to say. I see everything the same as it's been for a long, long time," she answered sadly.

"From where you are, can you see the...graves? Sorry to ask."

"Yeah."

"They're on your right side, correct?"

"S'pose."

"To the left of them, what can you see?"

"Same as always; the cave wall."

"What! That can't be... Sorry, sorry, didn't mean to sound like I don't believe you. Okay, if that's true then the window doesn't appear on your side for some reason. Have you ever tried touching the wall there or tried digging into it?"

"Why would anyone do that? What window?"

"If you'll listen, I can try to explain what happened to me?"

"If I do, will you help me get off Mars?"

"I'll do my best. Maybe between the two of us, we can figure a few things out, what do you say? My name, is Adam Harrow, as you know. I'm twenty-five years old..."

"What do you look like? Are you handsome, like my Daddy was?"

"Um, well, I guess I'm not ugly. I have long blonde hair and brown eyes, like my father. I'm average height, I suppose. I keep relatively fit when I remember to do my exercises. I...that's about it, I think. Anyway, when I left home to go exploring topside..."

"You lived belowground as well?"

"Yes, we had to."

"Why?"

"Safety. Look, that's a whole story on its own and a complete history lesson which I don't think I'm up for at the moment. I've been awake all night studying the professor's notes from the beginning. They started in 2019, by the way. That's twenty-seven years ago, two years before I was born. Like I was saying, I was walking around topside which was just...breathtakingly beautiful despite the starkness of it all. It's arid and desolate up there but I found it to be the most exhilarating experience of my life, sleeping under the stars for the first time, seeing the sun, running, jumping, free..."

"You weren't free before that?"

"No, I was trapped, much like you for all my life. Then a week after walking around touching everything, smelling the soil, the flowers, the trees, I found a huge fenced off paddock with all these identical dunes. They didn't look like a natural part of the landscape so I wanted to investigate. When I touched a piece of metal sticking out of one of the mounds, it started a landslide which saw me ending up in an old opal mine by the look of it.

"We moved to Cooper Pedy, in central Australia, you see? Before the beginning of the dark days."

"Dark days? Did the lights go out?"

"Expression of the times rather than an accurate description of the scenery topside. No, they were dark for reasons of utter sadness and hardship. I'll come to that eventually but not now. Right now, I'd like to explain how I got to be here, talking to you and what I discovered after all that reading last night.

"I slid down a long incline on my arse..." Adam heard Penelope giggling, which made him smile. "When I landed on the bottom, everything behind me and above me was blocked off. I couldn't see anything at first because I went from bright sunshine to total darkness. I was choking on the dust and had no idea where I was. When I located my portable lantern I found myself in a long tunnel with no exit that I could see. But it was still very dusty and I couldn't make out much at all. Without any possibility of an exit behind me, I had no choice but to move forward..."

"What's an...opal mine?"

"An opal is a semi-precious stone here and people used to dig tunnels underground to find it."

"What for?"

"Well, to sell it mainly, to make a living. Can we leave the questions for after, please?"

"Mama always said if I didn't know something I should ask a question."

"As long as you don't keep interrupting me, I don't mind if you save them for later. Anyway, I'll skip some parts. I ended up finding the Professor and his students in a dormitory of sorts. They...had all passed away a very long time ago, I'm sorry to say. I ended up finding some provisions which I transported to the main chamber where I saw all the old tech. and mech."

"Tech and..."

"Holy Pando, stop with the...okay, okay, sorry. Tech. for technical stuff and mech. for all the hardware, the mechanical stuff. There was a bunch of old computers and monitors as well as a whole heap of what looked like medical equipment to keep track of the subjects...er...people in the study. Parts of the tunnel kept caving in, so I had no option but to close off this chamber and stay here.

"The bit of metal I touched up top? It seems that was part of a solar farm for collecting energy from the sun. I figured out that it was there to charge the huge number of batteries I found in the main chamber here. There are two huge metal doors that I can't open next to a large pane of glass which was opaque at first. Next to that window was a set of electrical type switches. When I flicked one of them on, the window cleared and I saw what I believe is the colony site. Your colony site. I saw the red-stained chutes with the hatches on the outside leading to what appeared to be habitats built into the cavern walls. I saw the graves..."

"Could...it have been a large monitor that you saw?"

"Well, I won't say it's not possible. Doubtful, but not impossible. I hadn't considered that until now. I think we can find out, though. One other thing that struck me when we began to communicate made me think you might not be where you said."

"Oh?"

"Lag. Or lack thereof," he answered cryptically.

"What are you talking about? What's a slag?"

"Lag. Time lag. Mars is a bloody long way from Earth, Penelope. If you were truly there, we wouldn't have been able to talk in real-time like we are now. There would have been long delays between our communications, up to 20 minutes depending on Mars' position relative to Earth at the time."

"How, how far away is Mars?" she almost whispered.

"At its closest orbital point to Earth, around 55 million kilometres. About 400 million kilometres at the other end of the spectrum. According to Donny, that is. I can only go by what I've been taught. A space flight there would take somewhere between six and eight months with the technology of the day."

"You remember things like that? Things like numbers that your father taught you?"

"Yeah, numbers stick in my head for some reason."

"I don't trust you and I don't want to believe you."

"You really should want to believe me. If what I'm saying is true then you have a chance at freedom. If you're on Mars, unless I'm clueless about the current affairs of planet Earth, you have zero chances of getting off there any time soon, if at all."

"If you're stuck where you are how do you think you can help me?"

"A very good question. Now, according to you, there does not exist either a large window or a huge set of double, stainless-steel doors in your compound?"

"No."

"All I can say to that is there must be a covering of some sort on your side of it, to give the colonists the impression of a real-life situation on an alien planet with no means of getting away. What I think is, there has to be an exit in there somewhere with you. I've exhausted all possibilities on this side. The way I came in is a no-go. I wouldn't even contemplate trying to excavate the amount of rubble that's covering that up. If I've learned anything from Donny at all about the way governments work, is that there is always a redundancy plan, a contingency, a back door in case things go south. Well they've reached the south-bloody-pole here and I have only one option left, and that option is behind door number two."

"What does that mean?"

"Which bit?"

"All of it? The last bit especially, about door number two?"

"It's just something Donny used to say and a game we played sometimes."

"Where is he?"

"Who?"

"Your father, dummy."

"He...never mind. I don't want to talk about him."

" Every second sentence is Donny this and Donny that. Now you don't want to talk about him? Who's being childish?"

"I'm not the one coming out with 'liar-liar-pants-on-fire'."

"Well, if that's the way you feel you can talk to yourself."

"Penelope? Princess? Damn!"

Adam was too exhausted to argue. He was also too pissed off to let it go by allowing the brat to have her way. He marched over to the breakers and turned them all off. Then he moved to his cot where he curled up in a ball and went to sleep.

PROOF

The irritating sound penetrated his dreams. It started as Donny lecturing him and whining about his laziness. The horrible whingeing grated on his nerves, slowly transforming from the well-known voice of his father to a female tone. Adam had an inkling where the voice came from, even in his sleep. He ignored it and attempted to recapture the pleasant dream he'd been enjoying before the rude interruption.

It stopped after a few minutes, only to begin again later. By then Adam felt rested enough to rise. He only half-listened as the owner of the pathetic voice cycled through the gamut of emotions he fully expected to hear, including an impressive list of unflattering adjectives aimed at him. From apologies to invectives and everything in between.

He set about preparing some breakfast. He'd made a crude damper during the evening which he baked in a camp oven he'd procured from the kitchen when it was accessible. After peering through the hatchway after he woke, he was dismayed to see the rubble tight up against the porthole. He'd slept through another shift in the earth's movement. The only way out was forward and he saw no way of going forward through the security doors.

*Hell, there may not even be an exit in the other chamber...*her*...chamber. Miss Liar-liar-pants-on-fire's chamber!*

Just his luck he supposed. Out for only a week before becoming trapped again with a juvenile delinquent rather than a Miss November. Adam sighed, then smiled. At least he had food, lots of delicious food. Every day a new surprise to behold in the canned goodness he'd salvaged. *Curried beans! Oh, my, what a delight. Not exactly for breakfast, though.*

He washed it down with a can of fruit juice, pineapple juice (*what a strange name*), that was over twenty years old. It tasted nothing like apple juice, nor the least like anything associated with pine trees as far as he could tell. Once he'd satisfied himself with his meal and relieved himself of his nightly accumulation of waste products, he settled down for some more reading on the computer.

He hoped he might find some information on the tech. aspects of the chamber's infrastructure. Somewhere amongst all the files there had to be a set of drawings and specifications for the installation, with, he hoped, some pertinent details about the doors.

The annoying voice returned each hour on the hour, to make his reading unpleasant. He wanted bloody Princess Penelope to stew in her juices for a while to teach her a lesson in manners. Adam knew it was beneath him to act that way. After all, she was his only chance at companionship and she may well be the last living soul he ever spoke to. It would behove him to nurture the friendship rather than destroy it. He was guilty of being an overbearing and misguided landlord by cutting off her power supply.

He felt guilty. If she was truly just a young girl living alone, having dealt with the death of everyone else in the project, even having to bury them herself, he should cut her some slack. Reluctantly, he ventured over to the breakers, the levers of which he thrust into the ON position once more. He stepped sideways a couple of paces to the window that had instantly cleared again allowing him to view the interior of the adjacent chamber. A flutter of movement in one of the portholes caught his eye briefly then vanished. He wondered if he was imagining it.

Adam considered the fact that he may be already dead and experiencing the fabled 'life' on the other side his father spoke about once. A place where you go before a decision is made about a person's character or something along those lines. *Purgatory!* That was the name of it. A holding area. Donny read from a large book Adam didn't remember the name of about those things. The ideas and concepts within the book seemed absurd at the time and remained so in Adam's opinion. Donny was not a fan of it but declared it wise to at least inform Adam about alternate ideas of origins and life. The contrite voice broke through his reveries once more.

"Thank you, Adam. Please talk to me...I'm scared."

That was a new one. She'd been trying every other tactic in the handbook. Why not give the sympathy angle a try? Penelope Archer was nothing if not persistent and relatively predictable.

"You couldn't know this but you probably saved my life when you turned on the power. No matter how long I pedalled, I couldn't keep up with the needs of the botanical section. I've been pedalling for five hours or more every day just to keep the batteries charged enough for the lights to make the gardens grow. Every year I see more and more losses as the periods of light I can regenerate for the gardens gets less and less. Without that power, everything dies...including me. As it is, the less food I get, the less energy I have to pedal for as many hours as before," she explained with sadness.

"Can't have been me if I'm on Earth and you're on Mars," said Adam laconically.

"I said I'm sorry. What more do you want?"

"What more do I want? I want out of here, is what I want. I want back up top where I can see the sky, breathe the fresh air and go wherever I like in any direction. I want life to make sense again, as it was before with..."

"Donny?"

"Yeah, I miss him. He's all I had in my whole life. I guess he loved me...in his way. I wanted so much to be held as a kid, to be told it was okay, that everything would work out, you know?"

"I know exactly how that feels. We aren't that different, Adam."

"Sounds like you managed to get those hugs and kisses you needed. Doctor Sheba Thomas had a remarkable career before volunteering for the project, along with a host of incredible references for her personality. Her aptitude rankings for the project parameters were off the charts. She must have been one hell of a mother, I reckon."

"Yeah, she was. They all were, at first, according to Mama."

"What happened, if you don't mind me asking?"

"Everyone ended up getting sicker and sicker until they died," she said quietly.

"Do you...I mean, did they figure out what caused it?"

"Mama said it was from the water they found."

"Water? You do know that's probably impossible if you're on Mars, right?"

"Mama said all the signs point to Mars having water at some point in its history. When the supplies of bottled water ran out, and the gardens no longer produced enough condensation to produce drinking water, Doctor Farr said we should drill for water. Mama said they found some and soon after, everyone started to get sick."

"You never got sick?"

"Not like them, no. Mama told me never to drink the water they found even though she couldn't prove it was the cause of the illness. She stashed away some of the bottled water for me. She said it was our secret and that we should never tell anyone about it. Mama had no choice about drinking the water if she wanted the others to believe they had run out of the bottled stuff. I was the only one not to drink the water, but I'll have to start drinking it as well, very soon."

"Why?"

"I have two five-litre bottles of water left. That won't last me very long, because the body absorbs and uses most of the liquid it receives. Only a fraction comes back out again as pee-pee which I can recycle. Fortunately, I won't need as much if I'm not pedalling for five or more hours every day. That's thirsty work. I was drinking tons when I had to do that."

"Oh, sorry. I wouldn't have turned the power off if I'd known *that*. I just wanted to make you see that you couldn't possibly be on Mars."

"Wouldn't there be a way to cut off the power for the settlement from an Earth-based headquarters?"

"Still convinced you're on Mars, hey?"

"I don't know what to believe anymore."

"Your mother and father never spoke to you about any of it, about the project, about the study?"

"Only when I was very young and didn't understand. They spoke to Professor Simpkins about some things which made them all very sad. Eventually, no one spoke about anything like that anymore."

"I think I know what they discussed with Professor Simpkins that made them sad. He wrote about several meetings he had with the project's leaders a year after the start date. The original timeline was a duration of two years minimum to five years maximum. The 'colonists' were provided with enough food and water to last them for that period and longer. The botanical section was headed up by Doctor Maynard Foster, chief botanist, to provide basic fruit and vegetables as well as breathable oxygen."

"Why do you say you know what they discussed that made them sad?" she asked carefully.

"One year after the project was started, the world experienced a catastrophic event, a modern-day plague called Covid 19. According to Donny, by mid-2020, the globe was in the thrall of a major pandemic, wiping out millions of citizens, mainly older and more vulnerable types. According to Professor Simpkins' notes, it was agreed that the safest place for the project's inhabitants was to remain where they were, completely isolated. Everyone involved with the project had committed to a maximum of five years in any case, so no one needed to leave at that point.

"What was it, this Covid?"

"A coronavirus. A virus that originated in an animal and was transferred to humans. It was believed to have started in China at a wet market in the city of Wuhan. The entire globe went into many lockdowns to prevent the spread of the virus. The economies of several countries teetered on the brink of bankruptcy close to the end.

"Mutations of the original virus were popping up as the world poured billions, trillions of dollars into vaccine research and eventually distribution when a few had been developed. That went on for many months with the Wu-flu, as they began calling it, undergoing mutations into more virulent and infectious strains, taking many more lives than was ever predicted."

Adam hung his head for a moment as he tried to control the depressive onslaught from taking over. Over the following hours, Adam filled Penelope in on the salient points of history delineating a dark stain on humanity's report card. Most notably, because he had inside intelligence handed down to him by his father who ranked highly in the Australian government at the time, Adam was aware of the reasons for much of the devastation felt by Australia as a consequence.

A young Australian with a Chinese heritage managed to infiltrate a scientific institute at the heart of the rumour mill, touted by a brash American President as the cause of the global pandemic. The Wuhan Institute of Virology, located near the Wuhan markets was suggested as a possible cause for the virus when it became known they were dealing with and experimenting with coronaviruses at the institute.

Mnim Hing Lung penetrated as deeply as possible into the institute's hidden layers of secrecy. He became aware of a fellow scientist, Dr Wing, whose wife was among the first people to contract the virus in Wuhan. She was a fishmonger dealing mainly in frozen products which she sold at the Wuhan markets. Mei Wing died as a result of her infections. Dr Wing tested negative for the virus when he was tested ten days later. It was said the delay in testing the close contact of an infected patient was the reason a connection was never made.

In a very minor incident at the institute days before the first cases appeared, and unknown to Doctor Wing, he acquired a needle puncture to his hazmat suit during his working day handling very dangerous pathogens, which allowed several viral particles to enter his suit. Showing zero symptoms, the doctor was completely unaware that he had contracted a coronavirus and that he had infected his wife as a result. His wife went on to transfer her particles of contaminated breath and hands to the fish she handled, then sold on to her customers.

The connection between the doctor and his wife was never put forward as he had tested negative ten days after she passed away and the world became aware of a new coronavirus which the Chinese government tried to blatantly conceal.

Australia had soured its relations with China later when it called for an independent investigation into the virus. China, to save face and possibly avoid recriminations or worse, compensations, to the world at large, puffed out its chest and began slapping tariffs and embargos on many of its Australian imports. The seed had been planted then for the series of unfolding events.

The virus mutated again and again with ever-more aggressive strains and variants until vaccines that nine-tenths of the global population had accepted, became useless. Worse than useless in fact, because many people died as a result of vaccines that were rushed through too quickly to ascertain their efficacy or long-term safety.

A leaked top-secret Australian document reached the eyes of Chinese Communist party officials, describing Australia's intention to publish its findings throughout the globe, placing the blame for the pandemic squarely on China's shoulders. The threat of worldwide condemnation and the possibility of crippling compensation suits being brought upon them prompted Beijing to act; with a devastating nuclear assault.

For only the second time in the history of the world had a deliberate nuclear detonation occurred during a conflict. China unleashed its formidable arsenal against Australia, daring the United

States, Australia's closest ally to retaliate in defence of the small country. Bogged down in the political rhetoric of diplomacy, the USA did not intervene until it was too late.

The two superpowers exchanged several nuclear blasts to minor cities, then everything fell silent with no one emerging as a clear victor, though both sides claimed it. Australia had been the clear and certain victim, losing most of its cities along the eastern seaboard as well as central cites, like Alice Springs. The nuclear fall-out affected most of Australia and their close neighbours, Papua New Guinea, The Solomon Islands and New Zealand, with some Indonesian islands affected as well.

"Was that it?" asked Penelope respectfully.

"Not by a long shot. The virus was still rampant when the bombs fell. Millions of Australians died as a direct result of the bombs landing on the major cities. Tens of millions more died from the nuclear fallout, radiation poisoning, which I suspect made your project peers sick after tapping into a contaminated water source. Then came the nuclear variant, the virus to end all viruses. With a fatality rate of 100%, and the aerosolised virus capable of indefinite sustained life in the air, Australia was closed down to the world. Nothing came in or left from that moment.

"Donny saw the writing on the wall when he found out about the results of the infiltration. He urged his fellow politicians not to act on the information until measures had been taken to ensure the safety of the country, to ensure American forces were stationed in Australian waters to ward off any pre-emptive strikes by China. They wouldn't listen.

"He went off to purchase a block of dirt in Coober Pedy, somewhere an almost certain conflict was not likely to reach. He knew China was ready to flex its muscles. He knew they could not afford to lose face in front of the global audience. They would act without any notion of guilt or remorse. Donny finally moved them away, when my mother fell pregnant with me. I was born at the end of 2021, one of the Pando-babies. By the end of 2022, Australia had been all but wiped out by the nuclear version of Covid. If they didn't perish from the contamination in the air and water, they died from the super-virus.

"Last Donny knew, America had suffered casualties but was regrouping well. The rest of the world was getting on top of the normal virus and China was sitting, grim-faced, at world conferences, seemingly unaffected by three of their cities reduced to nuclear rubble during the brief conflict with the USA. Russia and North Korea were in an alliance with China against the democratic countries. It was a stand-off that no one wanted to upset. The globe teetered precariously on a knife-edge. Australia was declared a no-go zone by the United Nations. Containment of the super virus being everyone's objective. With a vaccine probably not possible or years in the making, they couldn't afford for it to get loose.

"I don't know if anyone is left alive out there. I want to get to the east coast to find out."

"No one has tried to contact you?"

"Everything's gone. The infrastructure, the main power grid, something called television, radio, and the internet, everything. Not a word in all the time I've been alive according to Donny."

"Are you alright? You sound...strange?" she asked with sincere concern.

"I-I get so damn sad when I talk about this or even think too much about it. I suffer bouts of chronic depression, Donny says. I get over it soon enough but I feel like dying when it comes over me. Like I can't face another day of the terrible circumstances we live in. It just gets...too much for me and my mind takes a holiday."

"Wow! Sucks to be you."

"Says the chick who thinks she's alone on Mars! If the world has cut Australia off completely, how do you think you rate your chances of getting away from there? If the Americans are aware of your circumstances, which I doubt, they're hardly going to mount a planetary rescue mission for one fucked-up kid stuck on Mars, are they? I'd say it sucks to be you more than me. Well, it would do if you were on another planet. Fortunately for you, I don't think you are. I reckon you're right here next to me in the same opal mine. That's the good news. The bad news is I haven't figured out a way to get in there with you yet, and I believe it's my only way out of here. So, more bad news would be that I make it into there and find there's no exit. Or worse, we don't get out in time before the whole thing comes crashing down around our ears."

"I don't have much longer before I have to start drinking the water we found."

"What were the symptoms shown by your group?"

"They all started the same with nausea, vomiting, headaches and runny poo-poo. Everything gradually got worse until they started bleeding in their vomit and their poo-poo. They usually died soon after that. We didn't have any meds left for the later ones and they died in horrible pain. Mama...Mama was last to go. After the great quakes we all sort of..."

There goes that weird childish talk again; poo-poo? This is either a very young girl or one fucked-up adult stuck in a child's mindset.

"Great quakes? What's that?"

"Mama said we went through a series of disturbances. She said they felt tremors for days and weeks. It knocked out all communications with base, Mama said, and our power."

"That more or less coincides with the immolation of our cities by the nukes. Don't you see? Everything ties in with you being here, on Earth in this old opal mine? You were born after the project started, after the virus began. They elected to keep all of you underground at the beginning to avoid your being infected.

"I suspect the professor and his crew caught the super virus because it doesn't seem as though they had enough time to arrange for your release or to get themselves topside. The super virus takes only hours to infect a human and fill the lungs with fluid, destroying all the major organs which then start bleeding internally. Donny said the virus killed as quickly as three to four hours after exposure. They wouldn't have been able to call anyone because communications were mostly down by then and no one would have responded because they were either dead, dying or didn't care. I think it's a pretty good guess that you aren't on Mars, okay?"

"What's going to happen to me? Am I going to die then?"

"Don't give up on me too soon. Just, don't drink that water you found. Do anything you can to produce some water now that the power is back on. You don't have to expend as much energy because you don't have to recharge batteries anymore. In the meantime, I'll be doing everything I can to get in there."

"How can I believe that?"

"What motivation would I have for lying to you?"

"People have all sorts of reason for lying, don't they? Mama had her reasons, so did the others."

"They were probably trying to protect you from having to worry about the situation. Donny didn't tell me a lot of what was happening in real-time until he felt I could handle the truth emotionally. Until I was mature enough."

"I've seen the shows, you know? I know about surviving by forming alliances and that, doing whatever it takes, lying, cheating, anything at all."

"Okay, I have no idea what you're talking about now. What shows?"

"Doesn't matter," she said snipped.

"No, really, what shows?"

"Never mind," she quipped churlishly.

"Wow, you sure get upset easily. All I can say is, I'm trapped down here and the only way forward is through to what I assume is your compound on the other side of some bloody big steel doors. I have no way back the way I came. I'm learning about all this stuff, the project and such from what I've been reading. So, I am just as much in the dark about all this as you've been. Hey, answer me this; if you truly were stuck on Mars knowing everything you know now, would you even want to stay alive there? I know I wouldn't."

"Well, that's the name of game, isn't it? Survival?"

"This is no game and I have no intention of capitulating to anyone's idea of fun. I aim to get out of here and remain alive as long as possible in that hostile environment out there. I'm happy to help you in any way I can as long as it doesn't interfere with my main goal. We can't be together or anything because...well because we can't."

"Yeah, like that makes me feel better."

"Listen, Penelope. Like it or not, we only have each other. I need you to keep it together and stay alive in case I need your help on your side of the door. You need me to bring you suitable drinking water and to find a way out, seeing as your mob couldn't do it in all the time they've been there. Why wouldn't they try to find a way out, by the way?"

"On Mars?"

"Cut the crap! They knew they weren't on Mars. That's only you making all the wrong assumptions. Did anyone ever come right and say that you were all on Mars?"

"The Mars Colonisation Project," she said uncertainly.

"Yeah, I get that. Probably would have been called a mission, not a project if it was a real colonisation effort. I could even understand it being a precursor for an actual mission, but not the real thing yet. Not back then, and certainly not now. This isn't getting us anywhere. You have to start accepting what I'm saying so that we can start putting our heads together to think of a solution. Time's running out. This old mine is getting ready to collapse all the way. So, as far as you know, even though they were in there for much longer than they were meant to be, they never tried to find a way out?"

"They may have when they tried looking for water. I don't know, I was only little then and everyone got sick after that."

"I keep trying to think the way they would have. If I knew I was going to be part of a project to last a couple of years, maybe five, and it ended up being a decade or more, I would be starting to look for a way out. You lost all communications, power, and any hope of resupply. I guess, if you knew you had every chance of dying from either radiation poisoning or a super virus if you got out, it could explain it. Professor Simpkins may have been keeping them posted on current events until communications were lost."

"How do I even know you are where you say you are? You could be trying to trick me."

"Trick you into doing what?"

"You convince me to go out into the compound without a suit and I end up dying."

"Again, why would I do that? It doesn't make any sense for me to be anything but be honest. If we manage to get out of here, then I'll prove what I've said by showing you the evidence."

"What evidence?"

"A few kilometres back from here is a small township. Nothing but dead bodies in the houses and streets."

"Is everyone in the world dead, then?"

"No, not as far as I'm aware. Whether the original virus is under control out there, whether other countries were affected by the super virus...I don't know. In all likelihood, the rest of the planet was saved from the super virus by shutting us down. The UN sent a large joint armada to patrol our waters to keep everyone away and to make sure no one escaped."

"What are we going to do?"

"First thing is I have to prove to you that what I'm saying is true."

"How do we do that?"

"You have to take a leap of faith by trusting me."

"What do you mean?"

"I want you to walk out of one of those hatches without a suit. If you were truly on Mars, that wouldn't be possible, right?"

"I-I'm scared."

"I know that, and I'm asking a lot of you. What options do you have? If you are on Mars then no way is help going to arrive before you have to start drinking the water, even if it lifted off right now, which is never going to happen because we can't communicate with anyone out there. In the worst-case scenario, if you're right, then you help to bring about your end quickly rather than suffering a protracted illness."

"I can last a bit longer in here with what I have left."

"Granted. Not much good to me if I need your help out in the compound, though, and that may be the only way of us getting out of here alive."

"I don't know."

"Well, that's it then. I'll speak to you tomorrow..."

"Wait. Why are you going?"

"Nothing more to say and at least one of us has to keep reading and trying to figure some way of getting out of here. I have a few tech. manuals I haven't read through yet. I'm trying to find a set of detailed drawings of the installation. My priority is to get into the next-door chamber where I believe you are. This chamber may hold up longer than the tunnel did, but I don't hold much hope of it being secure for very long. Bit of bad weather like rain upstairs could spell the end."

"I'm ready."

"What for?"

"To do it."

"Really?"

"Said so, didn't I?"

"No need to get touchy. Do or don't. Your call. If I was in your position, that's what I'd do."

"Okay."

"Okay?"

"That's what I said," she replied irritably.

A SURPRISE

What he saw floored him.

It seemed an eternity from the time he moved away from the benches to stand before the big window. He waited impatiently for something to happen, for a sign of movement. The longer it took, the more concerned he became that he may have been wrong and had just sent a human being to their most certain death. Mars' atmosphere was too thin to support human life and long term exposure would lead to radiation problems.

It couldn't be, could it? No way this chick's on Mars. It just...

A flash of something behind one of the hatches toward the centre of the group, the same place he thought he may have detected a flicker of movement previously, caught his attention. When the handle on the hatch began to rotate, he held his breath. He was almost certain that he was watching something in real-time and not on a monitor, though he couldn't be 100% certain. His limited knowledge and experience with tech. had him at a disadvantage.

The hatch opened a crack with no immediate signs of the imagined chaos. Adam was unable to make out a person behind the hatch through the small porthole. The hatch edged open very slowly. That didn't make any sense to Adam, because the damage would already have been done if it was going to happen. Habitats on Mars had to be pressurised to sustain human life. It was an airlock system. The engineers who designed the installation attempted to mimic the conditions and infrastructure required of a Mars mission with great precision.

When she finally stepped through the hatchway, stooping slightly to get her tall frame through the low arch, his breath caught in his lungs. She stepped out onto the bare ground carefully. Adam stared at her, completely spellbound.

He raced back to the bench.

"Hello, Penelope? Can you hear me?"

"Oh, you're right, you're right. Yes, I have my portable ear set on. Oh, Adam, it's..."

"What's wrong with you?"

"Nothing, why? It's so...fantastic being out here."

"Why aren't you wearing anything, and what's wrong with you?"

"You told me not to wear the suit and nothing's wrong with me. Why do you keep asking me that?"

"You, you have the superbug, you're black, just Like Donny said about the victims of the super virus. They start bleeding internally and..."

"That's my natural skin colour, silly. My Mama was an African American and my Daddy was an Australian Aboriginal. As for the clothes, I don't have any of my stuff from when I was young that fits me anymore and Mama told me not to wear anything from anyone who got sick. Except for a spacesuit, I have nothing to wear. Oh, Adam, this is great. I feel so...freeeeeee."

Adam raced over the window to see Penelope dancing and prancing about the compound. He became mesmerised by the full-figured woman with long black hair flowing down her muscular back right up to the deep cleft of her firm bum cheeks.

"Well she was right about the titties and hair and everything!" he muttered to himself.

Adam continued to watch the lithe and spirited woman whooping and waving her arms as she ran and jumped around the compound. He estimated her age to be somewhere around her late teens or early twenties. The pure joy on her features told of her ordeal up to that point. It didn't explain her odd childishness, though. She was far more mature than her speech indicated. It may be that she was mentally impaired to some degree, or that she was very young when everyone passed away and hadn't had the benefit of an education. He thought that might be it.

He stared open-mouthed at her when she stopped suddenly to begin touching herself, the pleasure evident on her features. Adam raced back to the benches.

"Penelope, stop that!"

"What?"

"What you're doing."

"Why? It feels good."

"Well, yeah, but that's not the point."

"What is the point then?"

"Well, you should be doing that in private, Donny said...well he didn't say it was bad or anything, just said it should be..."

"Private?"

"Yeah, kept to ourselves."

"Don't you like what you see? Aren't I pretty? Mama said I was pretty and that all the men would be fighting over me when I got older. She even said some might like me before I got old enough. That's why we had to live alone."

"I wouldn't know about that. I haven't seen many females other than in a couple of magazines."

"Can I feel safe with you?"

"What do you mean?"

"Mama said men might try to take advantage of me, whatever that means."

"She was probably right but you can be sure your safe with me."

"Don't you find me...ooh, ah, mm. Oh, that felt good. Don't you find me pretty?"

"No, not really, no."

"Why?"

"Well, 'cause you're...you know?"

"What?"

"Well, you aren't the same as me."

"I sure hope not. I'm a woman and you're a man, so we can never be the same. Oh! Mama said sometimes men like other men instead. Is that why you don't think I'm pretty?"

"No."

"Well then?"

"Look, there's nothing to say I have to find you pretty, okay? I'm not comfortable talking about this. I don't like men in that way, not sexually. I just know I like someone like Miss November, that's all."

"Who's she? Sounds like a funny name."

"It isn't her real name, she...oh, never mind. Look, can we drop this?"

"I want to know why you don't think I'm pretty. Mama said everyone will think that."

"Well, she was wrong. I don't think you're pretty, alright? Just a matter of tastes and no need to be offended."

"I just want to know why that's all. I'm never going to learn stuff if I can't ask questions and get answers, am I? And I'm not going to be able to trust you if you won't be honest with me."

"It just isn't important. It doesn't matter if I find you attractive or not."

"So, I'm not that same as Miss November. How?"

"Not the least bit the same."

"Don't I have everything she has?"

"Mostly, I suppose," Adam agreed, squirming uncomfortably.

"What's different, then?"

"Well..."

"Adam, tell me. I have to know."

"Well, she isn't..."

"Isn't?"

"She isn't black like you. She's the same colour as me."

The silence lengthened into an eternity. When there was no answer, he moved back to the window, where he saw Penelope's head drooping and her shoulders slouch.

"Penelope? I, I'm sorry if I upset you. You asked," he said when he returned.

"Mama said that might happen someday. She told me that white folks kept black people as slaves in America, where she was from. Virginia, I think she said."

"Hey, no. That's not what I said at all. I know about that, okay? Donny told me all about the slave trade and that has nothing to do with whether I think you're pretty or not. If I don't find you attractive it doesn't automatically mean I think you are inferior."

"You just said that I didn't have the same colour skin as your Miss November. You just admitted it?"

"That's not... Alright, I said that but..."

"I understand," she said sadly.

"Why is it so important that I find you attractive? It doesn't make any sense. I don't have to like you to work with you or help or anything. I don't have any less respect for you because you're a different colour. I just, well, don't feel attracted to you in that way."

"What if we are the last two people in Australia? Or the world?"

"What about it?" he asked, cringing with the awkwardness of the conversation.

"I think I'm going to go back inside now. You..."

"Wait! Stop, Penelope. We can't be like this with each other. You want out of there, right? I want out of here, so we have to work together. Partners, friends, okay? I can be your friend if that's what you want."

"You're mean."

"You pushed for an answer and I was honest with you. I'm sorry if I upset you. I am. I shouldn't have to find you pretty, though. It isn't important. It doesn't matter anyway, we..."

"You're right, I suppose," she said with a heavy sigh.

Adam then heard laughter. When he returned to the window, he watched as she continued her leaping and bounding around the compound, judiciously avoiding the graves. He supposed nothing was going to prevent her ebullience for the time being, not even the threat of perceived racism.

As he stood there basking in the radiance of her innocent joy, he searched his mind to find the truth of her accusations. He studied her figure as he mulled over the connotations of his words. *Did* he see her as inferior because of her skin colour? He didn't think so. He hadn't had any occasion to form an opinion one way or the other. Donny had spoken to him at length about the slavery movement that started a civil war in the States.

He understood that most of the 'civilised' nations of the world had embraced slavery at some point. Even African tribes were known to practice slavery among themselves, often conquering their enemies and taking survivors as slaves. Did delusions of superiority among Caucasians filter down through the generations? Was Adam truly imbued with the same abhorrent and barbaric notions that saw him viewing a person of colour as being a lesser human being?

Seeing her prancing about the compound looking for all the world like a wild person did not inspire him with confidence. Yet, if he looked at her from another viewpoint he could see an innocent, child-like exhilaration in a person who had known nothing but restrictions and limitations to her freedom for most of her life. He suddenly felt ashamed. Had he not expressed similar feelings when he found himself in the open? Maybe he didn't whoop for joy or dance around like Penelope, but he felt it all the same.

He tried to view her with a more open mind as she gradually wound down her exuberance, almost out of breath. When she stood tall, surveying her world outside the habitat, with her ample chest heaving from the exertion, he saw a magnificent female form. Exemplary, in fact. He could not fault the curves or the magnificent musculature she displayed so openly. The sweat gleaming on her anthracite, smooth skin, and the proud lilt of the handsome face made Adam aware of a growing tightness in his shorts.

Maybe he did find her attractive? His body seemed to be telling him so. But then, that could be pure animal instinct coming out in him, something Donny said happens to males. He said there was a big difference between sex and love. His father said he'd had sex with quite a few women in his time but only ever loved his mother.

Did that mean Adam could be sexually attracted to someone without finding them...pretty? He didn't know. The bulge in his shorts gave him the answer but his mind baulked at the truth. Maybe he had behaved badly toward her? Maybe he should not have divulged what he believed was the truth? Maybe he lied to himself? Maybe he was doing exactly what Nietzsche had suggested would happen if you looked too closely at that abyss, that darkness within? He was seeing an ugly part of himself he did not want to face. He'd always been told he was a good boy. But he wasn't...in the end, was he? No, he'd proven that. He...

He wiped the thought from his mind. It wouldn't help to dwell on that notion. It didn't help his current situation and he had to concentrate on the present. He had to find an equilibrium, a balance between himself and the woman on the other side of the glass. They needed each other more than they knew. It would necessitate a cooperative relationship to see them both escape their predicament. Time was running out for her with only a small amount of drinkable water left, and the same applied to him for a different reason; the threat of an imminent collapse.

Adam moved over to the benches once more. He searched a drawer he had inspected much earlier. It contained an earpiece similar to the one Penelope wore. He pushed the plug into the monitor. The long length of cable enabled him to walk back to the window. He could hear the heavy breathing from Penelope as she remained rooted to the spot, marvelling at everything around her.

"Penelope?"

"Uh-huh?" she answered, hands on hips.

"I want you to come towards me. If you look directly to your right, that part of the cavern wall, and move in that direction, you'll be up against the glass window through which I can see you."

"Really? You can see me through the cave wall?"

"I think you'll find it has a covering to make it appear to be just another part of the cave wall. Professor Simpkins and his crew ostensibly wanted it to look like the real deal in there, making you completely independent and making it as easy as possible for the colonists to feel like they were on Mars...or below, I should say. That's it, now walk forward. Reach out and touch...that's it. See how it moved? Can you rip that covering down?"

Penelope tore at the gauze-like material used to camouflage the window. With age, it was brittle enough to come away easily. Penelope gasped when she spied Adam for the first time on the other side of the glass. She stepped forward to press her face against the glass, peering intensely at all the strange equipment on the other side and then turning her face to stare at Adam, making him a little uncomfortable, especially as she pressed her ample bosoms against the pane.

"So...it's true then. You weren't lying. I've been on Earth all along. Everyone here lied to me," she stated sadly.

"Probably not, Penelope. I think you'll find that if you remember what everyone said accurately, it will probably turn out they never stated that they were on Mars. You were born after every one on this side died. Your people would have been far too afraid of what was happening out here to want anything to do with it. They kept up the pretence of the project to make it simpler for themselves. Professor Simpkins will have informed them of the virus sweeping the globe and that they were in the best possible place to be.

"When the nukes hit and blew out communications, especially if the professor told them about the possibility of a nuclear conflict, they knew it could be worse for them than ever on the outside than where they were. I think they were content to wait it out, knowing they had enough provisions to see them living in relative comfort exactly where they were. Eventually, the world outside would settle itself and they would learn of the outcomes and possibly be set free. But it took too long and the solar panels above were covered by sand during the frequent sandstorms of the interior. You lost your power. I don't know, maybe the breakers were tripped before that even happened. Either way, it all started to go from bad to worse in there as water started running out.

"I see all the holes out there. So they tapped into a subterranean water table, only it was contaminated by radiation and everyone but you perished because of that. You have your mother to thank for keeping you alive. She saved your life by making sure she stashed away some bottled water for you. I have pellets with me for purifying contaminated water. I haven't needed them yet. There is so much bottled water in here, see it over there? I'll probably never run out."

"All that, so close, for all that time..."

"Umm, is there any chance you can put something on?"

"No," she said flatly.

"Really, just like that?"

"Yep. It shouldn't matter to you. I'm just a black person, right?"

"No, c'mon, don't be like that. You asked me to tell you why I felt like I did, and maybe that wasn't even the reason at all. I just...look, I'm sorry I said that alright? Can we get past that, or not?"

Penelope stepped back to look at Adam.

"Well, you aint exactly all that neither, Mr White Man. I coulda done a lot better you ax me," she stated with a soul-sister swagger.

"That would be your mother speaking, right?"

"Yo bet yo ass, Honky!"

"Cut that out."

"Oh? Ya'll don like somma yo own back at ya?"

"If you turn this into an all-out war between us we're never getting out of here."

"Oh, calm yo ass down. I just funnin' wid ya'll."

"And you can stop with the phony accent as well, otherwise..."

"What are you going to do? Tell me how unattractive I am some more? Sticks and stones may break my bones, but names will come back to haunt you."

"Maybe I'll turn the power off again?"

Penelope lost her smile all of a sudden. Adam regretted it the moment it came out of his mouth. He had no right to say that, no right to threaten her in any manner, least of all with her life at stake. He was proving how insensitive he was and probably a racist. What he intimated to Penelope was something someone would do to punish a subservient human or a chattel. Exactly what he had been accused of. Penelope turned and ran to the hatch of her domicile, tearing off the headset as she went.

TENSIONS

He felt miserable. For two long days, he was unable to reach Penelope to tell her how sorry he was, how disgusted he was with his behaviour. He hoped to explain that his life experiences left him with inadequate social skills bordering on non-existent. He'd seen no sign of movement, not heard a word and felt nauseous with guilt. What were once exciting food adventures whenever he opened a new can no longer held any taste sensations. He might as well have been eating sawdust or cardboard.

His exercise regime had lapsed into a pitiful lethargy threatening to overtake him. His depression deepened with every failed attempt at raising Penelope. His fears grew that he may have caused her to do something harmful to herself, maybe drink the contaminated water. He didn't know how long the remaining water she had would last. He also had no idea how long the chamber he occupied would hold up against the pressure being brought to bear by the tonnes and tonnes of rubble above.

He couldn't read anything of the last few files on the professor's computer terminal. No matter how hard he tried, the words meant nothing to him. It was like he was reading a foreign language. Every second breath he took, he peered longingly at the window, hoping like crazy to catch a glimpse of her. The sight of the desolate compound devoid of her exuberant cavorting left him feeling empty inside.

He destroyed the absolute joy she felt at being free from her restrictive home. How she was led to believe that she was on Mars in the first place was still a mystery, but that he'd crushed her happiness with one thoughtless comment was unforgivable. He went through the motions of subsisting. Eating, drinking and sleeping. All without a single drop of interest or benefit.

She was right. What if they *were* the only two people left on the continent? If Australia was still cut off from the rest of the globe and only the two of them were left alive, healthy, uncontaminated or deformed at birth, then the rest of his life would be spent in regret for that one stupid lapse in sensitivity. His monumental faux pas could cost him the only chance he may have had for some company.

Some female company. A most wonderful, glorious proponent of the female form, if truth be told. As virile and nubile as an African queen.

His dreams had been disturbingly filled with erotic images of her lithe and silky body entwined with his after dancing around the compound sensuously. Try as he might he was unable to rid himself of the lustful thoughts conquering his mind and his loins.

The trouble started when he became conscious of the dreams and began to alter the images, the outcomes, the colour of her skin. Instead of a magnificent and proud obsidian beauty, he would morph her into a version of Miss November. However, more often than not, she reverted to her natural state the longer he manipulated the images. It was becoming impossible for him to retain the version he thought he preferred.

Troublingly, further manifestations would see him exchanging loving glances, conversing happily and sharing experiences with her. He accompanied the woman from the mine to explore the landscape above as an equal, a life partner, and her pregnant with their child. Adam arose from those visions with a smile he was unable to remove.

He woke from that dream to another day trapped, by himself, in an opal mine. Stark, abysmal and boring. He thought of the laughter and the squeals of ecstasy Penelope displayed upon the discovery of breathable air outside her home for however many years she had been alive. The infectious delight had more of an impact on him than he was ready to admit.

He peered down at himself, at the rock-hard erection he woke with most mornings these days. His dreams were often so realistic that he found himself with dampness soiling his sheets as he rose. Even the act of relieving himself did little to quell the innate forces causing his nether regions to become engorged so frequently. Donny always said that any man between the ages of fifteen and fifty rarely had a thought that didn't start at their groin.

After Adam moved from the cot he caught the briefest hint of movement from the other side of the glass. When he rushed to the window he saw nothing out of place, nothing new to indicate she had been outside of her pod. He became embarrassed when he thought she may have seen him doing what Donny said others shouldn't see.

After a moment, he sighed, knowing it didn't much matter what she'd seen. After all, he'd seen *her* masturbating and it wasn't the dirty, disgusting thing his father made it out to be. Truthfully, he enjoyed what he saw immensely. So pure, so natural and carefree. He didn't understand how it could be seen as anything else.

He wondered if she crept out and watched him, or danced around the compound while he slumbered. Her stylised movements, tribal, primal, intense and highly erotic to observe. Nothing at all like a prima ballerina or a princess. More like a Nubian priestess glistening with sacred oils and perfumes. The lights were always on so she would have known he could wake up any time and see her.

She would be curious, he assumed, about all the gadgetry housed in the chamber with him. Adam imagined that the solar collector array aboveground had been mostly exposed by the shifting sands and the collapse of the mine because all the soldiers were fully charged, primed to execute their duties in the battle against darkness. Ready to illuminate his path to freedom, he hoped. At least keep the power on long enough for him to sift through every last piece of reference material left to him.

Adam had to get his mind off the problem of the exasperating female and her influence over his loins and dreams. He had to concentrate, get back to his mantras of living in the present, to tackle and solve one problem at a time. No good attempting to eat one's elephant in one sitting. Piece by piece, meal by meal, until the carcass was bare. That was the only way to move forward in life, one step at a time, be they baby steps or gigantic leaps. The journey forward...yada, yada, yada. He hated that he had been so indoctrinated by his well-intentioned father.

It was difficult to understand his own mind from the things he'd been taught; what to think, how to react, what to feel, how to behave. From the time he reached puberty, he had been at odds with most everything Donny shoved down his throat.

However, Adam had the intelligence to distinguish between fact and perception. He could not rely entirely on everything he'd been instructed to take for granted since the discovery that Donny had lied, but neither could he afford to ignore everything the old man said. He would do so at his peril. He understood that. Like testing, testing, testing. Failure to test everything *before* he touched, ate or drank it, could save his life.

Australia was a continent contaminated by radiation from the nukes. It affected everything from the water to the air and all in between. The gross deformities of babies experienced by the pregnant survivors taking the greatest toll on the psyche of those few who managed to avoid the initial pandemic. His mother counted among those to be irradiated by the fallout despite all precautions. Or so Donny said. It seemed odd to Adam that his mother had been contaminated during her pregnancy, yet he was born free of deformities like the others.

Then the virus became infected by radiation causing it to mutate once more into the deadliest variant of them all, the nuclear variant. The superbug to end all bugs. The possible cause of humanity's extinction unless it was contained. Donny said that even before he locked them safely underground after his mother died, people were dropping like flies.

100% contagion by anyone coming into a one hundred metre radius of an infected person, dead or alive, with the aerosolised virus capable of indefinite sustained life in the air, water or soil.

xcept for Adam Harrow. According to Doctor Donald Harrow, Adam held the key to humanity's survival in his genes. His immunity to the superbug would save the world! Adam still found it difficult to either believe or accept. Even if it was true, it didn't justify what Donny did to him all those years. The years of torture as he was subjected to one experiment after another, injected with all manner of evil concoctions that incapacitated him for months on end.

Adam cringed at the amount of bloody vomit and runny faeces he'd ejected over his twenty-five years. All in the name of science, a cure, a way for mankind to survive the ravages of the nuclear variant which would have no option but to escape Australian shores eventually. Prevailing wind conditions would see the virus spread to our Pacific neighbours and from there to the rest of the globe. Donny said there was no way possible that the entire globe would not be infected.

There was no means to contain it, suppress it or avoid it. He said the only hope for humanity was in a vaccine that no one had yet found. Only he, Donald Harrow, who had a wife deliver a son to him with a certain degree of radiation-affected chromosomes, could develop a serum from Adam's contaminated blood. Within his body, his cells, his haemoglobin, he held the key that every nation on Earth would need. It was his duty, his sole responsibility to deliver himself to the survivors in authority, probably somewhere on the east coast.

It was a tall order and a bitter pill to swallow after all the other pills and injections he'd been administered during his life. To carry the weight of such inordinate responsibility left him breathless at times. It became too much of a burden for Adam who suffered terrible bouts of manic depression. He didn't want it. He couldn't bear the load for long intervals. He fought with Donny long and hard to remove the onus from his shoulders. His pleading fell on deaf ears. His arguments were ignored. His life worth nothing more than the salvation it carried.

Donny had told him that there was more at stake than their simple lives. If that was true, then why did he keep changing the departure date one year after another? *If he was so bloody important to humanity's survival then why the delay, huh?* Adam could not figure that one out and Donny wasn't able to or refused to tell him in the end.

All those years of failures and Donny cursing his experiments. The continuing blood withdrawals, the injections of dubious compounds derived from that blood. The aches, the pains and the gut-wrenching agonies he'd suffered to finally procure that all-important success, only to have him be told that he couldn't have his freedom yet. Not for another year, or another, and on it went until Adam could not stand it any longer, until he felt his mind snap one day. But he hid it. He hid it extremely well.

Adam knew he had to bide his time, act as though nothing was amiss, continue to act normally, which included the occasional fight. It wouldn't do to trigger the alarms by suddenly becoming fully compliant. No, Adam had to play his cards just right to convince his father that he was going along with the insanity, his mad-scientist theories and experiments.

It worked.

Yep, Adam had it all figured out so that he could escape. Escape, he did, only to end up down another hole in the ground with some fruitcake as his only companion. A *black*, fruitcake. A black fruitcake of exceptional proportions and unblemished skin. Of long silky black hair flowing to a well-rounded, firm bum. Of graceful curves and muscular legs, the longest legs he'd ever believed possible. Of absolute perfection, if only he had the good sense to see it.

She was right, he was a racist. He had judged her by the colour of her skin, something Donny had lectured him on during their studies of American history and culture. He had indoctrinated his mind with prejudices filtered down through him by biased readings and teachings, from a white perspective. He'd fooled himself by insinuating to her that she was simply not his type, that he wasn't attracted to her because of simple chemistry. There weren't any sparks; if he could defer to that ancient axiom of love.

Who the fuck was he kidding?

Was he mentally deficient? Did he have rocks in his head? Along comes a magnificent specimen of the female form, youthful, buoyant, vivacious and alluring, ready to become his friend if he managed to convince her of the truth, and he casually states that he isn't interested, that he isn't attracted to her! He truly was a dumb-arse racist, sexist, chauvinist pig.

There was the other thing to consider, though. The reason for Donny's reluctance to set him free. There was that. He needed to at least consider that possibility. Donny didn't lie about *everything*. Unfortunately, Adam had only one method of proving him right or wrong and he wasn't sure he should apply that method, if it was worth the risk. He wouldn't be able to live with himself if he miscalculated by taking the risk and it proved to be correct. The results would be unbearable if Donny was right.

Again Adam chastised himself for losing himself in introspection. He would end up in the loony bin as well if he kept it up...if they still existed. He shook his head to rid himself of the confusing and irritating interruptions to a routine he had set for himself. He had lapsed into depressing lethargy and his body was letting him know that it was suffering.

Adam retreated to a corner where he could not be observed from behind the glass. There, he undressed hurriedly before washing himself thoroughly with soapy water. He had to wash the few items of clothing he possessed before they began walking around on their own. He smelled better afterwards. He felt invigorated. He had pushed some of the darkness from the forefront of his mind. After a full and hearty breakfast, he hit the computer with gusto, forcing himself to concentrate on the reports, on the technical manuals of everything about the chamber.

He wore only a towel around his waist as his clothing dried nearby. It was pleasantly cool underground, far from the searing temperatures above. He'd retrieved a few discs from the students' belongings before being denied access to their dormitory, Adam pulled these from his backpack, read some of the labels and frowned at the unfamiliar artists and tracks.

He placed one of the randomly selected CDs into the receiving tray of the nearest tower. Using the same speaker through which he heard Penelope, he turned the music to full volume. Immersing and losing himself in the pulsating rhythms and baseline of the tunes. Before long he was tapping his foot vigorously in time to the mesmerising beat while losing all track of the manual he was supposed to be reading. The beat quickened and his pulse with it. The foot-tapping became urgent and irresistible, his body twisting and swaying upon the seat.

Adam wasn't sure how he'd moved from the chair to the centre of the clear floor, how his towel had fallen away or quite why he found himself jumping and moving in time to the music. He just knew he'd been transported out of himself by the infectious base notes and the electric guitars screaming out their accompanying chords. Whatever words there were to go with the music were largely unintelligible and meaningless even when he picked up a word or two. It didn't matter, he was in it, with it, alive and exuberant for perhaps the first time in his life other than the day he found himself topside.

He was screaming for joy when the final notes sounded and the track finally ended. He was exhausted and exhilarated. He knew exactly how Penelope had felt. He understood her joy and her need to dance, jump, shout and run. It was a complete abandonment of the senses, a capitulation to pleasure, to happiness.

She was at the window staring at him when he turned that way. She had on a strange arrangement resembling a cross between a bikini and toga. He recognised parts of a spacesuit she'd butchered for the outfit which covered the salient parts of her to protect her modesty...or his would be more accurate. She was wide-eyed and peering...downward.

When Adam followed the direction of her eyes he discovered the cause for her attention. The one-eyed trouser snake had once more risen to the occasion. His rigid member stood out from the thick nest of dark pubic hair ever-ready and alert for the hand that would sate its hunger.

At first, he was deeply ashamed, ready to flee back to the discarded towel laying nearby. An impulse overcame the embarrassment he felt. He raised his eyes to look straight at her. She responded by peering back at him. His right hand moved across his body, gripping the solid shaft firmly. With his eyes glued on hers, he began to manipulate it back and forth. Her eyes grew wider if that was at all possible.

She quickly unfastened the ill-constructed garments, discarding them at her feet while her free hand found the moistness between her legs. With neither of them constricted by shame or guilt, they found themselves acting in unison, in harmony, feeling the sheer joy and pleasure that any young human finds with another. They imagined performing the wonderful feats on the other. Imagined their hands exploring the maddening heat and the hidden pleasure points.

Their pulses quickened, their chests heaving in time, their eyes locked and their lips wide. Together they finally gasped as the climax was shared. Though smiling fit to burst, Adam, nonetheless felt rather shy afterwards, like he'd been caught in the act. He felt sensational but he held those guilty thoughts with him. He made to move towards the towel. She shook her head vigorously. She pointed to her ears, then at him.

Adam could see she wore the headset. He guessed that she wanted to hear what he had been listening to. He nodded his head. He walked over to the place another single CD by the same band into the tray. After flicking the switch to ensure she heard the music, he pressed the play button.

With the first incredible guitar riff ripping through the silence, she almost shrieked in panic, never having heard such a thing, he presumed. He couldn't hear anything she said over the loud music. Once she relaxed enough to take it in, she began the same rhythmic gyrations she had seen Adam perform. Before long they were both swept up in the primal, carnal beat, naked, alive and vital.

COMPANIONSHIP

Over the following days, they spent every waking hour together in earnest and honest conversation. Every so often they would share those special, intimate moments as the feeling took them, abandoned, free and wonderfully happy. They enlightened one another with the gaps in their histories. Only Adam held back with revealing his entire life's story. There were some matters he was unclear of and did not see any point in divulging his concerns until they became clearer or relevant.

Penelope had never been awkward or shy, to begin with, and Adam soon learned to overcome that indoctrination by Donny to feel less shy about being naked in her presence. He ached for the day he might touch her in the flesh, feeling the warmth of her smooth skin against his as they kissed for the first time. They quickly developed a strong affection for each other with all the animosity they once felt melting away like last year's snows in the high ranges.

They shared joy for music and watched borrowed movies together on the laptop he had taken from Donny the day he left. Adam had set his cot up beside the window on those movie nights, with a table placed at the foot of the cot. Penelope had constructed a similar cot arrangement on her side of the window. On the table, with the laptop angled slightly toward the window, they would watch the movies with the lights turned low. They each wore the headsets to listen in and discuss the movies as they played. Finally, falling fast asleep as they tired.

Although Adam continued to read the rest of the available material to him, most of his time was spent engrossed in friendship, companionship with a person of similar age. He taught and played her tic-tac-toe on the window, chess, once they managed to find two boards, one for his side and one for hers, draughts and card games, strip poker being among their favourites. The days blurred into one happy moment after another. Two young people engaged in the business of falling for one another, though neither was ready to admit or commit to an official relationship. It lacked the final inclusion of tactile intimacy to cement that bond. Everything had occurred behind the transparent barrier only ten millimetres distant from each other, yet further apart than they could bear.

"Adam?"

"Yeah, Pen."

"What's that you keep holding and staring at when I'm not looking?"

"What?" he asked, startled that she had seen him with the vial. Then he relaxed and smiled, seemingly arriving at a decision. "Okay, I guess you have every right to know. That, my dear Penelope, is the answer to the world's current crisis." He retrieved the stoppered vial from his backpack. He held up the glass vial with the milky-coloured liquid for her to see. "Inside this vial is the cure to the plague that ruined civilisation as we know it. At least, in Australia at any rate. We don't know how the rest of the world fared with the superbug because all communications were lost."

"I don't understand."

"Well, my dad was a top virologist/epidemiologist and a cabinet minister in the Australian government. He had the inside track on what was happening with our spy sent in to investigate the Wuhan Institute of Virology. He spirited away a wealth of equipment and samples when he believed that China would react swiftly and decisively before Australia released the results of its findings to the rest of the globe.

"He began new experiments after the nukes hit, contaminating most everything aboveground. When he got word of the superbug caused by the irradiated virus, he changed...Oh..."

"Adam, what is it? You've suddenly turned even whiter if that's possible," she asked, half-smiling at her feeble attempt at humour.

"I just realised something truly, truly horrible. It always bugged me and I never got it. Fuck you, Donny, fuck you, you malevolent bastard! How could you?" Adam railed at the air while storming about the chamber.

"Adam, please, what is it? Tell me," she pleaded.

After he'd ranted for a while, he eventually calmed himself, nodding as he added a few vital pieces of information together in his head.

"My whole life was one big experiment, Pen. He used me as a guinea pig for his studies into a possible vaccine for the superbug. Once he was underground, though, with his wife pregnant, he had no further access to the subjects he required to complete his mission. Shit! Fuck! He needed access to the pregnant mothers who contracted the superbug, giving birth to the deformed babies he had been hearing about. He always said...lying cunt, that my moth...mother accidentally became infected by drinking some bottled water he hadn't got around to testing and purifying.

"He lied Pen, he...lied. The bastard infected her. He deliberately gave her the superbug while she was pregnant with me. I wasn't born deformed. *I* was born with natural immunity to the superbug. He kept me locked up in a laboratory while he conducted his experiments on me to provide a vaccine derived from my blood. He subjected me to unimaginable horrors and torture. All in the name of science. He killed his wife! MY MOTHER! He experimented on his son for twenty-five years, Penelope, me!"

Adam broke down and wept hard and long.

"I'm so, so sorry, Adam. Please keep going. I know how difficult it is, but I'd like you to explain the rest, the vial?"

Looking at her through the glass with a tear-streaked and dirty face, Adam pulled himself together. He nodded solemnly.

"Well, the rotten bastard did it. He managed to create a vaccine for the superbug, though it had yet to be tested. He had complete faith in it, he said. It cost him a wife...and a son because I now hate him with every ounce of my body. He said everything he did was geared for the day I would finally leave the lab and the underground bunker to give the cure to the world. He trained and taught me everything he knew so I would be prepared and able to make my way once I was topside, to get to the east coast and find what was left of life and his name would go down in the chronicles of history as its saviour.

"Only, he kept delaying my release for some reason. He studied my blood samples day and night and kept shaking his head, refusing to tell me why he lied, why he changed his mind. He kept me behind glass, Pen. All my life, I never had the benefit of another human touching me. When he did enter my room through the airlocks, he was dressed in a full hazmat suit. Mostly, he would use a pair of thick rubber gloves attached to the plexiglass shield to handle me when I got older. I was isolated. Alone

"Well, I made up my mind, Pen. The world isn't going to get the first crack at the bloody cure if I make it out of here."

"No?"

"No."

"What then?"

"You."

"Hey? What about me, Adam?"

"I'm going to give it to you, Pen. You aren't immune to any of it having been locked up down here all that time. Not the original Covid 19, not the first variants and certainly not the superbug. I've made up my mind, Pen. You deserve a shot at real life when we get out of here and there's only one way that can happen."

"I'm flattered, honoured really, but..."

"No, Pen. You can't feel guilty. You and I have both been brought up in a bubble and we deserve our chance. We didn't ask for any of this and..."

"What is it?"

"Well, I couldn't bear to be without you, Pen. Penelope, I love you."

Adam peered at her through the glass completely besotted by his first love, never conceding for one moment that his limited experience might be exaggerating his feelings. He believed his feelings to be reciprocated. When he did not hear the response he expected, his eyes grew moist.

"Oh, Adam, don't look at me like that. Of course, I love you too. I would have thought you could see that."

"You do?"

"Sure, I said so, didn't I? Only..."

"What is it?"

"Well you aren't doing much to get us together, Adam," she stated with a pout.

"Pen, I've tried everything including attacking this glass with what I have. I don't know what else to do. I'm out of ideas."

"Yeah, I get it. I know. Pity, we could have had a great life and made lots of babies if we were together. I'd like to have a baby...with you."

"Not so sure about babies, Pen. You really want to bring a life into that mess up there."

"It can't be that bad, surely?"

"Well, right above here is okay if nothing has dramatically changed since I left. It's all the rest, what we may come across if we try to make it to the coast."

"You want to go ahead with that plan of your father's. I thought..."

"Don't worry, you get the vaccine, Pen. But we owe it to the world to at least try to get the cure to them."

"How would that work?"

"I have all his notes on a memory stick and they have me to draw blood from."

"You'd allow them to use you the same way your father did?"

"Not the same way, no. They could draw blood from me in staged intervals but nothing else. Besides, they wouldn't need to do it all again if they have Donny's notes. He documented everything he did, all the sequencing, numbered experiments, the lot. He did all the work. They only have to duplicate the serum and synthesize it or grow it or whatever it is they have to do to mass-produce it. Only, I'm going to take Donny's name off it. He doesn't deserve the accolades for the torture he put me through, for murdering my mother. His name will never be known for anything but what I tell them about him, and that will not be complimentary."

"You want me to go with you?"

"Of course, Pen. I don't know that I'd want to go on without you."

"So why aren't you doing anything? I find it hard to believe what you say when..."

"Pen? What's wrong?" Adam sensed a sudden wave of sadness descending on her.

"I, I've probably got about one or two days of uncontaminated water left."

"Holy Pando!"

"What is that you keep saying?"

"Well, I'm a Pando baby, right? Born during the pandemic?" She nodded uncertainly. "Well, when I was young, Donny had these recordings of a very old show, in black and white. I forget the name of it now, some kind of superhero thing. Well, the hero's sidekick always came up with these lame sayings which reflected on each crisis at the time. I came up with Holy Pando and it sort of stuck with me. Donny used to laugh every time I'd say it."

"Adam?"

"Yeah, Pen?"

"I'm scared. Won't you do something?"

"Yeah sure, I'll just pull a magic wand out of my arse and get us free."

"So much for loving me!" said Penelope as she stormed out of the compound, straight into her domicile.

"Pen? Come back. I-I'm sorry okay? I'm as frustrated as you are. I don't know what else to do. It would take some sort of natural disaster to...budge...doors..."

Adam's voice dropped as a new thought engaged him, a distant memory of something he'd read in the manuals. Something about natural disasters. There was a contingency in the event of an earthquake or flood. He couldn't bring about an event like that but he might...get the tech. to think it was happening. He'd fiddled around with tech. often enough to have a basic understanding of the coding. Donny always said he was gifted in that area. Adam was told that he'd most likely have become a tech person if the world hadn't gone to crap.

He needed to access the mainframe, the back end. The professor's terminal probably had the authorisation to get into the coding...he hoped. He jumped from the cot to race over to the terminal. He swept away an accumulation of food containers and rubbish he'd neglected to clear away. He'd been sloppy. Penelope was right, he hadn't been trying hard enough to get them out and remain positive. He'd allowed himself to get carried away with the new friendship to the exclusion of all else, including the cleanliness of his environment and his hygiene.

He looked about him. The chamber was a mess. He couldn't believe he had let it go so far. Before he sat down at the terminal to attempt anything, he mustered his resolve to clean everything up. 'Clean workplace, clean mind', said Donny all the time. He was right about a lot of things and that was one of them.

An hour later, Adam had the chamber ship-shape once more. He'd had a full body wash including shampooing his hair. It was growing quite long since he'd been away from home. Home? He couldn't possibly think of the cold and stark laboratory he'd lived in as home. He brushed aside those thoughts, knowing what a monster his father truly was, hating him for it and the place where he'd grown up. He felt wonderfully refreshed, free from body odours and sex. How he reeked of that after spending every second with Penelope in carnal bliss. Even the thought of that brought on a reaction below, which he dismissed immediately.

Adam donned clean shorts and a T-shirt, with open sandals on his feet. His long hair, he tied back with a band. He had shaved as well. His straggly beard had finally gone. He felt kilograms lighter. His mind had also been cleansed to a certain extent as he concentrated hard on the task before him. He sat at the computer terminal after consuming a full, cooked, delicious meal. With a strong brew of coffee to sustain him, he began.

The hours quickly rolled by, merging as the day passed into night. Refuelling himself with meals, water, coffee and toilet breaks, Adam worked on. Several times he'd heard Penelope try to reach him. He ignored her entreaties, knowing he had nothing to confer. If he couldn't make it work, he would have to inform her sooner rather than later, but for the time being, he held back. He was vaguely confident in his plan. He had to relearn much of what had been forgotten, making many errors on a sample program he'd duplicated from the original.

Lines upon lines of programming operated the automatic doors. He read through it all to familiarise himself with the code. Then he experimented with it. If he hadn't duplicated the original coding he'd have messed up royally. As it was he saw the program crashing many, many times. It was either a catastrophic failure or nothing at all happened. He spent many hours re-reading every line of code, testing its functions, testing its parameters.

He had opaqued the window to prevent himself from being seen and also to stop himself from being distracted. The voice through the speaker grew more and more desperate, more frantic with each attempt to reach him. He finally turned off the speaker altogether. She was beginning to annoy him. Her wheedling and begging, interspersed with bouts of ferocious outrage, followed by tears began to seem a little contrived to Adam. He was possibly being unfair. After all, she was running out of drinkable water and her life was in the balance. She had every right to be fearful. It was just the manic and volatile temperament that worried him. She cycled through such a gamut of emotions and vindictive curses that he couldn't be sure exactly what he felt towards her anymore.

By the second day, he was exhausted but mildly confident in his plan. He would have to lay it all out for Penelope. She would have to play a part if it worked. She would have to be prepared to receive him...and get the injection. He would have preferred to delay it a little longer so that he could get some sleep. He realised that wouldn't be fair to Penelope who might already be suffering dehydration on the other side.

When he cleared the window, she was right there, with her face pressed against the glass desperately hoping for a glimpse. He pointed to her head, indicating she should get her headset. He watched her bare behind as she rushed off to her domicile. She was, without a doubt, the sexiest person on the planet as far as Adam was concerned. He sighed.

"You bastard!" she spat when she returned.

"And then some," he replied.

Adam allowed her to vent for a short time.

"I think I've found a way," he managed to squeeze in hurriedly when she stopped to take a breath.

"What do you mean?" she asked cautiously.

"First, you need to get some clothes on so we can discuss what's going to happen."

"Why don't you just get on with..."

"No, Pen..."

"Don't you be Pen-ing me!" she warned.

"Alright, alright. I was about to say, 'don't get your knickers in a knot', but that wouldn't have worked." He smiled at his attempt at humour. Her scowl told him she was having none of it. "Okay, sit down...Penelope. Sit, please?"

"Just tell me okay? No more bullshit."

"Whoa, ratchet it down a notch or two. Firstly, it is one mother of a security door with all sorts of identifications required to open it. Eye scan, breath analyser and voice analyser by the look of it. After all that, you need a card and a ten-digit code. I don't have any of that. Only the professor and one or two others are authorised to open the damn doors. I saw some names that I didn't recognise in the coding, probably government."

"So, how do you plan to get around all that, Mr Smarty Pants?"

"Hey, you're the one who stormed off remember? Having a little tantrum every time something doesn't go your way will not help."

"If you loved me you wouldn't say such mean things."

"Stop it, Pen! Stop challenging the way I feel all the time. I've been doing the best I can regardless of my feelings for you. After all, my life hangs in the balance here..."

Just to justify where his statement was headed Adam felt a tremor beneath his feet.

"What, what was that?"

"Just a bloody reminder that time is running out. Listen, we only have one chance to get this right and there's a strict sequence of events that needs to happen for us to pull this off."

"I'm listening," she said enthusiastically.

"I think I've figured out a way to trick the system into believing we're suffering a natural disaster."

"How is that going to help us?"

"The doors have a failsafe in the event of a disaster. For a flood, for instance, the doors will open for sixty seconds before slamming shut again."

"Why so little time?"

"I guess it's to prevent the floodwaters from completely swamping whichever area is unaffected. It allows sufficient time to get people out of the area being flooded then safe again when the doors close. Sure some water will get through but not enough to drown anyone. Always assuming the flooding is a slow process and not a sudden inundation of the entire chamber. I think I've found a way to convince the system that it is being flooded."

"How?"

"Well, it all runs on lines of code, so I just enact the line of code that calls for the flood protocols to take effect. That's the simple version anyway. It took a long time to get to that. That's what I've been doing since you ran off."

"So, what happens?"

"Well, this is very important, okay?"

"Sure."

"We have one minute from the time the door opens. The second it does, I will hand you a syringe filled with the serum. You have to inoculate yourself first, and very fast. In the upper arm, just jab it in and plunge. That easy."

"Oh, Adam I appreciate you wanting to protect me and all..."

"No, Pen, you have to do that first before anything else can happen. Promise me you'll do it."

"Really?"

"You have to promise me."

"Okay."

"Okay?"

"Said so, didn't I? What then?"

"I'll have a pallet with all the food and water and whatever else I think we might need on top. That will be waiting outside the doors. Once you've given yourself the jab I'll pull that through with your help. It'll be bloody heavy and the rough soil over your side will be difficult to move the trolley jack on. That's all we'll have time for before the door closes again. I can't get that bit of coding to change. We have one minute and not a second longer or less. Then we'll be together, Pen, and we can find a way out together."

"Sounds too simple."

"Best plans are the simplest."

"If they work."

"Have some faith in me, okay? I'm a bit of a whizz when it comes to tech. I have to get all the gear ready on this side before I can hit the execute order for the program to activate. You don't need to do anything at all except sterilise the area where the injection will go. You think you'll be able to do it on your own?"

"Do I have a choice?"

"No."

"Can't we jam something between the doors to give us more..."

"Too much hydraulic pressure behind the doors for that. They are designed to save lives in the event of a catastrophe. The doors will close after sixty seconds. That should give us plenty of time Pen."

"Couldn't we..."

"No. I've thought of every possible contingency, checked every line of code three or four times. I've tried adjusting the times, believe me. The program crashes if I mess with the times. If I crash the actual program and not just the duplicates, everything shuts down and locks up for good. We can't take the chance. It's that or nothing."

"No other way?"

"Not that I can think of and I reckon we're running short on time. That last tremor was probably the precursor to another imminent collapse. If I'm caught on this side when that happens, we both die."

"When?"

"When will I do it?"

"Yeah."

"As soon as I've packed the pallet and moved it with everything we need. You need to run and sterilise that arm. Do you have a disinfectant wipe or something?"

"In the first-aid kit probably, if there's anything left in it," she stated sadly.

"Yeah, I get that. Sad times, huh?"

"It was terrible. It sucked being me then."

"Go do that, Pen. We need to hurry up a bit. I don't trust this mine at all. I'm very glad you ran off in a huff, by the way. It got my arse moving and thinking."

Adam smiled as he watched her rush off to her domicile again, admiring that beautiful bottom with the defined muscles rippling through it as she ran. *A divine bottom, to be sure*, he thought.

It was all business thereafter, with Adam racing about his chamber to gather everything he thought may be of use. Mostly, it was provisions like water and food. He had everything of a personal nature in his trusty backpack, which he placed on top of the pallet. He dragged the heavily laden trolley jack to his side of the enormous double doors. He quickly transferred the contents of the precious vial into a syringe.

H shook his head in wonder as he finished with a full syringe in his left hand. Donny would not be a happy chappy at all. He'd drilled it into Adam all his life that they were nothing in the scheme of things; that humanity, the species, needed saving rather than a few individuals. It was so much more than their meagre existence. Donny's entire life after the super virus hit had been to save the human race. His dedication, his obsession would be nullified in one simple gesture by Adam when only one person would benefit from that particular vial. He couldn't be sure how long it would take survivors to manufacture more once they were given Donny's notes and access to his blood.

He shook off the question. Penelope deserved the jab. She'd known no other life either. They both deserved a chance at happiness. He comforted himself with the knowledge that he and Penelope would seek out the right people, responsible people, who would use the notes to bring about hope and a future. The only problem he foresaw, was a lack of skilled survivors having the ability to make use of the instructions left by his father. Giving it to just anyone would be as bad as Adam having a crack at it...

Well, it wasn't such a far-fetched notion, was it?

What was to stop Adam from trying to duplicate the serum from his father's notes? He was possibly as skilled as most when it came to virology. After all, he'd been schooled in it all his life. He didn't hold any qualifications. How could he? The universities were gone. Didn't mean he lacked the expertise. He had practical experience up the wazoo! All he lacked was an official record of his learning. A bloody useless piece of paper to say that he was qualified in virological research. He was, though. He'd been taught by one of the best.

He broke off his thoughts to concentrate on the present. He felt immensely relieved about his decision to use the serum on Penelope. He felt confident that he could duplicate his father's research to create another. Donny had kept him apprised of every stage of the research. He was his father's protégé after all. Dear old Donny had imbued in his son all the skills and knowledge required to duplicate his efforts.

Nodding his head, Adam ruminated on the information he fed himself, testing its veracity, its likelihood, and ultimately, his ability to achieve that goal. All while struggling with the trolley jack to get it into place. Last-minute searches provided extras he hadn't thought about, with one final memory bubbling up to the surface; toilet paper!

He recalled a very interesting and disturbing fact Donny had relayed about the first things humanity thought of when facing a pandemic. It wasn't precious memories like photos or home movies, not gold and jewellery, nor even food and water. No, it was toilet paper! That was what disappeared from the supermarket shelves first when the lockdowns were announced. Fights even broke out over the common commodity in the supermarket aisles. Adam could not credit it, and he refused to believe Donny until he was shown some recorded footage of people devolving into fisticuffs and animal-like behaviour over bloody toilet paper. So, the first and most important thing anyone thought of during a crisis? Shit!

Adam and Donny laughed about that often. It was pathetic considering the lockdowns were not total incarceration. Meaning that folks were allowed to attend to normal activities like shopping, caring for others, receiving care, or some basic exercise. It was madness, pure madness, but Adam made sure he included some toilet paper in his bug-out pack, all the same, smiling as he did so.

Penelope stood ready at the window, dressed in her primitive Amazonian outfit of shredded reddish-white spacesuit material covering her bosoms and groin area. He didn't understand why Penelope didn't simply borrow some clothes from one of the other female 'colonists' instead of resorting to such flimsy ware. Then he remembered that Penelope's mother had warned her daughter not to use anything from the persons who died, fearing contamination by radiation. Adam grew excited as he thought about greeting her for the first time, in the flesh. It would be a momentous occasion for himself, never having met another human apart from his father.

Penelope had the distinct advantage of growing up with a host of other humans, albeit only a short time and at a distance once they became ill. Presumably, her mother protected her by keeping them isolated once symptoms began showing up. Not immediately knowing that radiation caused the illness, Doctor Sheba Thomas would have assumed it was the virus she'd been informed about by Professor Simpkins.

Still, Penelope had enjoyed some contact with other human beings while Adam had not. Why then did she revert to such childish behaviour at times? Did her mother and the others teach her nothing, not disciplining her when she acted up? Was she allowed free rein as she grew? There were still many unanswered questions he had for Penelope Archer. He wasn't overly concerned. They had the rest of their lives to get to know everything about each other, including the not-so-good stuff.

"Okay Pen, are you ready?" he asked when at last he thought he might be finished.

"I think so."

"Good. Now, I expect an alarm or two to go off after I trigger the calamity, so you have to be prepared for that, okay?"

"Gotcha."

"Okay. Remember, the second the doors open I will stick my arm through the opening. You grab that syringe and plunge it into your arm where you've just sterilised it. Then we grab the trolley jack together and pull like crazy. Got it?"

"Hm-mm."

"That didn't sound very confident. Have you got it?"

"Yeah, yeah, okay."

"I have to walk over to the benches to activate the program. I managed a small delay before it executes to give me enough time to get to the doors with your jab. Ready?

Penelope nodded her head.

"See you soon," said Adam with a grin wide enough to take in a banana sideways.

He rushed to the bench where he hit the 'enter' key to activate the program that would fool the computer into believing a natural disaster was taking place. He grabbed the syringe from his pocket as he raced to the doors, waiting for the few seconds it would take before it happened.

The loud shrilling, wailing sirens took him by surprise despite being prepared for them. The cacophony within the reverberant chamber was shocking and deafening.

"FLOOD WARNING, FLOOD WARNING," came the amplified voice. "Sixty seconds to evacuate, sixty seconds..."

Adam was almost overwhelmed by the debilitating noise and the whirling, spinning, coloured emergency lights. He braced himself when he saw a slight shudder in the massive doors. With a slow and ponderous rumble, the doors made a move to part. Before Adam had the chance to thrust the syringe through the opening, he saw a tube reaching through the crack, followed by a buzzing, crackling noise accompanied by sparks, then a sharp pain before the lights went out.

TRUTHS

Adam was awake and feeling pain all over his body. He found himself disoriented and in unfamiliar surroundings. He recognised the area only once his head cleared, by the sight of the dirt mounds to the right of the large window he faced. The opaque window. His mind went swiftly to the doors. They were shut tight. He was on Penelope's side of the window. She was nowhere to be seen.

On the ground before the immense doors sat a small pile of provisions and his backpack beside the light covering that camouflaged the doors. He shook his head to clear the cobwebs, the fuzziness he felt there. He was lying on the floor near the provisions. He rose painfully to his feet. His chest felt on fire. There was a scorch mark on his T-shirt where he'd been...electrocuted? Zapped! He'd been tasered, he supposed, or incapacitated by the homemade equivalent of the commercial product.

What on Earth? Adam could not understand what happened or why. The ear-set that Pen wore sat atop the cot below the window. He walked over to it, clipped it on and called her.

Nothing.

He sat on the cot shaking his head in confusion. What happened? Did he imagine it? Was he asleep on the other side dreaming everything? Did he take that nap after all? It didn't make any sense.

"Shit!"

Adam removed the Geiger counter from his pocket, testing the entire area for any high concentrations of radiation. A reading of 1000mSv could see him being sick. Over 10,000mSv could see him die.

The instrument barely registered at all. He was safe for the time being.

"Hello, I did it, where are you?"

"Hello, Pen? Hey, what happened? Are you alright?"

"Come on, I did it, I won!"

"What do you mean? Won what?"

His questions went unanswered. She was tuned to another channel by the sound of it. She couldn't hear him. He was receiving her but couldn't transmit. He was unable to see through the window, had no idea what she was up to. She had no idea...

"Oh, Pen. You stupid, stupid girl. You have...damn! If what Donny said is true... I hope he was wrong, for your sake."

He peered about the compound with a sinking feeling, his gut was churning like he'd eaten spoiled food. The hatch to one of the domiciles hung open, probably Penelope's. He decided he should check it out, if for no other reason than to get his mind off the horrible possibility that he'd been betrayed. Only, she didn't realise yet how badly she had miscalculated. *Oh, boy, was she ever in for a surprise.*

Adam could not figure why she might have done it, what she could hope to gain. The lion's share of the provisions, to be sure, but at what cost? Wouldn't do her much good. If he was correct, she wouldn't require a fraction of that for the time remaining to her.

The hatch squeaked with age as he swung it open. Moving through the air-lock to the inner hatchway, he noticed how very authentic everything appeared. No expense had been spared in creating an environment that mimicked the conditions and the habitats they would require on a real Mars expedition. It was clever to base it underground as well. Too risky to consider flimsy habitats on the surface of Mars where a single storm could last for weeks, months, or even years.

Placing a colony in one of the gigantic caves discovered in the walls of the Valles Marineris, the solar system's largest canyon, descending some eight kilometres below the surface of Mars, made a lot of sense. Easy to replicate those types of conditions here in the opal fields of Coober Pedy. Still, a monumental effort with an exorbitant price tag, thought Adam as he nudged open the inner hatch.

The stink caused him to back off a pace or two. It was the stench of extreme body odour, urine and human faeces blending into one foul miasma. He wondered if maybe Penelope had done him a great favour. The utter chaos he glimpsed through the hatchway led him to the conclusion that Princess Penelope Archer was most likely slovenly, something that bespoke of a great rift between them had they cohabited.

While Adam was not innocent of the same charges throughout his lifespan, he knew he had to make an effort at some point to clean himself up, as he'd demonstrated so recently to himself. The stench was an assault on his olfactory senses in the extreme. The shambles defied the belief that anyone could exist in such a state. He doubted he could navigate his way through the rubbish and overturned...everything.

It was clear to Adam that Penelope had a very long history of tantrums where she ripped everything to pieces, overturned and broke furnishings, clothes and linen, all of it. No wonder she had no clothes to wear. He would probably find the same conditions in all the domiciles. Five of them in total, purportedly housing twenty colonists each. That meant they extended for quite a distance into the walls of the chamber. Twenty sleeping pods per domicile with a communal living area and a separate dining area. The kitchen, or preparation bay, being nearby in the main area beyond the inner hatchway according to what Adam had read in the professor's notes.

He knew he would have to explore them all at some point if he hoped to find an exit, but just couldn't face the prospect feeling the way he did presently. He backed out of the tube to return to the compound. He walked over to the miserable pile of provisions he'd been left with. A few packs of bottled water, an assortment of tinned foods. He supposed he still had his portable cooker in his backpack. He would use that if he couldn't face going into one of the domiciles to cook food or make...

"Holy Pando...please tell me...ah. Thank you, thank you, thank you. You at least remembered to leave me some coffee. Bloody hell, Pen! Why? This is insane. Why, why, why?"

Adam shook his head in disgust. He thought about drinking some water but changed his mind. He was tired. Exhaustion enveloped him suddenly. He recognised the onset of one of his dark moods descending on him. He couldn't fight it. He felt such a deep and sad loss that he wondered if he would ever resurface from the abyss into which he was slipping.

It was a physical shroud that covered him within its misery and weighed him down like it was made of pure lead. His breathing became laboured, he shook with dread and sweated profusely. He wondered if perhaps he had acquired the virus, such was the severity of the symptoms. But he knew better. He was succumbing to the desolation of his mind, the self-pity eating away at him until Adam no longer existed. His eyes remained dry despite his wish to cry. He felt only the advancing waves of doom crushing his spirit, tearing at his confidence, levelling his self-esteem, grinding it to nothingness. The onerous juggernaut advanced, bulldozing any attempt to stand against it, crushing every molecule of positivity. Had he ever believed in religion, he would have believed he was sinking into Satan's lair.

He staggered over to the cot below the window where he curled up into a foetal ball and drifted away into his personal asylum. All thoughts were banished to the nether regions of his mind as he fell victim to the crushing and devastating onslaught of despair.

He hadn't realised he'd fallen asleep until he awoke several hours later. At first, he did not recognise where he was. When it all came back drifting slowly back to him, he sighed heavily and stood up. His head-set had come off during his slumber so he didn't hear anything coming through to him. The window was clear again with Penelope thumping against it with her fists in a demented rage.

With his back to the window, he could hear a very faint sound coming from that direction but paid no attention to it. He had a feeling he knew what it was. He didn't care. Nothing mattered anymore. He was hungry but didn't want to eat. Thirsty without feeling like drinking. In all honesty, he didn't feel like breathing. He wandered aimlessly about the expansive compound. He ventured over to the Rover. He cast his eyes over the vehicle without much interest.

His mind required more sleep even though his body was well-rested. Adam opted to explore one of the other domiciles in the hope of finding a clean one in which he might grab a few more winks. Away from...everything. He opted for the farthest one on the left. Number one. When he entered the inner hatch he was pleasantly surprised to see it largely intact and relatively free of clutter or smell. He walked through the communal living area, down the main hallway to the line of sleeping pods he knew would be there. Ten to a side, just as he'd read about. He opened the first on the left.

The stench hit him the second the seal of the door was broken. The putrescence was overpowering. On the cot against the wall lay a corpse in a state of extreme decomposition. He barely managed to back out of the pod without throwing up. He should have known. He cursed himself for not realising that there weren't enough graves outside to account for the one hundred people involved in the experiment.

Penelope told him the power had gone out. That meant her mother couldn't charge the Rover, which meant she would have had to dig the remaining graves by hand. It would have taken too much energy to pedal her way into recharging the Rover. Or she just wasn't bothered any longer. He would make sure to look through the small windows first before opening any more hatches. If the hatch windows were covered, he would not enter and just assume it contained a dead person.

Of course, if he failed to find an exit anywhere, he would be forced to inspect all the sleeping quarters. If he felt it was worth his while to continue with his quest, that is. He may just opt to find the contaminated water and drink heartily of it. He didn't know what he wanted to do. Didn't know what he was doing. Didn't care.

He walked back outside where he saw Penelope through the window. She was peering upwards, talking or was it a pleading of sorts? He couldn't be sure. She turned to face him when his movement caught her eye. She raced over to the half-destroyed benches, to turn a dial. She then pointed to Adam, for him to put his headset on.

Adam looked at the shambles in the other chamber. Her rampaging had upturned almost everything. There was a jumble of wires and broken monitors littering the ground, overturned chairs and even a couple of benches and shelves had been upended. The area was littered with cans of food and bottles of water. Cyclone Penelope had really done a number on the joint. Adam sighed and placed the headset on. He watched her come forward with her provocative walk, silky smooth and sexy as all get out.

"Where are they?" she asked as she approached the window to stare at Adam with piercing brown eyes.

"Who?"

"Come on, I won. Last one. I deserve the prize. What is it, by the way?"

"I have absolutely no idea what you're talking about," said Adam shaking his head sadly.

"Come on Ad..." she cleared her throat. "Come on Adam. It's over, I won, damn it."

"Won what?"

Cough, "I'm the last one," she said touching her throat.

"Oh, yeah, I get that. You're the last one left from your experiment, so what? Do you expect a medal for that or something? What did you do? Why?"

"Oh, don't give me that look. You knew it had to be this way. I had to be the one, the last one."

"I meant nothing to you? It was all...bullshit?"

"What? Expecting happily ever after or something? Only works in the stories Mama told me way back when."

"So, nothing, then?"

"I did what had to be done to play the game to its conclusion."

"That...that sounds like a well-rehearsed line."

"I said it good, didn't I? Been practising that one."

"Why, Pen, why?"

"Oh, would you stop pretending already? You know why otherwise you wouldn't be here. You're the last minute-ringer sent in to upset the apple cart. Took them long enough, though. I figured it out. I'm smart, see. I seen all the moves and all the schemes. Lucky, otherwise I woulda fallen for it. Fallen for your whacky story."

Cough, cough.

"What's the matter, sore throat?"

"Just a bit scratchy."

"Wait! Did you... Penelope, did you inoculate yourself?" asked Adam in a dreaded whisper.

"Not yet. I have plenty of time for..."

"NO! Damn it, Penelope, damn it!"

"What?"

"You don't have time."

"Might be a while before I get topside and if what you said was true and there is a virus up there then I'll be safe if I give myself the cure before they get here."

Adam walked away from the window, shaking his head. "You've just signed your death warrant. The inoculation wasn't for if we made it topside. It was for me."

"You?"

"Yeah, Penelope, me. It was to safeguard you against *me*. The whole reason Donny wouldn't let me out when the time came was because I was not only immune to the superbug, I was also a super-spreader. I didn't believe him at first. Then he got sick after exposure to me. I hoped it was just a coincidence, but I wanted to play it safe with you all the same. You had to inject yourself immediately. It's too late now. It's not a cure, Penelope. It's a preventative, a vaccine. Its efficacy is redundant after the fact. In some ways, it may be worse. It may delay the end for you, something you do not want."

"Crapola, you're just playing the game again..."

"What the hell is this game you're talking about?" he said whirling around to face the window, furious with her.

"Please tell me the truth, I think I deserve it now, after playing the game for all these years. When will they come for me?"

"You're not making any sense. Who? Who do you think is coming for you? What game?"

"You aren't the only one who watched old shows with your parent, Adam. I saw them. All of them. My Mama had all of them recorded for her. It was her favourite she said. Only, I knew it was more than that. She was trying hard to tell me something without admitting it outright. She was preparing me by showing me the old recordings. I finally figured it out and knew I had to start playing the game. I learned. I did it. I survived. I am the last survivor to leave the island. My flame was never extinguished."

Adam looked at her with a growing realisation. She had spent far too long on her own. Her mind was going, if not gone. He understood that Penelope was stark-raving mad, bonkers. He had no idea what she was waffling on about. He remembered she had mentioned some show soon after they met. Having never seen whatever show she spoke about, he had no reference point on which to engage.

"Penelope, listen to me. I wasn't lying about anything I said to you. Everything happened exactly as I explained it. I stumbled into all of this by accident. It wasn't by grand design, not a conspiracy to do you out of anything you perceive to be happening. This...game you think we're playing, I haven't heard about it, or know anything at all about it. I'm not a part of it. All of this, the professor and the mine and the habitat here on this side of the glass, I knew nothing about it until I started reading. I was the one who figured out you weren't on Mars, for fuck sake!"

"Oh, you're good. You are so, so good. You almost had me believing. Almost. You even created tension points to get me going, to make me believe it wasn't an act. The whole racist thing was a good one. If you'd simply gone along with everything, if you were totally nice then I would have had you sussed from the get-go."

Cough, cough.

"You're sick, Pen. You have the superbug and you're going to die a horrible death. The cough is the first symptom. Have you eaten any of the food in there yet?"

"Yeah, what is it with that. It all tastes the same, like nothing. I opened three different cans and..."

"It's another symptom of the virus; loss of taste and smell. You could eat shit right now and taste nothing."

"Bullshit!"

"Alright, you could eat bullshit right now and taste nothing."

"Very funny," she said without smiling.

"You aren't laughing, though, are you? You already feel the sore throat. You probably feel a little feverish already. I see the sheen on your skin, Penelope. You're hot aren't you?"

"Yo bet yo ass, ahm hot, honey!"

"Joke all you want, but the signs are there. You're breathing is going to get more and more painful. Like breathing razor blades Donny said."

"What?"

"Oh, yeah. Judging by your hairy legs, you have no idea what a razor blade is, do you? Um, like swallowing sharp knives."

"No, no, this is more of your trickery. It won't work on me Adam, I'm too smart."

"Smart? Far, far from it. But then you wouldn't know about that, would you? A dumb person probably doesn't know they're dumb. You especially, having lived alone for most of your life; no one to compare yourself to."

"More lies, tricks and mind games..."

"No, I'm not trying to convince you of anything anymore. You'll find out soon enough. It took Donny a day to die a very painful death, gasping for air, bleeding from most orifices. Internal bleeding as well. That's why they turn black, you see? All the major organs begin to break down and bleed out. In your case that won't show, I suppose. That's why I thought you had it at first. Never saw a black person in the flesh before you. I should have followed those first instincts and had nothing whatever to do with you. Should have stuck to being a racist."

"Ooh, that's mean."

"Says the bitch who suckered me into believing she cared for me? Led me on in any way she could, just so I could figure out a way for her to get into that chamber after electrocuting me?"

"Don't be so melodramatic. It was just a jolt to knock you out for a while."

"What was it?"

"Just something Mama made when it looked like some of the men were looking to take over. Things got pretty rough down here for us."

"All that pretending to get *into* the chamber I was trying to get out of. Doesn't make much sense."

"When they come..."

"Idiot! There isn't anyone left up there. They're all dead, you dingbat! Even if there were a few odd survivors up there walking around a desert for no good reason, they have no way of getting in there with you because the tunnels collapsed. Which part of that didn't you get? You felt the tremors the same as me. Look at the dirt build-up behind the hatch over there behind you. Tried getting out that way yet?"

"You can't fool me. I know they're coming. I won," she said with a manic zeal that left Adam with very little doubt that she had diminished possession of her faculties.

"Yeah, Pen. You won...the booby prize."

"I don't need no boobs. I got my own. You didn't seem to mind them, staring at them all the time."

Adam shook his head sadly while removing the headset. He had nothing more to say to her for the time being. She was incapable of rational thought or discussion. He was a fool. He'd been played like a cheap instrument. He felt nothing but shame for the way he'd behaved and how he'd fallen for her like the gullible idiot he was. He watched as she ranted and raved at him, probably ordering him to put the headset back on so she could further humiliate or berate him.

DESPAIR

The only domicile without a body rotting away in it was Penelope's. The other twenty inhabitants of her wing were presumably interred, one or more to a grave, in the yard. He'd explored every centimetre of the others, including the ones with corpses, his face firmly ensconced within his face mask while he searched. He was very thankful that Penelope had left him with his precious backpack. It held all the essentials for keeping himself safe topside. Though his hopes of ever reaching the surface again diminished with every hour spent in fruitless searches, he persisted.

His severe bout of depression had abated sufficiently for him to continue. He peeked through the large window each time he exited another domicile, witnessing the slow and inevitable decline of the woman he had professed to love. He saw her sweating and breathing hard as she lay on her cot for much of the time. The pain in her lungs would be excruciating as she struggled to find enough oxygen to keep her alive.

Even the ordinary virus, the original Covid 19, could fill the lungs with fluid similar to pneumonia. Millions of humans across the globe were hospitalised with the modern plague during its first year. Then the variants arrived. By the fifth or sixth variant, the first vaccines were no longer effective, forcing the medical researchers back to the labs. When the nukes fell and the virus became a superbug, the symptoms grew worse, the sickness became quicker to contract, quicker to debilitate and totally lethal. No one survived the superbug.

Except for Adam.

Having a mother who was infected by the superbug while he was still in the womb meant he had developed an immunity while other Pando babies were born with horrific deformities. He found out that Donny had given him high doses of his mother's infection, through water, blood, saliva, any means available to him. Donny said her body was kept in the chamber with him for months when he was a baby. When she was no longer of any use, he removed her and incinerated the remains in a purpose-built, gas-fired kiln.

He didn't know he was a carrier, a super-spreader until he finally pushed his father into revealing the truth behind his reluctance to set him free. Even then Adam knew there was more, that Donny was not telling him the entire truth. He only found out after his escape, when Donny lay on his deathbed, his breathing laboured. When Adam explored the underground bunker he discovered the horrific truth that Donny was making arrangements to destroy his son, the super-spreader, for the benefit of mankind. That was when Adam unleashed the beast within, tearing his father from limb to limb, smashing his head to a pulp and inflicting him with hundreds of stab wounds.

It resembled a slaughterhouse once Adam had finished venting his accumulated wrath upon the sick and hapless monster that dared to call Adam his son.

To get out of his prison bubble, Adam feigned the symptoms of acute appendicitis, requiring Donny to don his suit and enter the enclosure. At the very least, even if what he claimed was false about Adam being a super-spreader, he knew his father believed it enough to use it to his advantage. He secreted a small shiv he'd fashioned from some rock samples he was allowed to keep in his collection. While he writhed in perceived agony upon his cot, Donny entered in full hazmat gear, coming closer to Adam than on previous occasions.

Adam made a big show of slicing the flimsy suit open so that his father would understand clearly what he had done. Once Donny was distracted by blind panic, Adam made good his escape, locking his father in the same prison in which he'd kept his son his entire life. It was ironic that the scientist had not thought to vaccinate himself first with his miracle elixir. He lacked the resources to produce quantities of the vaccine. He valued the fame of being the one to save humanity over his safety. His arrogance had cost him both.

Adam vowed he would tell the world nothing of his father. Partly through his shame of committing patricide, mostly because he hated him enough to withhold the one thing the old man valued above all else. His guilt gnawed at him regardless. What he saw when he stared into the abyss and it stared back, was a monster, no better, no different than his father.

A casual glance through the window had Adam rushing to place the headset on.

"No, Pen, no, don't do it," he urged.

"H-have to do...something," she gasped between laboured breaths.

"Don't inject yourself now, Pen. It's too late. It may just prolong your agony. Better to go quickly."

"Fuck...you! M-my life."

Adam watched in dismay as Penelope thrust the needle into her upper arm, depressing the plunger. Donny assured him it would not cure, only prevent. Adam supposed there was always a chance the man was wrong. Penelope may have a chance at surviving in that case. Who was he to stop her trying at least? Only, if it failed and extended her life rather than succeeded in killing the bug, she was in for a dreadful time.

Adam tried convincing himself with the argument that the vaccine was untested for either application, in which case there was always a remote possibility of it being a cure. He hoped so for Penelope's sake. He wouldn't wish the virus on his worst enemy having witnessed some of what Donny went through. In a way, he helped his father by killing him prematurely, giving him an end to his suffering. He couldn't do the same for Pen. She had seen to that.

Adam turned away from the window, staring unseeingly at the compound with its graves, and all the...holes? Something didn't add up for Adam when he followed that train of thought. He'd been all over the compound and examined all the domiciles except Penelope's sleeping pod. He hadn't been looking for it specifically but knew he'd not come across anything like it during his searches. He removed the headset again. He inspected the compound with greater focus.

"What's going on here? Doesn't...make sense," he said scratching his head.

Leaving the compound, he headed towards Penelope's domicile where he battled through the mess to arrive at the sleeping pods. All the pods were empty, in great disarray, littered with empty plastic bottles, food containers, scraps all shrivelled up and desiccated until he arrived at the last one on the right. That one was clean as a whistle. The cot was made, the shelves were intact, though they held little. He walked over to the cot, which was simply a box-like construction made of lightweight materials with a foam mattress and some space-age type sheets in silver.

He assumed it was Penelope's sleeping pod but he had no way of confirming that other than the fact that the rest of the pods were in such bad shape that sleeping in them would be next to impossible. He sat heavily on the cot. The absolute silence was a physical presence, onerous and forbidding. He wasn't sure what he was looking for exactly. It didn't add up. His mind wouldn't accept the logic of her statements until he'd found some evidence of it. He sat quietly, regulating his breathing, attempting to find a state of peace.

The smallest sound eked its way into his consciousness, breaking his momentary trance. He wasn't sure he hadn't imagined it. He had to still his breathing again before he could hear it once more. It was there, extremely faint, but registerable in his mind, in his hearing. Peering about the small pod, he saw no indication of a reason for the sound. Rising to move around the pod made him lose track of it. It was beyond his hearing almost everywhere except when he sat on her cot. He lay down on the cot to close his eyes and concentrate.

Adam opened his eyes suddenly. He turned on his side with his ear pressed hard up against the flat pillow. He rose from the cot, lifted the mattress away and lay on the bare base, repeating the action of placing his ear to the structure. It was there. Still faint, but there. He rose again to stand by the cot. Reaching for the opposite side, he tilted the cot over toward him, then slid the top across the tiles to allow him access behind. The plastic tiles that covered the entire habitat's flooring had been disturbed under Penelope's cot for some reason.

He leaned down to inspect the loose tiles. Placing his finger under one with a raised corner, he uncovered another sheet of something laying beneath the tiles. He removed an entire section of the tiles until he uncovered the sheet. Upon lifting the thin, hard plastic covering he discovered a hole. The sound became much clearer once the hole was exposed.

It wasn't a large hole. It had the ends of an aluminium ladder resting against the inner rim. He didn't think he would be able to squeeze himself through. Not big enough for most humans.

Big enough for a child!

"Oh boy! Are you Penelope or Alice I wonder? You went down there, didn't you? That's where the water came from. I can hear it trickling down there. They didn't find it while drilling, you found it while exploring. Only...that wouldn't explain... I don't know what it means. This is getting weird, or I'm losing my mind."

His brain raced over all the possibilities as he wandered into the compound again. After checking on Penelope, seeing her sleeping fitfully, he walked over to the storage area behind the Rover. He'd spied some implements in there earlier, near the botanical habitat, which would assist him. Back in Penelope's sleeping pod, he hefted the mattock to begin widening the hole. He was careful not to remove too much too quickly, fearing another cave-in. He gently worked the instrument to wear away the edges of the hole to make it as big as he deemed necessary for him to fit through. Though the interior of the hole registered on his Geiger counter when he tested it, the levels were within a safe range.

Shining a torch beam down the hole assured him that it wasn't very deep, only a metre, perhaps two. Once the hole was large enough, he retrieved his backpack. He wasn't all that certain why he'd felt the need to bring along the pack. He decided that he didn't trust the integrity of the entire structure. Figuring if he managed to get trapped in the hole, he at least had his pack with him. He could survive a short time with the basic rations he had, and pellets for purifying the water, a gas mask if needed and his manually rechargeable lantern.

He questioned why he was risking going down the hole at all. Then he answered himself; that he hadn't identified any means of exit above. Not that he believed the hole led to an exit either. He was just running out of options and time. Sooner rather than later, the whole lot would collapse and he didn't want to be there when it did.

One last check of Penelope indicated that she was getting worse, not better, in Adam's opinion. She was bathed in sweat and struggling to breathe. Although he couldn't hear her, he guessed she was crying out with the pain. He felt a stab of regret for... he didn't know quite why he felt the way he did. He had nothing to feel guilty about. He supposed he felt that way because they'd shared a few intimate moments with her, even if he was the only one being honest about their feelings. He regretted the way it turned out.

Tearing himself away from the morbidity of staring through the window at her discomfort, Adam withdrew to Penelope's sleeping pod where he readied himself to descend into the abyss once more.

He wondered what might be looking back at him the second time around. He shuddered at the thought while turning to descend. He placed a miner's torch, he'd found among the stuff in the storage locker, on his head to leave his hands free.

He immediately recognised the hollow beneath as belonging to the network of tunnels created by the miner. His torch beam illuminated the same glinting mineral patches in the walls; potch. The tunnel extended for some distance beyond the reach of his light. It was high enough for him to stand at a stoop and wide enough to relieve any concerns he had about claustrophobia. He heard the tinkle of water in the distance. It wasn't a two-way tunnel. It dead-ended at Penelope's sleeping pod.

Adam assumed that a small hole had formed in the floor beneath Penelope's cot, allowing her to hear the water during the silences of the night when everyone was asleep. When she discovered the hole after investigating the sound, she made it big enough to allow her through.

What he found when he came across the source of the sound proved his theory correct. Scattered about near a tiny pool of water, which came trickling through a small hole in the tunnel ceiling, were several hand-made child's toys. A rag doll, some stone pebbles and keepsakes, as well as some crude, childish drawings.

Adam tested the water. It registered high enough to convince him it was dangerous. If ingested, it would cause severe harm. His breath caught in his lungs when he lifted his head to look further along. A considerable stack of bottled water sat on the tunnel floor in its original shrink-wrapping. Other open packs sat next to them. The seals appeared to be intact and the bottles were all full, though they appeared to have a pinhole at the top, under the cap. He tested the contents of a bottle after opening it. It gave a high concentration of radiation.

On a hunch, Adam tested a bottle after removing one from its shrink-wrapping. No sound from his instrument. The water was clean.

"Oh, Pen. What did you do? It had to be you because no one else could fit down the hole. Holy Pando, what an evil little bitch you are! You made them all sick. You killed them, including your mother. You kept enough water to sustain yourself for quite a while down here. You painstakingly removed the clean water from bottles by syringing it out, then replaced it with the contaminated water the same way. What the heck for? Why, why, why, Pen? When they all died you didn't need to come back down again and grew too big for the hole anyway. Shit! How old were you when you did that, Pen? Couldn't have been much older than six or seven I reckon. You're bloody lucky you didn't die yourself without some... Ah! You did have protection. You used those heavy-duty rubber gloves I see there for filling the bottles."

Adam was impressed and horrified at once. *An evil mind lurked in the body of a very young girl who figured out how to kill everyone without anyone knowing. They wouldn't have been able to figure it out without the right testing equipment. Don't suppose anyone thought of radiation poisoning. The holes topside weren't for water exploration at all, just routine core sampling like you would do on Mars, part of the experiment*, thought Adam.

"You were running short on water but only because you couldn't get back down here, eh girl? No, you would have known to make the hole larger just like I did. You weren't running short on water. It was just another ruse to get me to find some way of reaching you. Well, it worked, Pen. Only, you went off the rails, didn't you? A few roos short in the top paddock, eh? I reckon we're both fucked anyway, mate. This is a dead-end as well. The only thing getting out of here is that..."

Water!

It was dripping steadily from the roof, pooling at the bottom but not overflowing. That meant it had to be going through. There were a couple of possibilities he thought. There might be yet another tunnel beneath the one in which he was standing or the water might be draining into a natural subterranean water table. If that was the case, he might be able to follow it out. Donny gave him a map of the area to study once. He remembered seeing quite a few small waterways, and even a lake or two. Whether the water reached that far was another question. Knowing his luck it would probably end up in some sponge-like geology after only a few metres.

Adam changed tack with his thinking. He wasn't being logical. It was dirty water, contaminated, enough to kill him if he was exposed to it for long or ingested it. Then he recalled the one-time emergency jab. Donny told him only to use it if he had no choice if he became irradiated. It would damn near kill him anyway according to the old man. Donny wasn't even 100% certain it worked. Adam blanched. He'd found the syringe when he rummaged through his father's lab. It had a needle on it like something you would give a bloody horse. It had to enter his chest, directly into the heart to get into the bloodstream.

He retreated to Penelope's sleeping pod. He would have to bring some tools down the hole if he hoped to follow through with his plan. He would need to re-pack some provisions in his backpack.

He was purposely avoiding thinking about Penelope. There was nothing he could do for her and she didn't deserve his moral support. He was lucky he wasn't killed by the sadistic bitch! *Total fucking psychopath!*

Adam breathed a big sigh of relief when he understood just how close he'd come to the Grim Reaper's emissary. He shook his head in wonder at the brazen audacity of the girl at such a young age to figure it out and follow it through. Adam couldn't remember what he was like at that age, but he didn't come close to having a skillset as she possessed.

"Hey, I *had* to kill Donny! That wasn't the same! It... You're arguing with yourself, Adam. Who's the loony?"

Penelope was sitting up looking like death warmed up when he returned to the window. Reluctantly, he placed the headset on.

"...cough..doing?"

"What am I doing?" he asked to clarify what she'd said. When she nodded, "Same thing I've been trying to do all along; find a way out."

"No...way...cough."

"Maybe. Although you look like crap, you must be feeling a bit better to be able to sit up?"

She nodded.

"I have to tell you, Pen, that is not the good sign you see it as. If the vaccination has had an effect, it will only lessen the symptoms to a certain extent over a longer period. The result will be the same. Then again, it isn't proven one way or the other. Only theoretical. I suppose miracles do happen."

She coughed some more before opening her mouth to say something when a glob of clotted blood exploded outwards, spraying the cot red.

"I hate to say this, Pen, but I think you're going to turn black."

He smiled weakly and shrugged. She managed a smile in return.

"You killed them all, didn't you?" he asked, frowning. She turned from the window. "Why, Pen. I don't understand. You all could have lasted for a lot longer in there."

She turned back to face him, shaking her head vigorously.

"No...had...to...cough, cough...win."

"Win what, Pen. What was it?"

"Go...go...my pod. S-see...r-recordings...Mama's."

Penelope laid back down on the cot, exhausted. Adam could see she wasn't able to remain awake.

After removing the headset, he made his way back to Penelope's pod. He spied the folder of CDs tucked neatly into a storage unit. He retrieved his laptop from the backpack, finding an outlet into which he plugged the cord. He hadn't thought to recharge the batteries in some time. The CDs were all numbered in sequences of seasons and episodes. He started with S1E1 in the first pocket of the folder.

After watching several episodes he thought he might have understood the principle enough to make some staggering assumptions. It didn't seem possible to him, but then, he hadn't lived the life she had, hadn't experienced what she had been through. It was still difficult to accept. When he leafed through the rest of the folder without paying much attention to it, a single sheaf of paper wafted out and landed at his feet. It was very wrinkled and creased like it had been handled and scrunched up into a ball many times.

My Dear, Sweet Princess,

I had no idea how this would all turn out when I volunteered for the Mars Project. It never occurred to any of us that we may be marooned and alone here for the foreseeable future. I'm so, so sorry, my love, for bringing you into this alien environment. It was very selfish of your Mama to do that. I fell in love with your Papa and we couldn't help ourselves, I'm sorry to say. Not very professional of me as a lead scientist, was it, Pet?

You have been the shining light of my life, Princess. Watching you grow from a baby has been the single most enjoyable experience of my life and if I had to do it all over, I wouldn't change a thing.

You've sat with me watching all my favourite shows since you were old enough to sit. If you take away anything at all from watching them, take away the instinct to survive at all costs my, sweet, sweet child. Life is just one big game and the end goal is always to survive. So, survive, my girl, survive. I'm so sorry I won't be there to share in your life, watching you grow into a beautiful woman.

All my love, now and always,
Your Mama.
Doctor Sheba Thompson.

Adam supposed Doctor Thompson had written the note to her daughter when the communications died and the power went. The last thing she knew was that Professor Simpkins had told them Australia was being nuked by China. They assumed the worst when they were left alone for more years than they planned.

Then death struck in the form of a seven-year-old girl who discovered a method of eliminating the competition, including her parents.

"Wow! What a crazy world you lived in, Pen. Your mind is out there, truly, out there. You believed it was real, a game of Survivor, and that the last person left would win the prize? What? A million bucks, or something? That is...fucked-up, girl! I thought I was turning into a bit of a head-case but I'm only an amateur screwball compared to you."

ESCAPE

Progress was slow in the confining conditions. It was difficult for Adam to swing the mattock properly without catching the ceiling every time. He supposed the original miner must have been relatively short, never considering that it may have been excavated by machine. He dug around the pool with a small spade first to widen the hole into which the water drained. The pool emptied. He wore all the protective gear he could find to avoid the radiation. It wasn't certain yet where the hole would lead or whether he would have to immerse himself in the water to follow it.

He wondered just how deep underground he was. It didn't bode well for the idea of getting topside, that was for sure. It defied common sense in a way, to be digging down to get up. However, he needed to remain as positive as possible in the circumstances. His life depended on it. He hoped beyond hope that the subterranean watercourse would eventually find its way out somewhere.

He'd checked on the patient before descending once more. She was restless and sweaty as she tossed about on the cot, heavily stained with blood and other body fluids. He felt a smidgeon of sadness for her even though she was a psychotic, evil bitch. He still marvelled at the boldness and tenacity of the young child committing so many murders for the sake of a game, all in her head!

A deep tremor interrupted his digging and postulating. The hole he was digging suddenly fell away in one big soggy lump. The dust settled all about him from the tunnel in which he stooped. Creating a major cave-in was something he was expressly hoping to avoid. He stood in readiness, arms akimbo, waiting for the world to collapse on him.

Relaxation only came when the dust settled and no further tremors occurred. He angled his head with the attached light downward, through the hole. As he'd suspected, another tunnel crossed beneath. Adam knew that his inadvertent brushing of sand from the corner of one collector topside did not cause the chain of events that led him deep underground, but he couldn't help feeling like it did. Major, major coincidence for the entire underground system to have lasted that long only to collapse the second he brushed some sand away. That was just the way of things. If he had played a part in that occurrence, then it was probably just meant to be. More than likely his footsteps had already disturbed the delicate balance of all the components synergising to keep the mines intact...or not.

There was a little greenery around so maybe recent rainfall had loosened everything to a point where it was ready to go at the slightest footfall. Adam shook it off. Didn't pay to think too much on coulda, woulda or shoulda. He guessed he was deliberately delaying something with his wandering mind. Making the final choice to leave the area would ensure the woman above died a horrible, lonely death. If their roles were reversed he would think it very unkindly of her to leave him dying alone.

He couldn't think of leaving immediately at any rate. He needed some well-earned rest after a decent meal and a wash. He'd been awake for a long time and was feeling the tug of exhaustion in his limbs.

In the compound, he saw to his gastronomic requirements as well as some brewed coffee. He felt much better after washing himself with some of the clean bottles of water from Penelope's stash. He emptied all the other bottles containing the contaminated water down the hole he'd made. He washed thoroughly, ensuring he scrubbed every last trace of possible radiation from his skin. He threw away the clothes he'd worn, dressing in another clean pair of shorts and a T-shirt.

He took his mug of coffee over to the cot by the window. Penelope stirred when she detected movement, placing the headset on. She sat up wearily, grimacing at the effort and the sight of the cot.

"How are you holding up?" he asked, genuinely concerned.

"Did...cough...you see them?"

"Some."

"And...let...letter?"

"Yeah, the letter too."

"See?"

"I can see what you manifested from that."

"Don't...cough, cough...know what...that means."

"Didn't understand the words or the inference?"

"Don't under...stand that neither," she said testily.

"You need to stay calm or you'll go into another coughing fit. Look, Pen, I don't want to upset you any further. You're sick and..."

"Tell me....what...mean."

Sighing, "I can see how you might have misconstrued... Sorry, I'll try this differently. You made an assumption based on what you saw and what your mother wrote. Somehow your young mind merged the two things to arrive at a conclusion that...well, wasn't right, Penelope. I'm sorry. Even if you *were* somehow part of an elaborate game based on that show, it didn't give you a license to kill. No one on that show killed anyone by the look of it. I didn't see all of them but I can feel pretty confident that murder wasn't part of the game rules."

Her eyes bore into his with a fire that made him squirm. If looks could kill, he'd have been toasted to cinders. He could almost taste the ire boiling up in her. He waited for Vesuvius to explode. The veins in her long neck pulsed with the blood pumping wildly through them. The muscles there were tense and she was scowling. They locked eyes for an eternity before he finally looked away.

"I'm leaving after I've had some sleep. I hope I don't have to return."

"You...you're leaving...cough, splutter...me?" she whispered the last word.

"I can't stay much longer. Did you feel that last tremor?"

"Not, not sure."

"I see you were at the hatch? You couldn't open it with all the dirt behind, could you?."

"Weren't...cough...lying, were you?"

"No, I haven't been lying about anything, Pen. Especially the way I felt about you."

"Black...black woman?"

"Look, I've apologised a million times about that. It was a stupid and racist thing to say. You were right about that, okay? I was being a naive jerk. I thought we'd moved past that but you didn't, did you? You were the one lying. It was you that felt nothing for me, stringing me along."

"Had...to...win," she said as she looked down into her lap.

"This isn't a game. Not for me. You're right about one thing. It is about survival, but not a game, and certainly not some gladiatorial combat to the death. I don't know if I was being totally honest with you, Pen. I've never been in love before. Never known a woman before. I may have been feeling lust or puppy-love, infatuation. I can't tell anymore. I'm sorry for the way it turned out. I would have liked to spend some time getting to know you properly and sharing ourselves physically. Shit, you may be the last woman left in Australia. Beggars can't be choosers, eh?" He smiled. "Pen, I think we had something whether you acknowledge it or not. It could have worked. We could have made it work together."

"Would have...gotten sick..."

"No, Pen. If you'd given yourself the injection immediately, you would have avoided getting sick. The virus wouldn't have had the time to infect you. Mind you, I might not have found out your secret. You would have done almost anything to prevent me from finding that, wouldn't you? Pretty clever, I must say. Bloody brilliant actually, for one as young as you were. That's how I hope to get out."

"Dead...end."

"I found another tunnel underneath the pool of water. I'm hoping it leads to a subterranean watercourse that eventually flows out somewhere. A lot of 'ifs', but I don't have many options."

"Leaving...me...for dead," she whispered.

"Come on, who left who for dead?"

Penelope didn't answer, simply nodded her head in acceptance of his statement, then removed the headset. She mouthed the words, 'you win' to him before laying back down. She was bleeding from the nose.

He didn't feel like a winner. He felt like shit. The guilt gnawed away at him as he tried to sleep, causing fitful dreams. He had moved to Penelope's pod where he righted the base of her cot. He couldn't bear being under the window, knowing she was right next to him, dying slowly and painfully. He wouldn't hear her but he could imagine it after watching his father go through some of it before he...ended it.

They were both victims of the abyss. Or rather, they were both monsters if they looked closely enough at themselves, into their souls. He was no better than she, just fewer victims attributable to him. He wondered what Donny would have done if he were in Adam's shoes. Heck, that was an easy one to answer. Donny would have done everything and anything he could to bring the vaccine to the world no matter how many dead bodies he had to stand on to get there. 'The plight of the many outweigh the few', Donny was known to quote.

Donny regarded himself as altruistic and noble in his efforts, whereas he was an egotistical, deluded and murderous fiend. Using his wife and child as a medical experiment was abominable. An abhorrent act for which there was no forgiveness or justification. Adam hadn't volunteered, nor had his mother. Donald Harrow was a scientist first and a human second. He was never a father or a husband in Adam's opinion. He questioned his mother's sanity in marrying the evil bastard. There had to have been earlier signs of his deranged personality.

Or did that only appear when the world upended with the modern plague? Did Donny succumb to his insanity while he was trapped underground in a bunker with his pregnant wife? Did he assume his deity-like status as the saviour of humanity by being confined like a trapped animal? Adam thought not. The evilness had to reside in the man first. Whichever way that was released in him, whatever the catalyst, he had it there to begin. So did Adam. He proved that when he tore his father apart in a bestial rage.

Adam was truly surprised when he finally gave up on sleep, to find he had been tossing and turning for almost eight hours. He didn't feel rested. He felt worse than before. He had a headache starting. He hoped it was not the onset of a migraine. No auras, no shimmering waves or twinkling stars that would normally precede a migraine, made an appearance. Those precursors might have occurred during his troubled dreams.

There was some aspirin in his backpack. He would have to find them before the migraine took hold. Although the simple medication would not eradicate the headache, it would dull it to a level that he could bear.

He was stunned to find Penelope sitting up in her cot eating from a bowl of food that had steam rising from the contents, obviously heated or cooked. She appeared clean and calmer. Her cot had been remade with relatively clean sheets. When she turned to face him staring at her, she beamed her pearly-whites at him. They both donned their headset simultaneously, excitedly.

"Hey, Pen. How're you doing?"

"Better, much better."

"You sure look it. It might be the calm before the storm, though."

"What does that mean?" she asked tersely, not wishing her good mood to be ruined by him.

"Never mind."

"No, that's even worse. Tell me what you meant."

"Donny said that when people get sick, gravely ill, they sometimes get better before..."

"Before they die?" Adam nodded. "Sucks to be me then," she said lightly.

"I don't know what to say, Pen. If Donny was wrong about the vaccine, I... Well, it will suck to be you. It would have been better to go swiftly than hang around waiting for the walls to cave in on you."

"They may not."

"Gee, that sounds so much better then, doesn't it? You get to hang around on your own until your food, water or air runs out. No telling if the solar array upstairs will stay put and remain functional, so the lights and power may go out before then."

"Are you trying to scare me?" she asked with a fierce gleam in her eye. "You aren't getting out either."

"I've got something I can try. Any avenue of exploration is a better proposition than none."

"Please take me with you?" she begged pitifully.

Adam saw through the ruse. He was becoming inured to the ways of the femme-fatale. She was able to change personas in the blink of an eye and Adam would have none of it. He was done with her manipulations.

"You want to tell me how *that* could be achieved, Princess?" he asked with a sneer.

"You're the smart one, you'll figure it out. Don't you want to be with me?" she asked suggestively, coming closer to the window with her bare breasts.

"Fool me once, my bad. Fool me twice, my death!"

"I'll be good."

"Knock it off, Pen. I'm not going to fall for it again. There's nothing I can do from this side in any case. You saw to that."

"You can talk me through what you done? I'm smart, I could learn?"

"Too late. Once I triggered the doors to open for an emergency flood, the doors locked again afterwards to prevent the floodwaters from inundating both chambers. There is no opening them again." Adam thought for a moment, "There is a very, very slim possibility that the tunnel I discovered might lead beneath that chamber but I won't be pursuing that. You sealed your fate when you tricked me. You chose wrong, Pen. I would have done everything I could to get us both out if you'd trusted me."

"Oh, Mr Goody-Two-Shoes, huh?"

"Far, far from it. I'm guilty of patricide so I'm no better than you."

"What's that? Patri..."

"Patricide. I killed my father, Penelope. Not only did I unwittingly infect him, but I also murdered him brutally, in a fit of rage. Tore him apart and smashed his head in. When I found out what he intended to do with me I lost it big time. The acorn didn't fall far from the oak I fear."

"What?"

"Oaktree. The acorn is the seed. So the analogy is that I am a lot like my father, an evil prick!"

"See, I'll never get to experience any of that, an oak tree, or any tree for that matter."

"No, you've had it tough, I'll give you that. So have I. We aren't that different at all in our shared experiences, both trapped for all our lives."

"Not you. You say you've been...up there."

Sighing, "Yes, Pen. For one very brief week, I was alone in paradise. Adam in the desert of Eden."

"What..."

"Never mind. A reference to an archaic book that Donny read to me in an attempt to further my spiritual education. He named me Adam for that reason, being the first man, the man to bring the cure to the masses. Everything he did was aimed at bolstering his vision and his ego. You could have been my Eve, my partner in Eden."

"Can't I be?"

"You already know the answer to that."

"Then what good are you? Get out of here and leave me alone you bastard! You shit, bum, prick, cunt! I hate you, hate you..."

Penelope flung the remains of her food and the bowl against the window. She flew into a demented rage where nothing was spared her wrath. Adam could not watch any longer. She was a lost cause as far as he was concerned. She was mentally unstable, a true psychopath capable of heinous acts and volatile mood swings.

Adam gathered the rest of his belongings that he deemed important enough to tuck into his backpack before heading back to the tunnel under her bed. One last look at the window before he left saw Penelope flush up against the glass, pushing her sex toward him lasciviously. Her eyes were completely glazed over as her fingers thrust deeply into her vagina. He turned from the window for the last time, leaving the madwoman to her fate.

Pushing all thoughts of her from his mind, he made his way down the ladder into the first of the tunnels. Taking the ladder with him, he placed it into the hole he'd made below the pool of water. Carefully, he climbed down the ladder. The only light he had was the miner's light on his head and the rechargeable lantern he carried. Some of the other stuff like glow sticks had been removed by Penelope for some unfathomable reason.

He had a choice to make. Left or right. Left could lead towards the chamber in which Penelope was trapped. That alone was a good enough reason to choose the opposite. Although he had a compass with him, it was of no use. He had no way of knowing which way led to a possible exit. His only reason for selecting right other than heading away from Penelope, was the trickle of water sliding down the wall, continuing its journey to the right in a small runnel that ran through the compacted dirt floor.

The meandering rivulet cut a shallow swathe as it zig-zagged across the tunnel floor, altering its course whenever it came across a large rock. Judging by the pitiful amount of water trickling along, it would have taken many, many years for the water to erode the small ditch. Adam squared his shoulders, bumping the ceiling as he did, then trundled forward, crouched low.

Before he had reached ten paces the earth shook and rumbled sending dust and small pebbles down on him. Once again he needed to don the gas mask he'd used previously. The rumbling continued behind and above him. He didn't think he could change his mind and go back. It was either move forward or perish. He felt a slight pang of...guilt...for Penelope's fate?

Surviving the superbug only to be crushed by tonnes of soil did not seem to be a fitting end for such a strong and tenacious individual. Despite her many flaws, he couldn't help but admire her. She'd endured when all the odds were stacked up against her. He had done whatever was necessary to do the same thing. He couldn't very well stand in judgement.

"Let he who is without sin cast the first stone," he mumbled into the mask.

With a tinge of regret, he moved along the dusty tunnel with his headlamp nearly blinding him as it bounced off the billowing dust clouds. He made sure to avoid placing his foot in the water draining slowly by. He hoped that the flow may cease if the newest collapse halted the source. If he needn't worry about becoming contaminated by the water he could feel less anxious.

A thought struck him quite suddenly. He had completely missed it after discovering the truth. How did Penelope know the water was contaminated? How could she have figured that out by herself, without any instrumentation or testing equipment? That was a mystery he may never have an answer for. Too late to go back and ask her.

He supposed and conjectured several explanations as he progressed. More to take his mind off the imminent threat of being buried alive under tonnes of rubble than for procuring a definitive answer.

Professor Simpkins will have informed the project members of the nuclear threat. They will have understood that the percussive blasts they felt shaking the earth would have been the result of those detonations.

They were scientists...or Doctor Thompson, Penelope's mother, was. She would have understood the implications. Adam followed through with that line of thought for a moment. He imagined young Penelope sleeping in her pod and hearing something during the dead of night when everyone was asleep.

he probably would have mentioned hearing water to her mother. If her mother knew her stuff, she would have warned her daughter not to go anywhere near it if that's what she heard, knowing it could be contaminated, explaining that to her young daughter.

The mother would have thought nothing more of it if her daughter never raised the subject again. The adults of the project had far more on their minds at the time than the inane ramblings of a juvenile. The idea festered in the young mind, conjuring a method to eliminate the other players in the game.

Whether Doctor Sheba Thompson cottoned on to the fact after her fellow project members became ill, will probably never be known. In all likelihood, if a mother suspected her very young child of such a despicable act, she was not likely to broadcast it. As far as the project members were concerned, they were doing nothing different to make them sick. They all drank only bottled water and none suspected it to be contaminated. They had no means of testing it in any case. Adam seriously doubted that they were supplied with Geiger counters as part of their equipment.

Poor, twisted, demented soul. Adam shook his head in wonder at the weakness of the human mind...or the strength, depending on which camp you were in. What that young girl concocted was nothing short of evil genius. Adam was satisfied that he had arrived at the most likely explanation for his query. It may never be proven but he was happy with his deductive processes and he had advanced some way along the tunnel in the meantime.

The dust had settled enough for him to remove the restrictive breathing apparatus. He removed a bottle of water from his pack to quench his thirst when another sudden thought halted him mid-lift. He quickly removed the Geiger counter from his trouser pocket. He waved the instrument over the bottle, listening with a sinking feeling to the ratcheted sounds indicating a non-safe level of radiation.

"You evil bitch! You replaced my water bottles as well. I didn't think to grab some fresh ones from your stash to replace the ones in my backpack. I...shit! If I've had some of this contaminated stuff already, how come I'm not sick? How much does it take? Do I somehow need higher doses if I'm a nuclear baby? Fuck you, Penelope! I should have known, I should have tested everything. Idiot, Adam, idiot."

Adam had to calm himself down to think properly. He couldn't remember consuming any of the water from his backpack. He had washed using the water he pre-tested from Penelope's stash of unopened water. He'd made his coffee with one of those bottles as well. The bottle he had in his hand was the only one from his backpack that he had touched and, thankfully, had not consumed. With a sigh of relief, he wiped the sweat from his grimy forehead.

With the first dilemma sorted, he set about remedying the

second. He opened his backpack again to take out a collapsible container. Into that, he poured several bottles of water, after which he added one of the precious pellets for purifying contaminated water. Donny told him it would decontaminate the water to a safe level for consumption within a minute of the pellet dissolving. Testing the water first would be his most pressing priority, not trusting his life to anyone's say-so ever again.

It was inconceivable to him that such a sadistic and mentally deranged person as Penelope existed, let alone that she should want to harm him. He had done nothing but offer his help and his friendship. He admitted to being rather prudish and even racist at first, but that was hardly enough to warrant his death sentence in his opinion. A very painful and prolonged death sentence.

After a minute had passed, Adam tested the water. A few arbitrary sounds but nothing more; nothing to set the alarm bells ringing. The water was now safe to drink...unless his instrument was defective? He was suspicious of her having tampered with the device. He put nothing past her. Unfortunately, he had no means of testing the device for a malfunction. Sighing with the impossibility of it all, he poured the cleansed liquid back into the bottles using a small funnel.

All of his bottles were treated to his satisfaction before attending to anything else. The battery in his lantern needed recharging, everything settled comfortably into his backpack, before heading off, semi-crawling once more.

More rumbles and heavy disturbances ensued behind him. The path backwards would not be available to him. There was only the path ahead to follow, avoiding the small narrow stream running through the tunnel floor. The earthen disturbances had not affected the water flow to that point. The fact that it was still trickling along indicated a natural declination in Adam's mind. Gravity never lied. For that constant, he was very grateful. In the ever-changing and threatening environment in which he travelled of late, he was thankful for such scientific constants keeping him grounded.

Although he loathed the man for all he was worth, Adam had to credit Donny for being a skilful teacher. While it may not have seemed to him that he was highly educated at the time, when compared to Penelope, Adam knew he had a vastly superior store of knowledge. Not her fault, though. She simply didn't have a lengthy period of learning under an educator who dedicated his life to the pursuit of knowledge who then passed that down to his son. Her time with her mother was cut very short...by her hand presumably.

He was saddened by the thoughts of Penelope. She'd been born into a bad situation made worse by battling elements within the small community it seemed if her mother had to fashion a homemade cattle prod. It was bound to happen of course. It would be damn-near impossible to get one hundred people to get along for years in a highly tense atmosphere of doubt and fear.

Adam had read a few books in his time, mostly fictional accounts, of the way people can change dramatically when placed in certain environments and situations. *Lord of the Flies* came to mind in particular as a good example of self-governing going terribly wrong. He supposed that was what the project was all about, measuring people's reactions in a simulated colonisation experiment.

Given enough time, alpha males were always going to start exploiting their perceived authority, gathering their minions to bolster their egos and their power base. Penelope hadn't mentioned how her father died. His life may have been taken defending his family from the warring factions or some aggrieved male venting his dissatisfaction with the status quo. Greed, power, lust, all vying for supremacy among a group forced into an intolerable situation by the vicissitudes of nature and human tempest.

While Covid 19 and its variants scourged the planet, all due to China playing with the virus in their labs, the Mars Colonisation Project remained safely underground, even when the nukes started falling. When they were cut off from all communication and saw their power dwindling with the shifting sands of time, the community began to alter, to morph into a new society based on some primal, survival-of-the-fittest, concept.

Adam saw how it could have unfolded over time. In only a few short years all semblance of normal and democratic principles were swept away when human emotions took control of a few disgruntled subjects unhappy to continue taking orders. Envy, jealousy, corruption; all part of the heady emotional make-up of the human condition when left to revert to their baser instincts. Penelope being a prime example. Born into the volatile muddle had set her mind on a deadly path of anarchy.

Of course, Adam understood that she was not of sound mind. Whether by nature or nurture was yet to be determined and possibly a blend of both. He seriously doubted her ability to ever successfully integrate with other humans, not without some serious intervention.

He wasn't trained enough in psychology to loosely diagnose her problems. He assumed she might be suffering from some form of schizophrenia. She was paranoid about everyone and everything, non-trusting and capable of instantaneous mood swings, often volatile. Donny had him studying any number of medical manuals during his education, hoping his son might follow in his father's footsteps.

It was not to be. Adam chose a different path as he matured. He had discovered many truths about his parent, none of which impressed him. He felt nothing but contempt for his father's ambitions. He did not want to become a healer. If healing meant inflicting despicable acts upon his fellow humans, he wanted nothing whatsoever to do with it. He didn't know what he wanted to do with the rest of his life if truth be told. To live, to be, he supposed, was the ultimate goal.

Topside, however! He wanted to live topside in the open air, under the stars. He never wanted to see another underground installation for as long as he survived. Once he had tasted that heavenly elixir of freedom, it was all he wanted. He could have seen himself sharing that life with Penelope before she revealed her hand. However, he was immensely grateful for having discovered her true nature before committing himself to her.

He had, hadn't he, though? He had committed himself to her in his mind. Adam knew he was trying to distance himself from that fact, attempting to diminish his culpability in being played. Whichever way he chose to spin it, he had fallen for her ruse and was ready to commit the rest of his life to her in the end.

They could have enjoyed a blissful life together if they'd managed to escape the mine. They had shared some wonderfully intimate moments separated by a wall of glass. Together, in the flesh, there were no limits to the joy and pleasure they could have found. The possibilities were boundless. He still felt an overwhelming sense of grief when he explored that train of thought. *Such a waste*, he thought.

Returning to the task at hand, Adam found himself staring at a dead-end. The water flowed through the wall at floor level. He had come across a few niches cut from the main tunnel but no offshoot tunnels. A touch of anxiety tickled his stomach when he thought he may have missed a side tunnel during his ruminations instead of concentrating. He couldn't hope to dig without the aid of the mattock he used before. He could backtrack and hope he had missed something.

He was feeling hungry, thirsty and tired after the long expedition in a crouching trot. He didn't know if he'd walked far or not. He berated and cursed himself for allowing his mind to wander. He sat down heavily. He tore open the packet of a dehydrated meal, electing to eat it un-reconstituted and cold. It tasted foul. He still mistrusted the water but drank anyway. Before long his eyelids fluttered and closed.

RUDE AWAKENING

He was taking a ride on something, something he didn't recognise. Up and down it went at dizzying speeds. A vague recognition played at the edges of his mind. Rolling along tracks...in a carriage of sorts. Donny told him about it and he was thrilled at the telling of it. He had never experienced such exhilaration as described by his father when he was still very young. It came to him in a flash; a roller coaster.

When Adam woke suddenly with a bone-jarring jolt to his lower back, he found himself in total darkness. Fumbling for the switch on his light, he was almost at the point of panicking when the lamp wouldn't turn on. Then he remembered he had probably fallen asleep with it on and the battery had run down. It required charging.

The light came on after he wound it, snapping the darkness back into the recesses. Gazing upward, he noted a rather large hole above his head. He recognised the tunnel up there, the mine shaft. Peering about the level on which he found himself incurred a groan. More of the same, just one level lower again. Was there no end to the warren of shafts? At least he determined that no single miner could be held responsible. It was unmistakably a former commercial enterprise with some serious mech. involved to move the tonnes and tonnes of dirt and rock associated with the network of shafts.

He'd landed painfully on his coccyx. The struggle to rise was compounded by a head that was being pounded by a sledgehammer. The effort proved too much, forcing him to slide back down to sit with his head in his hands. Dust still swirled about from the collapse. If he thought about it, he might have concluded that the small rivulet of water had weakened the floor of the shaft above considerably, causing it to collapse once Adam added his weight to a small area on the floor above. He'd fallen asleep and remained in the same spot for quite a while until the ground gave way beneath him.

Knowing how it happened did not help him one whit. He found his store of aspirin within his pack. Taking two of the capsules with water, he rested with a sigh, trying to calm his mind and ease the ache. The water bottle was thrown aside after he'd emptied it.

Considering how deep he'd ended up, if he sank any further he would end up in China according to the tales. *Right in the lap of the enemy*, thought Adam. If they were still an enemy of Australia. After all his years underground with no news from topside, anything was possible. For all Adam knew, they might be the new rulers, spreading their Communism across the Antipodes.

There were no signs of occupation on his previous visit to the world above ground. Ostensibly, that was due to Donny's perspicacity in choosing such an out of the way location for the bunker. Donny deliberately chose it for its worthlessness in the eyes of a would-be attacker. Avoiding major cities or populated areas being the main criteria for the selection. Wind patterns and climatic conditions being the next.

Hoping to find some of the answers to his questions gave Adam the impetus he required to attempt rising again. The pills had taken the edge off his headache and he was ready to tackle the next obstacle. The shaft intersected the one above at right angles again, just like the one above that.

Unable to see much beyond the reach of his weak lantern, Adam shrugged his shoulders and departed the area in whichever way came first to him. There was no rhyme or reason to his decision, just a need to be moving again. It didn't matter what direction he chose anymore. There seemed to be no hope of him ever reaching the surface. Instead of laying down and simply giving in, Adam chose to do something. Quitting was never going to be an option for Adam Harrow. While breath and mobility remained, he would always choose action over the opposite

The air tasted foul and smelled worse. It was probably stale, or even toxic. Being many metres under the earth, possibly as deep as a kilometre, would not allow fresh air to penetrate or circulate naturally. While the mine was in use it would have had air pumped in from above. Were it not for the fact that the collapses meant a certain amount of breathable air from above had entered the shafts below, Adam may well have perished already. The further he advanced and the deeper he went, the worse it would be. He refrained from using his mask for the moment and it would probably be of little use in any event.

A glint of reflected light caught his attention. Where a small section of the shaft's wall had peeled away with the last subsidence,

Adam saw an exposed surface of vivid colour. The kaleidoscopic array of rainbow colours against a black background made the wet mineraloid stand out against the pale yellow and mustard coloured walls. It was a mesmerising piece of the highest quality black opal, not usually found in Coober Pedy. More commonly located in Lightning Ridge, the amorphous form of silica was highly prized by jewellers across the globe back in the day.

The gem was about the size of a goose egg, rounded mostly with one face cleaved off the end to show the spectacular colours within. Ruby red, and sapphire blue, mixed with green, purples and flecks of gold. Truly a dazzling specimen. Adam manipulated the gem from the wall of the shaft in short order, pocketing the prize, never knowing how rich he would have been in days of old for such a find. Of course, in days of old, he'd have probably been arrested or shot for trespassing on a commercial mine and stripped of anything he'd found!

The ground shook and rumbled again causing him to lose balance, falling on his backside once more. The acute pain ran straight through his spine, disabling him for several seconds. The pain was excruciating. He lay perfectly still, not daring to move or even breathe too deeply. Inside, he was screaming at himself for once again touching something that caused the land to shift beneath him. Anyone would have thought he'd learned his lesson after the first time!

Ooh, shiny things. You bloody idiot Adam! Look what you've done to yourself over a bloody rock.

Everything shook about him sending more and more dust and debris on top of him. The trembling tumult soon caused the ground beneath him to heave and tear. Cracks appeared everywhere in the walls of the shaft, the ground, and most ominously, the ceiling. Adam sighed inwardly recognising the end of the road for him. He had gone as far as he was able and would soon die when he was crushed by the mountain of earth above him.

He felt the ground giving way under his arse, though he had his eyes closed, for the time being, not wishing to witness his demise. His back ached intolerably with every shift and movement beneath him. While he still had feeling in his lower back and legs, he was unable to make the supreme effort to move them. He felt the ground giving way under him slowly but couldn't be bothered trying to move, accepting his fate.

Incredibly, before the widening hole swallowed him, he felt his arms being grabbed by something, hauling him away from the opening. The clouds of billowing dust obscured everything. The pain as his body was dragged roughly backwards saw him screaming, swallowing great mouthfuls of choking dust. The pinched nerve in his lower back finally righted itself just when Adam believed he could take no more of the agony cascading through his body.

Then the entire world seemed to collapse at once.

When he next opened his eyes, believing himself dead or dying, Adam was amazed to see a very bright shaft of blinding light. A stiff breeze was filtering away the dust clouds. Incredibly, he lay at the lip of an opening at the edge of a vast depression in the earth. When he leaned forward to peer at it, he saw a massive crater before him, possibly hundreds of metres across, maybe as much as a kilometre in diameter.

At the bottom of the crater was a muddy lake. A few metallic structures broke the surface of the lake. Adam recognised the solar array he had discovered a lifetime ago, topside. He grinned despite the ever-present danger of further disruptions. He was alive. He'd made it after all. He had a chance. Slim though that may still be, he had a chance. It was a bloody miracle. The entire area had been so honeycombed with mine shafts crisscrossing the landscape, in combination with the water seeping into it, it had slowly eroded the integrity of the remaining ground, causing everything to collapse into an enormous sinkhole.

Then Adam had the notion to question *how* he'd made it. He'd been pulled from the lip of the abyss as it opened up beneath him. Looking into the shaft he could see very little but dirt and floating dust particles. On the ground was a shape he did not immediately recognise. He saw the mound of dirt rising periodically, then deflating. Shuffling over to the mound he began wiping away some of the dirt to find a warm, soft surface beneath. Further exploration revealed legs.

With growing alarm, he realised it was probably Penelope. The rise and fall of the chest covered by dust and dirt indicated life persisting. He had no way of knowing if she was injured in any way. Still not able to make the effort to stand, he crawled up to her head which was partially buried. He wiped away all the soil from her face. He understood that she had difficulty breathing, that she was probably choking on the dust.

He removed a few bottles of water from his backpack in a panic, splashing the water haphazardly over her face. He opened her mouth to remove any soil that may be hindering her attempts to breathe properly. He scooped out globs of mud mixed with blood and saliva, though very little of the latter. He gently poured a little water into her mouth. She reacted violently, turning on her side, heaving and gagging on the elements invading her throat, finally vomiting great wads of congealed blood, dirt and water.

Adam helped her wash away the remains of the vomit and smut on her face while assisting her to take small sips from the water bottle. Slowly, she regained her senses enough to recoil at the sight of the water bottle so close to her face.

"It's alright, Pen. The water is okay. I purified it all. I have pellets with me to do that. You need to drink, but slowly. Blow your nose with this," he suggested, handing her a pair of cotton undies from his pack.

Penelope recoiled further until Adam took a sip from the water to demonstrate the safety. She accepted the proffered jocks with which to blow her nose. She was greatly relieved when she could finally breathe through her nose again. She sipped more of the water, relaxing appreciably.

Adam laughed as he crawled to sit with his back against the wall of the shaft, peering out at the great expanse of clear air in front. Sunlight poured in from the outside bathing them in its glorious warmth. It would soon be too hot for them possibly, but for the moment he luxuriated in it like it was an intoxicating balm. Despite her condition, Penelope managed a smile as well. Her brilliant white teeth shining through the ebony, dust-streaked face, made Adam laugh harder.

He slapped the ground in jubilation, whooping for joy. Penelope moved gingerly to join him with her back against the wall peering out at the strange and magnificent vista, experiencing sunlight for the first time in her life. She was amazed and frightened by the realisation that a huge wide world existed beyond the chamber in which she'd grown. It was scary and exhilarating. She joined Adam in laughing, though periodically stopping to cough and splutter.

Adam turned to her after they both quietened down.

"Thank you for saving my life, Princess Penelope Archer."

"Thank you for saving mine, Adam Harrow, "she answered with difficulty.

"Does that mean you'll stop trying to kill me?"

"Maybe."

Adam smiled and stared back out at the most beautiful panorama he had ever seen. He couldn't wipe the sheer joy from his face. They sat together in silence taking it all in.

"I don't know about you, Pen, but I still don't trust that all this has finally ended. I think we need to get out of here while we can, don't you?"

"Can we?"

"Not sure how well I can walk. How are you feeling, by the way? You don't sound as though you're dying."

"I'm sore all over, including inside. My throat..."

"Yeah, you should try not to talk too much."

"You asked..."

"Yeah, that's okay, my bad. The less you try to talk the less you'll aggravate your throat. I'm not saying you should be a mute, just be conservative with your speech. I'll try to limit my questions to yes and no answers which you can indicate with your head. Okay?"

She nodded.

Adam raised himself slowly from his seated position. While his back no longer felt as though the nerve was being compressed between vertebrae, it was still very tender. He let out a slow groan as he stood, still with a slight crouch. He advanced to the lip of the opening, peering all ways to discover a route out. When his eyes adjusted to the glare, he saw they were halfway up the sloping wall of a crater formed by the collapsing mine shafts. There was a distance of around a few hundred metres up or down.

A slight stumble as another piece of the edge crumbled under his weight warned Adam of the need to somehow keep moving. He stepped back one pace to feel a little safer. He didn't want to tempt fate by carelessly losing his footing. To the right of his position, he noted the only means available to them for leaving the area. A thin ledge spiralled halfway around the crater. It ended a metre or two below the lip almost opposite their position. It didn't look safe.

Staying where they were would not be any safer and possibly far worse. Anything was better than getting trapped below ground again.

"Pen? There is a bit of a ledge we can use to try to get up top. I don't like it much..." he shrugged his shoulders, wincing as a spasm caught him unawares. "You'd better... Why are you looking at me like that? No, don't answer that. Look, Pen. I'm not trying to trick you. I want us to get up top, both of us, to be free. I waited twenty-five years to be free and I'm sure you want the same. I know you don't really trust me, so why save me then? Huh? You could have let me fall down there while you had the chance. Something has to be telling you that I'm not your enemy. I tell you what, once we reach the surface, all bets are off and you can do what you want. Go, stay, attack me, whatever. I can't be fairer than that, surely?

"You need to get some clothes on, though. You won't know this, but that sun can burn your skin, even black skin like yours. I have a long-sleeved shirt in my pack and a pair of jeans that might fit you if we tie some rope around your waist. My belt won't fit you, too big."

Penelope agreed reluctantly to Adams suggestions. The feel of strange fabrics against her skin felt restrictive and annoying. When she stood at the edge of the shaft the way she'd seen Adam do, she understood what he meant when she felt the full effect of direct sunlight on her bare skin. She was very scared and way out of her comfort zone. Though she had wanted nothing more than to be free all of her life, the suddenness of that freedom and the yawning expanse frightened her more than she would admit.

She stood and watched as Adam rolled up the legs of her jeans so she would not trip over them. She also watched in amazement as he placed on her feet a pair of something called sandals. She gave him an odd lilt of the head.

"These are to protect your feet, Pen. Not only from sharp rocks and such but from the heat. The sun can heat the ground to a very high temperature, especially rocks. You have soft feet that have never experienced the rough, stony earth and this mad heat. They'll soon blister and bleed. If I had gloves I would give you those for protection as well. You're going to be using your hands against the walls to brace yourself as we move along the ledge. If you don't press too hard you should be okay."

They drank some water and ate some food. Adam noted that Penelope was quick to tire. He worried that she had not survived the superbug at all. He was concerned that the vaccine had only sent her into a type of remission. Regardless, she had not fully recovered if it had cured her. Her breathing rattled in her throat and she grimaced often when inhaling.

"Now, Pen. I'd like you to take a proper look out there before we head off."

While Penelope was standing near the edge inspecting everything outside with a look of concern on her features, Adam stood behind her.

"Now, up there is the surface. It's practically a desert. Nothing but rocks, dirt and stunted trees. Once we make it up there, you can go off on your own if you prefer. What I want you to understand is, it isn't a game and there's no one waiting up there to congratulate you or give you a prize for making it. If we make it in one piece, that will be your reward, surviving. Though you deserve all the accolades in the universe for making it, there won't be a single person around to give it to you.

"Everything I told you was as I've been told. My information may be flawed and for that, I apologise in advance. It isn't an attempt by me to fool you. I hope you can trust me at least that far?"

After taking one final look at the alien landscape, feeling very much out of place, Penelope nodded.

"Do you want to go first or after me?"

She shot him a look of suspicion. He shrugged to indicate there were no hidden agendas and that he was giving her a choice to alleviate her concerns. She stepped aside to let him go first. Facing the wall of the crater, Adam sidled out of the shaft opening onto the narrow ledge after testing its stability. Satisfied that it would hold his weight, he inched forward.

As it was not a sheer vertical wall, they did not feel quite so vulnerable, allowing them to sidle along the shelf more quickly after a short time. Adam reassured himself that the worst that could happen was for them to end up sliding down the wall a short distance to end up taking a swim...

A couple of very troubling thoughts occurred to him. First and foremost was the fact that neither of them could swim. If they plunged into the water and it turned out to be anything deeper than their necks, they would drown. Secondly; the water was most likely contaminated.

Note to self; don't fall in the water, thought Adam. He was about to warn Penelope to be careful when he clamped his mouth shut, feeling rather foolish for nearly blurting out something entirely stupid. She was old enough to be aware that danger existed. He could see her being very cautious. Adam had to remind himself that everything was new for her. She could become overwhelmed at any moment. A sensory overload brought on by him uttering useless cautions could certainly prove fatal to one or both of them.

The sun beat down upon the pair as they gradually worked their way around the crater towards the ledge's highest point. What they would do when they arrived was yet to be determined. Thinking ahead made Adam squirm uncomfortably. About the only method he could think of for reaching the top once they came to the end, was for Adam to allow Penelope to climb on him, up to his shoulders to reach the surface. He would then be left completely at her mercy. If she should fail to reach down and assist him up, he would be left alone on the ledge. The soil seemed far too loose to gain enough purchase with which to hoist himself up and over the rim.

The thin, brittle ledge felt to Adam as though it would give way at any second, hardly capable of bearing even the lightest weight, yet it held relatively firm as they made their way around. Several times, Adam had to gently coax Penelope forward, easing her fears and calming her nerves. In the stark sunlight, her skin appeared darker than anything he could ever have described. Her hair was blacker still, though lustreless and drab because of the film of dust coving every strand and the fact it had not seen a comb or brush in a long time.

He touched the hand extending towards him, clinging fearfully to a small outcrop of sharp rock. They were both facing and hugging the wall as closely as possible. Had it been any more vertical, they would not have been able to maintain their hold, gravity simply plucking them away from the wall effortlessly. Penelope stared at his eyes, finding some comfort there. He could see that she was exhausted and that her limbs were trembling from the exertion after her recent debilitating and potentially lethal illness.

"Rest for a moment, Pen. If you go on like you are you'll shake yourself off the ledge. Breathe steady, in and out, rhythmically, naturally, calm, serene..."

"What...are you...babbling about?"

"It's a calming technique Donny always used on me. Believe it or not, I had quite a temper when I was younger."

"You?"

"Yes me! You think you have the market cornered on temper tantrums? Been there, done that. I gave as good as I got. I..." He was about to say he had matured and grown out of it, learned patience, but thought better of it. She might misunderstand. "Let's just say that I calmed down a bit over the years and learned to focus that energy into more constructive pursuits, like educating my mind and training my body to stay fit and healthy."

"I...just need to get angry...otherwise I feel bad."

"I get that. Sometimes it's good to release, to vent. Other times it pays to conserve that energy for better things. Picking and choosing the times that suit you, is part of gaining control over your emotions rather than the other way around. You strike me as a person who likes to be in control," Adam shared with a smile. It was met with a loud harrumph. "Okay, so much for that tactic. How about we keep going?"

He removed his hand from hers to continue edging his way along the thin track that mountain goats would consider a highway. Judging by the angle of the sun, or the lack thereof, it was around midday. Not that Adam had much practical experience in judging the time by the sun's orbital position across the sky. He'd dug deep into his pool of accumulated knowledge imparted by the ever-wise Donny to arrive at the conclusion.

It was hot! Getting hotter by the minute. He should have taken the time and followed his advice to cover up his arms with a long-sleeved shirt also. His shorts allowed the sun to bake the back of his legs. His long blonde hair, soaking up the sun's rays, was slowly boiling his brains. Adam was not to know that the ambient temperature was a comfortable level for anyone acclimatised to that part of the world. He had lived in the open for a total of seven days before the world turned upside down for him. In Donny's bunker, the temperature was always even and mild.

They were both sweating profusely by the time they reached the end of the ledge. Adam groaned as he peered upward. The lip of the wall was unreachable by him, just as he'd suspected. He'd desperately hoped to be wrong about that.

"What, what's wrong?"

"Getting up there is what's wrong. I'm going to have to climb on top of you, onto your shoulders to be able to reach it."

"Are you crazy?" she asked, suddenly clear of the fug that fought to wear her down.

"I can't reach it on my own, Pen."

Penelope chanced a glance upward. She understood the problem immediately, though didn't agree with his solution one little bit.

"Nuh-uh, no way are you climbing on me."

"Can you get up there?"

"By climbing on *you*, yeah."

"Then what, genius?"

"Whatcha mean?" she said unkindly.

"It's like this Penelope, I'd like to get up there and live as well as you."

"Yeah, so?"

"How do I get up there once you are?"

"I..."

"Precisely! If I go up first, I have the strength to haul you up after me. Won't work the other way around."

"I could do it," she offered unconfidently.

"You just went through an illness that nearly killed you. Look at you, shaking from the exertion of a little trek around on the ledge. You're sweating twice as much as me."

"I can do it," she stated emphatically.

"I'm not about to risk my life to your stubborn refusal to accept facts."

"So we both stay down here then," she said with a tone of finality.

"Holy Pando, you're being stubborn and bloody childish," yelled Adam with frustration.

"So much for controlling the rage and focusing that wasted energy," she remarked dryly.

Adam frantically searched the area for some other avenue of reaching the top, which was so tantalisingly close. He knew there was nothing. He'd been looking at the same spot for the entire journey with no new routes or possibilities presenting themselves.

He wasn't being entirely honest with either himself or Penelope. He didn't want her to go up first because he didn't trust her. That was the plain and simple truth. He couldn't trust her, not ever again. She had proven herself to be a malicious and devious person capable of almost anything. He wasn't sure at all why she ended up dragging him to safety...

"Hey, I forgot to ask. How the heck did you get out of the chamber?"

"Fell," she stated sullenly.

"Fell?"

"Yeah, fell, through the ground. One minute I'm standing there having a drink of water, the next, I'm looking at everything from below."

"Just like that?"

"No, I waved the magic wand that came out of my arse!"

"Wow, nothing wrong with your memory, is there?"

"Why would...cough...there be?"

"Sorry. You better calm down a bit. You don't want to get a coughing fit standing on this tiny ledge. I just meant that I'd said something like that to you soon after we met and you remembered it, that's all."

"I'm going back..."

"Suit yourself, hothead."

"You, you're not coming back?"

"No point. If I'm going to die it may as well be here than there. No escape from the shaft and no telling how long it'll remain the way it is."

"Can't get much worse than that," she said leering downwards.

"Don't count on it. This whole area has been seriously undermined by a natural water table by the look of it. That and the honeycomb of mine shafts. I don't intend to be over there taking the chance. So, impasse."

"What does that mean?"

"An impasse? A stalemate. No one wins."

"Thought you said..."

"I meant in chess, Penelope. Don't take me so literally. I'm telling you for the last time, this isn't a game. We are facing life and death consequences and no one is going to end up a hero or get a prize."

"Not much point then, is there?"

"Life?"

"Huh?"

"The point is, staying alive. Getting out of this mess to begin again, start a life up there in the real world."

"Why?"

"You can't mean that, surely? Penelope, you and I haven't even tasted a fraction of life. Together or apart, we could have a happy, healthy and productive life. So much to see and do, and you want to waste that with negativity? Toss it all away? Give up? Well, I thought you were made of sterner stuff than that. I thought you were a fighter, a survivor?"

"You said it isn't a game."

"It isn't. It's about actual survival and living free, not proving yourself to a crowd or an audience. There isn't anyone up there, Pen. Donny drove his car hundreds of kilometres in all directions before he finally ran out of fuel he could siphon from other cars. Ghost towns, dead bodies everywhere. What the plague didn't kill, the radiation did. Then came the combination, the superbug. A virus mutated by radiation into a lethal, airborne pathogen capable of remaining alive in the air indefinitely.

"Get this into your head; we might be the last two people on the continent. We might even be the last two people on the planet! Probably not, but possibly. Donny didn't know because all communications were lost. The last thing anyone here knew, was that the rest of the world had cordoned off Australia and banned any visitation by penalty of death."

"Why?"

"To protect the rest of the world from the superbug. Whether they succeeded or not is anyone's guess. Holy Pando, it's hot! My bloody brain is starting to boil. Won't you please let me climb..."

She was shaking her head before he even finished the sentence. Tears of frustration and anger were welling at the corners of his eyes as he stared at her in pure exasperation. After weighing up everything, he finally concluded that he had no choice.

"Alright, alright. I give up. This is getting us nowhere and sooner or later you, me or both of us is going to either go for a swim once the ledge gives way, or get sunstroke if we stay here much longer. I'm going to flatten myself against the face of the wall here.

I'll hold my right knee out for you to use that as a step. You go from there to my shoulders. You have to go slowly and make sure you don't lean too far outwards. Neither of us can swim, so it pays not to end up in the drink. You think you can do that?"

She nodded. Adam resigned himself to the fact that he had little to say in the matter anyway. He nodded for her to proceed once he prepared himself. He placed both of his feet parallel to the wall to distribute the weight as much as possible onto the broadest possible surface of the ledge. Concentrating the weight on one small section would undoubtedly see the ledge crumble.

"Pen, I'm going to make another step of my arm. By placing as much pressure as I can against the wall to hold you up on my arm, it will alleviate some of the weight bearing down directly on the ledge. So step as quickly as you can from my knee to my arm, then take your time to get to my shoulder. Once your there, reach for the top and scramble up as fast as you can without causing a landslide. Ready?"

She nodded. Adam noted that she was shaking before she began, possibly from fear more than fatigue. It wasn't that far down to fall, but that was the end of the line if they did. The water would cushion their fall to an extent, however, they would drop like stones to the bottom unless the water was shallow enough for them to stand. Didn't matter. There was no way out from below. He'd seen that immediately from the opening of the shaft.

Despite her smaller size, she was not the lightweight he thought her to be. He felt his knee strain under the pressure as she mounted, the tread of her sandals biting deep into his bare flesh, already quite sensitive after the time spent in direct sunlight. He placed his right arm as low as he could, making sure to keep it bent to provide a crook for her to gain purchase. He grimaced as she stepped onto his arm, feeling it sliding downwards despite every effort to hold it in place.

When she slipped with her left foot, missing his shoulder, Adam thought they were done for. Her entire weight rested awkwardly on the foot standing on Adam's right arm. His muscles screamed at him to let her go, to allow her to tumble off into the lake below. Sheer willpower stayed his arm, even lifting it slightly to assist her to gain his shoulder. The event took less than a minute but felt like a lifetime when she finally stepped off his arm. Before Adam could say a word to make her reach for the top, her weight was gone.

For a moment, he was confused. Had she fallen? When he looked up, there was no sign of her. He looked below but saw no tell-tale splash or ripples in the water. The silence and her disappearance caused alarm bells to start ringing for him. Just as he was about to shout out his frustration, her head appeared over the lip of the rim.

"Pass me your bag," she said as she reached down.

"What? Why?"

"Well, like you said, I might not be strong enough to haul you up with the bag. Better to hand it up first, then I'll get you up."

Adam hesitated long enough to cause Penelope to screw her face up in disgust. Adam didn't think she was aware that she was giving herself away.

"No, no I'm not going to do that, Penelope."

"Why? It makes sense to make you lighter," she pleaded with a look of sincerity.

"I'll keep a hold of my bag, thank you. It means everything to me."

"Now who's being stubborn?"

"Come on help me up," he said.

"I can't do it, not with your bag as well. It would be too much."

"The bag stays with me," he said finally.

"At least pass up the water and the food in there to get some weight off?"

"Oh, why would that suddenly be important to you?"

"What are you talking about?"

"I'm talking about you making off with the only provisions we have and leaving me here to die."

"That's a mean and horrible thing to say. How could you think that?"

"How could I think you'd zap me with a homemade cattle prod and leave me for dead in the chamber you vacated? How could I think you planted contaminated water in my backpack? How could I think *that*, you mean?"

"Stay there and die then you bastard!" she spat with more venom and hatred than Adam had ever witnessed in his life.

Then she was gone.

FROM THE ABYSS

Adam couldn't credit his bad luck. He felt almost nauseous with the betrayal he'd experienced; twice! He understood why she saved him. It had nothing at all to do with either an emotional attachment or a change of conscience. She needed his pack to survive. He was the only one with provisions. Without that, she didn't stand a chance. He sought to believe she had acted nobly, sacrificing her safety for his. All along it was nothing of the sort. A ruse, another game/role-play in the sick, twisted mind of a psychopath.

However, she became a victim of her actions when she ended up choking on dust. He had stupidly saved her life after being rescued. He figured out a way for them to possibly escape their predicament only to face the prospect of frying like an egg on the side of nature's frying pan after being abandoned by the bitch of the universe. Adam found himself cursing her existence, cursing the mother that spawned the evil thing, and regretting having ever had the curiosity to touch something causing so much trouble.

His brain was still sizzling painfully. At least, it felt that way. There wasn't a breath of wind to diminish the furnace's temperature. Every time he laid his hand flat against the surface of the wall, he winced with the sting of the heated gravel. The water he could see below became very tempting to him, a solution to one problem at the very least. Somehow, he managed to turn around on the narrow ledge after shrugging out of his backpack, facing inwards. All he had to do was lean forwards, just a fraction, and he could perform a majestic swan dive into the beautiful cooling water below.

Not that he knew how to perform a swan dive, or any dive less fanciful or otherwise. He couldn't even... A sudden memory flooded his mind. A very old song his father used to play often when he believed Adam was asleep. He recalled one of the verses:

"I,
I wish I could swim.
Like the dolphins,

Like dolphins can swim.
Though nothing,
Nothing will keep us together.
We can beat them,
Forever and ever.
Oh, we can be heroes, just for one day..."

Adam smiled. Donny thought of himself as a hero, a saviour to the planet. There was more to the rather confusing song, but that was what he'd remembered as he stood on the thin ledge contemplating diving. The only thing that stopped him was his inability to swim. He was scared of drowning. It didn't seem a fitting end somehow. He hadn't fought so hard for so long just to wind up as pond scum.

Indecision and doubt clouded his judgement while the unrelenting heat scorched the cauldron walls in a concentrated fashion. The glare from the water below was blinding. The silt had settled, leaving a clear surface to reflect the high intensity of the sun's rays. Adam could see the bottom of the pool without being able to judge the depth. It could be one metre or ten, he had no way of knowing.

As he stood on legs shuddering with the strain of balancing precariously for so long, his hand was absently playing with the surface of the wall behind him, scratching away at the soil. When his mind eventually caught up with his activity, it sparked an idea. Possibly an insane idea, but an idea nonetheless. Far better than doing nothing, he thought.

Carefully, he turned to face the wall again, then donned his pack. He extended his hand as low as it would go on his right side. He began to scratch away in earnest, with purpose. His fingers hurt after only a very short time with almost no progress made. He searched his mind for anything useful in his pack. Nothing stood out except perhaps his last foolish find, the piece of opal he'd found. It was rounded on one end with a sharp edge where it had a missing top.

It wasn't easy to search his backpack to find the rock. On several occasions, he teetered precariously backward before righting himself in time. With the rock in hand, he aimed the sharper edge at the surface of the wall. He scratched and sweated at it for half an hour before he was satisfied with the result. He transferred the rock to his left hand, scratching and digging at a level about 300 mm higher than before. He tested the depth of the small holes he'd dug with a shoe from his pack. It reached about halfway in. He nodded with satisfaction before transferring the rock to his right hand once more.

Once another three similar holes were dug, the last one on the right at about head height, he thought he would test out his ingenuity. Gingerly, he placed his right foot into the first hole he'd scraped out to the right. Testing the integrity of the hole gradually to ensure he would not slip and fall to his certain death by drowning, he placed more and more weight on the right foot. He found the hole to be supporting him enough to attempt moving his left foot to the hole on that side.

It gave a little as he placed his foot into the hole. He felt the edges of the hole crumble while the inner section seemed to hold for the time being. Adam knew it would probably not last long, so he moved quickly to transfer his weight to the right foot once more. Two more steps up his roughly hewn ladder in the wall had Adam able to grip the rim with his hands. He found he could have used one more step to make it easier for him. Regardless, he climbed up and over the lip, lying face down on the ground with heaving sighs.

Applause broke the silence.

"About time you figured it out," said Penelope standing over him with a huge grin. She offered her hand to him.

Adam slapped the hand away angrily, rising quickly. His entire body down to the depth of his soul was shocked into defensiveness and outrage. His stance, threatening. He edged sideways away from the lip of the cauldron, never losing eye contact with the insane woman in front of him.

"Get away from me," he warned through clenched teeth. He had never felt more like killing someone than he did at that moment, setting aside what he did to Donny in a rage of madness. The fury he felt was pure molten lava ready to burst outwards like Krakatoa.

"What?"

"Don't you 'what' me you evil, psychotic bitch! Stay the fuck away, I'm warning you," he spat vehemently.

"What could I do? You didn't leave me any choice. You weren't willing to lighten the load so I could lift you, so I had to wait until you figured out a way of getting up. I knew you would because you're so smart and..."

"KNOCK IT OFF! I'm not interested in hearing your bullshit anymore. Get away from me," he insisted while fumbling in one of the pockets of his pack.

Penelope watched as he withdrew an odd-shaped metallic object from his pack. He seemed to be pointing it at her for some reason.

"What's that?" she asked innocently.

"It's a gun, you dumb bitch."

"What does it do?"

"Really? You don't even know what a gun is? It shoots bullets. It kills people!"

"That little thing?" she asked incredulously.

"I'm not going to waste a precious bullet to demonstrate it for you, so if you don't take my word for it, you'll find out the hard and painful way. I will not hesitate in killing you. I hate you more than anything in the world right now."

"Why?"

"Stop it! Stop the shit. I'm sick of your act. Everything that comes out of your mouth is some sort of trickery, manipulation, game advantage."

"That's not..."

The shot rang out, reverberating on the harsh landscape, causing a flock of raucous cockatoos to take to the air suddenly. A dozen of the birds had settled onto the single stunted tree surrounded by bare earth for many hundreds of metres. Penelope had taken a step toward Adam which caused him to fire the old weapon. His shaking hand had skewed his aim. The slug nicked Penelope's upper arm. Blood soaked her shirt sleeve, though she was too stunned to notice. She fell to her knees.

Adam backed away from her accusing stare. He kept backing away until he felt safe enough to turn his back on her and keep walking. He didn't care which direction he was heading as long as it was away from her. His temper had all but abated, shocked out of him by the loud blast from the weapon he had stolen from Donny's desk drawer. He'd read enough information to know theoretically how it worked, though never experienced one in the flesh. Donny showed him old movies where they used to carry the guns on their hips and shoot each other right there on the streets, with the whole town watching mostly.

He wasn't proud of what he'd done. Neither did he regret it. He had aimed for the head, at a spot between the eyes. That his aim had been upset by his shaking annoyed him a little. If he hoped to make it in the outside world, he had better master his emotions. If she had been more of a threat, that near-miss might have cost him his life. She wasn't to know that it was the only bullet in his pistol. He hoped to find more bullets on his explorations of abandoned houses, which was where Donny had found the gun in the first place.

He peered back over his shoulder a few times to assure himself he was not being followed by the sadistic bitch. He couldn't believe she'd sat just above him all that time waiting for her chance to pounce on him the moment he figured out a way to get up.

Donny told him once that cats were like that, sitting in place for extended periods until their intended prey either came close enough to pounce on or made an error. Adam hoped he wouldn't come across any of those. They sounded extremely dangerous to him, though he hadn't the foggiest of a notion as to how large they were or what they looked like. He admitted that there were large gaps in his education. He made a note to look up what a cat looked like if he came across any old reference books.

The last time he peered over his shoulder, his adversary seemed to be sitting in a daze. Adam walked faster to avoid any chance of her catching up with him. It was late afternoon and the daylight would be fading soon. He wanted as much distance as possible between him and her before he began looking for a place to settle for the evening. He knew he didn't have much energy left, though. He was feeling the fatigue in his heavy limbs after the exhausting strain of the day.

is throat was bone dry by the time the sun began to set. He found a stunted tree surrounded by thorny bushes. Once he was through the prickly barrier, he found a couple of loose, dead bushes to cover the breach in the perimeter defences through which he'd passed. He would make sure not to light a fire to give away his position during the night. He ate frugally and downed a full bottle of water before settling down to sleep after covering himself with a thin blanket, useless pistol in hand.

A few hours later a dark figure thumped down hard on the form under the light silver blanket with a weighty branch. She flogged the bulge under the blanket again and again until she was breathing so hard she could barely stand upright.

Slow applause broke the deathly silence and light brightened the scene.

"Congratulations Penelope, you just beat the living shit out of some brush under that blanket. Feel better?" He asked holding up the lantern.

She made to move back out of the surrounding thorn bush...

"Uh-uh, no you don't," said Adam holding the pistol where she could see it pointing at her chest.

"I, I saw you getting ready for bed. I saw you getting under..." she stopped.

"That you did, Penelope Archer. That you did. I knew you were following me. Don't ask me how, but I knew. Don't ask me how you managed it either. I thought for sure I'd put enough distance between us. Care to explain that one?"

"Daddy was a full-blood Aboriginal. He taught me a thing or two about bushcraft before he died. Might have been young but I soaked it all up. Now, you going to tell me how you tricked me? I saw you get under that blanket."

"That was key. You had to witness that for me to get away with it. I slipped under the blanket which covered me and a few dead tumbleweed-like bushes. That silver roll which you had your eyes glued on was enough to distract you while digging my way out from under the stockade of thorny stuff surrounding the tree.

"Nice dark night. I moved slowly and quietly enough to make sure you wouldn't know. Sat in a little hollow just over there watching every move you made like a hawk. I was bloody tired, I have to tell you. Almost fell asleep a dozen times or more until you finally made your move. It was worth it to see your face right now. Got suckered, girl, well and truly, by a white boy!"

"Well, aren't you the clever one? What now?"

"Want to get shot again?"

"No," she said touching the bullet graze on her arm.

"Then sit down right where you are, but first throw that big branch, way the fuck over there," said Adam, pointing with the hand holding the lantern.

After complying with his request, Penelope sat down hard in defeat.

"Can we start over?"

"No. I can't trust a word that comes out of your mouth. You would do absolutely anything to win this ridiculous game you think we're in."

"That's not true, I..."

"Save it. I saw the way you bashed that roll thinking it was me under there. You were trying to kill me and you'll keep on trying until you succeed. The only reason you saved me in that mine shaft was to get a hold of my backpack. I know that for certain. Again at the big hole in the ground, you manipulated me into allowing you to get up first so that you could get the pack off me. You're a psychotic bitch and a pathological liar."

"If all that was true you'd have killed me with that thing you're holding," she remarked with growing suspicion.

"This may come as a shock to you. Not everyone is a cold-blooded killer. I missed back there and only grazed your arm because I was shaking like a leaf. My conscience made that happen. My sense of right and wrong was battling within me to throw off my aim. I wouldn't count on that ever happening again if I were you."

"But you are like me."

"No, I'm not a psychopath, thank goodness."

"You killed your father," she accused.

"One person died at my hands compared to your hundred? Sorry, it's a no-brainer as to who wins the prize for being the worst serial-killing psychopath."

"Wasn't one hundred," she explained sullenly.

"Spare me the story of the one or two who may have died by natural causes, okay? I wouldn't believe you anyway. You may well have the dubious distinction of being Australia's worst serial killer, you know that?"

"According to you, there isn't anybody left to care about that or lock me up."

"According to me, huh? So, my word isn't to be taken at face value? Alright, I get that. It isn't even my word we're talking about, is it? It's his word. Bloody Donny's word that everything happened the way it did. He told me and I told you but he could have been telling me porkies, couldn't he?"

"Porkies?"

"Porky pies? Lies? It's rhyming... Oh, never mind. Lies, he

could have been lying to me about pretty much everything."

"Where does that leave us?"

"Good question. I can't just let you go or you'll follow me and clobber me when I'm not expecting it. Can't take you with me the way you are for the same reason. So, either I kill you now and get it over and done with or..."

"Or?"

"Or I take you prisoner."

"Huh?"

"Manacle and shackle you so you can't get up to mischief and mayhem. I have to keep you where I can see you otherwise I'll never feel safe. Just lucky Donny found something during his searches that I stole from him when I left."

Adam reached into his pack to withdraw a cloth bag containing something metal. He tossed the object over to land at Penelope's sandaled feet. Penelope peered at them with curious disdain.

"What are they?"

"Shackles and handcuffs were worn by prisoners that the police arrested. Push the curved bar right through until it revolves right around. Place the open section on your shin and push the curved piece closed again until you hear the ratcheting noise. Don't go too tight or it will be painful. Not too loose to allow your foot to slip through. Do one then the other. Donny found these when he raided a police station in Alice Springs. Unfortunately all the weapons were gone. One of his longest journeys. I was alone for a week that time."

"I won't do it?"

"That's fantastic news. I was looking for any excuse to shoot you dead and you just..."

"Okay, okay," she said in a panic as he raised the weapon to point at her head.

Adam waited until he was satisfied she had complied. Once the shackles were securely in place, her legs connected by the short chain, he tossed her a set of handcuffs.

"Those are for your wrists. Place one on your left arm, then go hug the tree."

"Hug the tree?"

"What, are you a parrot? Yes, place your arms around the tree once you have one on your left wrist. When your arms are around the tree, place the remaining handcuff on your right wrist."

"Around the tree?"

"Yes, Polly, around the freaking tree," he explained with a sigh.

"Polly?"

"Polly wanna cracker? Parrot? Never mind. Just do like I said. I need to get some sleep and I won't rest easy until I know you're secure. DO IT! I'm not joking or mucking around her," he warned, levelling the gun at her again.

"Alright, alright, I'm doing it, see?"

Adam approached her with caution. After inspecting the manacles and the cuffs, making slight adjustments to each, he was finally able to relax. He placed the weapon in his pack, shook out the broken bits of dried up weed from the silver blanket and foam ground cover, and laid down to go to sleep.

"Hey, what am I supposed to do? I can't get any sleep like this."

"Your problem, not mine. Now shut up so I can get some sleep."

"I'm thirsty," she whined.

"Too bad. Should have thought about all that before trying to kill me...again! Now shut it or I'll gag you as well. Your choice."

COMPANY

"**What's that?**" asked Penelope pointing wildly with her hands cuffed before her.

"You're kidding, right?"

"No?"

"You've never been taught about kangaroos by your Aboriginal father?"

"They weren't that common on Mars," she answered drily.

"You weren't on bloody Mars, remember?"

"Is it dangerous?"

"Only if you're wearing boxing gloves."

"Huh?"

Never mind. Keep moving. No, they aren't dangerous. They're an iconic symbol of Australia. A marsupial. Meaning they have live young they rear in a pouch. See the head of the joey peeking out from the midsection of that one there? When it's old enough, it will hop out of the pouch to graze while the mother stands guard. At the first sign of danger, the joey jumps straight back into the pouch. They bound away on those powerful hind legs, instead of running. Thought you said your dad taught you something about Australian bushcraft?"

Ignoring him, Penelope kept gazing at the small mob of roos as they walked wearily past. The vegetation became sparser as they ventured in the direction Adam believed would bring them to the coast eventually. He ordered Penelope to walk a distance in front of him, still shackled at the ankles and with her wrists cuffed. He was taking no chances with her. He had even seriously contemplated leaving her imprisoned at the tree. He changed his mind reluctantly when he couldn't face the guilt of leaving a fellow human to suffer in such a cruel manner.

They had been walking since daybreak beneath the unrelenting sun beaming down upon them. Adam wore a peaked cap he'd found among his clothes. They were following a dry creek bed in the hope it might turn into at least a trickle of water, or even better, a river, flowing with uncontaminated water, or lead to one of the small lakes or billabongs present in the area according to the map in Adam's memory.

Not long after, Adam spied a shimmering image of water in the distance. He thought he might be seeing things, like a mirage. Donny had taught him about the possibility of mistakenly seeing water in extreme heat conditions. The only reason he believed it might not be a mirage was the small copse of eucalypts defying the arid conditions. In a landscape denuded of vegetation, trees could only survive if they were close to a water source.

"Head towards that group of trees to your right. Your other right," he said after a moment. "Yeah, those trees, the only ones we can see?"

"I can hardly see anything for the glare."

"Yeah, I get that. Having never experienced sunlight, I can see how that would be a problem. Hit me pretty hard the first time as well. Donny told me to wear something called sunglasses, but I didn't know what they were or what they looked like. I didn't find any when I looked around the bunker. If we come across any houses or abandoned cars we can have a look for some."

"You thought of handcuffs but not some protection against the sun for your eyes?"

"Yep, came in handier than bloody sunglasses, that's for sure. Soooo, glad I found those when I was rummaging through Donny's stash of goodies."

"I could walk a lot faster without the ones on my legs."

"Yep, you sure could. Which is exactly why you're still wearing them. I wouldn't trust you as far as I could throw you."

"That's an odd thing to say."

"Another Donny-ism. It means I don't trust you very much. In fact, not at all."

"The ones on my wrists are getting hot, they're burning me."

"Alright, hold up a minute," instructed Adam as he retrieved a cloth tea towel from his pack. He placed it on the ground, then backed away. "Cover your handcuffs with that."

Penelope rolled her eyes and walked over to the dishcloth, which she placed around her wrists.

"Not sure what you think I could do to you to make you so scared of me," she explained.

"Not scared, just using an abundance of caution. Absolutely

necessary with you, as you've proven over and over. I don't feel like having my head bashed in unexpectedly by a demented psycho-bitch."

"Why do any of this then? Why take me?"

"Because I don't want you to die a horrible death of thirst or starvation. Might even be dingos around these parts looking for an easy meal of someone chained to a tree. Unlike you, I have a conscience."

"Oh, yeah, you're an angel for sure."

"Never said I was completely innocent, just not on the same psychotic level as you, is all."

"What's the plan, do you even have one?"

"Walking is the plan."

"I feel like I've been walking forever. I'm thirsty and hungry," she whined annoyingly.

"Keep that up and you'll get nothing till tomorrow morning and only then if you're good."

"What?"

"Oh, you think you have some sort of right to my food and water? Guess again, bitch. My stuff, and I'll decide who gets it and when, so you'd better behave and stop that bloody whinging. We'll rest up when we reach those trees. Nowhere else to take five anyway. Now move it, or stay here, I don't care. Just make up your bloody mind will you?"

"I'm going, I'm going. You're such a grouch."

"You get that when you're an intended murder victim."

"Wasn't trying to murder you."

"Were too."

"Not."

"Too."

They carried on like that for another hour until they reached the billabong. Penelope walked swiftly to the edge of the inviting pool before Adam called out.

"Hold up. I have to test the water first."

"Test it? For what?"

"What do you think?"

"I don't know."

"You are dense, aren't you? Radiation, nuclear fallout after Australia was nuked by China. Like the contaminated water you used to kill everyone? Any of this registering with you."

"I was only asking, don't be so mean."

"Let's get something straight. I can't trust you anymore and I certainly don't like you anymore. Get used to it. You can't expect me to be civil after you tried to murder me. If you don't like it, feel free to walk away and never come back. No, you can't do that because I can't trust that you won't return during the night to kill me again. Just shut up. I'm sick of all this. If you decide that you're unhappy with the way things are, I'll lock you up around a tree and leave you to your fate."

When Penelope closed her mouth to further comments, Adam tested the water with his device, registering only minimal sounds when he waved it over the surface.

"Great, we can refill our empty bottles with this water. Okay, we'll camp here for a day or two to rest. With any luck, we can kill some game when it comes to drink this evening. We could be dining on some roo steaks tonight."

"Are you crazy? We can't kill an innocent animal."

"You're asking me if *I'm* crazy? You're perfectly willing to kill a hundred people for a game yet baulk over killing an animal for our dinner? Man, you are really weird, you know that? Suit yourself anyway if you want some rehydrated goop or canned stuff. Might not get to kill anything anyway, so it's probably a moot point."

"Moot?"

"Not happening. You don't get an education from me. Now, drink from the water if you're thirsty. Splash some over your head to cool yourself down, then go sit in the shade up against the trunk so I can secure you."

"You aren't going to chain me around the tree again?" she asked with a sinking heart.

"You bet I am. You can have your legs around the tree or your arms. Choice is yours."

"You can't keep chaining me to a tree every night. That would be cruel."

"Coming from you that hardly qualifies."

When Penelope drank and splashed water over her head, she felt immensely relieved. Reluctantly, she tromped over to a tree. Adam asked her to place her cuffed wrists to one side of the tree, while he squatted behind the trunk. The second he released one of her wrists from the cuff, she made a sudden movement in the hope of escaping. Until she looked up to stare directly down the barrel of the pistol aimed at her right eye, causing her to remain perfectly still. Adam secured the wrist to the other around the tree.

"This is stupid, I can't sleep like this. What are you going to do with me?"

"You just proved how very not-stupid it is. Try that again and you'll regret it. What to do with you? Now, there's a question."

Adam contemplated the answer as he set about heating a can of food for them. He had his portable butane single-burner stove, onto which he placed the small pan with the contents of a can labelled, 'Braised Steak & Onions'. It did not look very appetising when he upended the contents into the pan. He was only half kidding about killing their supper. He doubted he had the stomach for killing an animal then attempting to butcher it.

After they had both eaten, him feeding her, he set the pot on to boil some water for coffee. Adam refilled the empty plastic bottles with water from the billabong. He peered at the water longingly. He'd never immersed himself in water before. He'd seen movies of people swimming, seen pictures in magazines of folks in the surf on glorious beaches, always hoping that one day he might be able to share in that experience.

He glanced at Penelope to assure himself that she could not possibly wriggle free. The tree was stunted but far too tall for her to do anything about scaling it or reaching over it. She would have to chew through the tree or her arm to get away. Neither avenue seemed plausible in Adam's mind. After finishing his coffee, the afternoon sun was still hot enough to burn his skin if he stayed in the open too long. Sweat poured from his sun-beaten face after drinking the hot coffee, despite being in the shade.

He stood up to disrobe. Penelope watched with growing curiosity as he stripped naked. She felt her groin moisten and tingle at the sight of his well-toned body, pale as it was with tan lines forming on his thighs around the hemline of his shorts. Oohing and ahhing as he stepped into the sunshine on the hot gravel, Adam made his way to the billabong. He stepped gingerly into the water up to his knees. He felt the mud squishing between his toes, a new sensation for him.

Penelope watched with pure envy as he walked further, then

bend at the knees to sit and soak in the cool water. She saw him wiggle his bottom with glee, imagining a smile plastered a mile wide on his face.

"What, what's it like?" she asked coyly.

"Like nothing else I've ever done. It's, it's unbelievable! Frigging fantastic," he replied tossing handfuls of water over his head.

"Can, can I have a go?"

"After your little stunt? Get real."

"What if I promise...?"

"Your promises mean nothing to me anymore. You've proven you can't be trusted, time and time again."

"I'll be good."

"You are incapable of being good. You're evil incarnate."

"What does that mean?"

"I don't really know. Just something I read once, I think. Tell you what, though. I've been thinking about your question about what I'm going to do with you. The world, if it still exists, if people are still alive out there, they need my father's research. They need to have a chance at combatting the superbug. I can't physically give it to them. I'm a super-spreader, just like Donny said. You caught it from me. You would have died if not for the vaccine which cured you. They don't need *my* blood anymore, they have you.

"So, here's the deal. We keep heading towards the coast trying to find a pocket of civilisation that survived. Once we find one, I will send you with Donny's notes and written directions from me for them to follow. Included in the package you deliver will be the keys to the cuffs which you will not access until you reach them. I'll be watching you closely, so no false moves.

"They'll need some of your blood. You may be required to stay with them for a time while they develop the vaccine. You'll be on your own after that. I can't join them. I can never be with another human until that vaccine is distributed."

"What if we don't find anyone?"

"Always a possibility. Not one I want to contemplate, though. That would be devastating."

"Where are we going then?"

"The closest big city to our position would be Adelaide. I don't propose going *into* the cities, though. They'll be too hot."

"Too hot?"

"Radiation. Probably won't be able to get near the nuke sites safely for another thousand years, at least. We'll stick to the perimeters of those places if they test safely. It should be easy to spot pockets of survivors by their campfires at night. We never go forward during the day until we have seen no sign of life the previous evening. Even meeting up with someone accidentally will be fatal for them."

"What are you going to do once you've got rid of me?"

"Why should you care?"

"Just curious."

"I intend to find a beach. If I find a house there I can use, great. If not, I'll build one and stay there until I pick up signs of people being immunised. I never want to see anything underground again. I may not even sleep inside my beach hut. I want to sleep under the stars out in the open for the rest of my life."

"You mean that? You'll let me go?"

"Yes, Penelope, I mean that. I am a man of my word. I don't know what else to do with you. I wish you'd died in that cave-in to save me the trouble, I really do. You've been nothing but a pain in the arse since I had the misfortune of meeting you."

"You lied then. You said you loved me."

"Stupid, stupid infatuation by a young, inexperienced man. I fell for your bullshit like some idiot thinking with his dick! I should have had the good sense to realise that. Call me a dumb arse if you want. I deserve it for even contemplating a relationship with such an evil person. I will always regret admitting that to you whether it was real or not."

"I, I'm sorry, Adam. I know you don't believe that, but I am. If you..."

"Give it a rest! I'm deaf to anything that comes out of your mouth," he stated bitterly.

"You wouldn't leave me chained to a tree, would you?"

"I told you what my plans are. Now shut up unless you want a gag. I want to enjoy this moment in peace. I feel as though every ache and pain is being washed away and cleansing my anxieties at the same time. Bloody paradise." Adam closed his eyes and ears to the world, submerging his head under the crisp, cooling water.

Penelope watched on in frustration and anger. If she wasn't

bound like an animal she would let loose with a mighty tirade to end all tirades. Instead, she took the man at his word that he would gag her if she opened her mouth again too soon. She couldn't blame him for feeling the way he did. She was so very, very confused by everything. Ecstatic about being free of the underground compound, to be sure, but essentially, still a prisoner.

She was so sure. Positive about everything until he came along. Then she figured out how he was a part of it; the game. He was the last-minute drop-in, the ringer, the game-changer, the foil to make her slip up. Then it all went wrong so quickly. She suspected him of lies and deceit. She fully expected treachery. Only, he didn't exhibit any of the tactics she assumed he would use. The game kept changing. Had she been wrong from the start? Was everything he said true?

She wasn't on Mars. He was right about that. There was nobody that came when she turned the tables on him to end up in the other chamber. No one to congratulate her, reward her, give her the acclaim she so richly deserved! She thought she had it all figured out and then he made her sick. He was right about that as well. He was wrong about the vaccine but he admitted that. It did cure her after a long and excruciating period. Breathing razor-blades he'd described it as. He wasn't wrong about that either if she had that pictured right.

They were on the surface, a blessed relief, she could see that clearly and there was no one around for as far as the eye could see. She hadn't seen any evidence of bomb-like devastation, not that she would know what to expect, and hadn't seen any victims of the superbug yet. That may only be because they hadn't reached any townships or outlying homesteads yet, she supposed.

Penelope hung her head as she mulled over all the conflicting messages and circumstances. Had her mother lied?

"It wasn't me," she blurted out suddenly.

"I thought I asked you to..."

"It wasn't me who killed them all," she said softly.

"What sort of game are you playing at now?"

"Mama told me what to do. She figured out how to do it when I told her about the water that I heard under my bed. She explained how to swap the water in the bottles for the bad stuff. She told me it was the game we watched and how we had to win it. She said the others were forming into groups and bullying everyone else. Men taking over everything and forcing women to do things. Daddy got killed when they ganged up on him outside our pod. Mama wanted to protect me. She said we couldn't let them win, that we were the ones who had to survive. It was Mama who buried them others. Then...then it was just a few of us left. One of the men, who was real sick, blamed us for what happened and attacked Mama. He killed her. I locked myself in my pod for days after that."

Penelope remained quiet while Adam tried to digest what she said. It made a certain amount of sense to him. He never fully accepted that a child was capable of what he'd assumed. She couldn't have known about the contaminated water unless her mother had told her, and probably wouldn't have come up with the diabolical scheme to kill off the opposition by utilising the water, by poisoning the others.

He shook his head in frustration and a begrudging admiration for the girl who went through all of that. It didn't forgive her actions against him after he was only being kind and helpful and he thought his feelings were reciprocated. He pushed those emotions back down again. It wouldn't help to get suckered again regardless of the truth. She could very well be spinning a whole new set of lies to trap him.

"Doesn't change or adequately explain what you did to me."

"I saved you, remember?"

"Only because you needed my provisions. Dragging me back into the shaft was your only way to get a hold of my backpack. If you hadn't succumbed to the choking dust I doubt we would be having this conversation now," said Adam sadly as he rose from the pool.

He sat in the sun on his T-shirt, facing away from her, to dry himself off.

"I wasn't going to leave you. I had nowhere to go anyway. You figured that way out of the hole. I don't think I would have been brave enough to try that on my own. You're very smart."

"Flattery won't get you anywhere. I'm immune to your feminine wiles now."

"What's that? Feminine...something."

"Wiles. The sneaky and devious methods employed by members of the opposite gender to lure their enchanted victims to their doom."

"I don't have any of them wiles you're talking about and you're too smart to fall for anything anyway."

"Oh, you have them in spades my dear Black Widow, and I fell for them, heart and bloody soul. Donny was so right when he warned me that could happen, most likely with the first girl I met. Oh boy! Clever, clever man and I just scoffed at him."

"You, you loved me? Truly?"

"Not straight away, that's for sure. I admit that the whole different skin colour threw me for a loop. I purposefully denied any connection that might have been forming for that reason. Then...well, it changed for me. I started to see beyond the outer layer. I think, I sorta fell in lust at that point. When we...you know, shared ourselves like that, it created a pretty solid bond. I found contentment and satisfaction inside, a calmness I had never experienced before. It felt right. I...I was at peace with the world for once. That grew into what I considered to be love. I was mistaken, though. It was probably just a youthful infatuation, a crush, like Donny said would happen. Thinking with my dick. See where that got me?"

"I'm sorry, Adam. So, very, very sorry. You were right. We could have had something really special. I'm a total fuck-up, aren't I?"

"Yep."

"You didn't have to agree so quickly," she said with a smile.

"Maybe."

Adam rose to dress in clean clothes from his backpack. He washed the few items he'd been wearing in the water with his bar of soap. His last one. As he hung his wet clothes on some low branches to dry, he thought about finding some more soap if he hoped to stay relatively clean. He planned to stay put for at least another day and night. He wanted to soak up the outdoors and luxuriate in the billabong once more before moving off. He supposed Penelope would need to wash and clean her clothes as well. It presented a problem he would have to face in the morning. She couldn't very well remove her clothing without being unshackled and un-cuffed.

A burst of raucous laughter startled the pair. Kookaburras, sitting in the upper branches of one of the eucalypts, raising a ruckus with their unique sound. Seeing Penelope quaking with fear...

"Just a pair of kookaburras. Birds, Penelope. Relax, they can't hurt you."

They listened to the unusual sound for a few moments before the birds flew off.

"I don't know if you took the time to gaze up at the night sky last night, Pen, but you should do it tonight. It's...mind-blowing. More stars than you could count in your lifetime I reckon."

"Sort of had my mind on other things last night," she admitted.

"Hmm."

Adam settled down on a rolled out ground mat, with his silver blanket at the ready should it get cooler later on. The sun was setting on the horizon casting shades of gold, orange and red across the heavens. The flat landscape took on a splendid golden glow. It was easy to assume that nothing out of the ordinary had occurred in Australia, that everything was just the way it had been before 2020, in a pre-Covid world.

DEATH

They had been scrutinising the house for signs of occupation throughout the evening. By dawn, Adam seemed satisfied that no one was living there or using the place temporarily. A couple of leaning fence posts and a few lengths of stray barbed wire were all that remained of the yards surrounding the old homestead. The near-petrified cow pats scattered about the area told of the reason for the home being out in the middle of nowhere.

Any grass that had once grown on the desolate earth had long since turned to dust along with everything else. The harsh, early morning sunlight blasted its heat down on the pair of observers stationed under the single tree half a kilometre distant. According to Adam's watch, it was only eight o'clock, yet his brow had already begun its day of extreme perspiration underneath the sweat-stained band of his cap.

Adam and Penelope had been walking for three days since leaving the billabong. Something neither wanted to do after tasting the sensations of bathing in the cool water. Adam finally mustered up the motivation to move when he saw their provisions dwindling far quicker than anticipated. Penelope was a voracious eater if left to her own devices. Fortunately for Adam, she was never left alone with the provisions or had a choice in the quantity they would eat.

Worst of all for Adam were the lingering effects the superbug had on Penelope who had a case of the galloping trots. Her rear end spray painted her patch of ground set aside as a lavatory after every meal. Adam had to curtail her use of toilet paper due to her 'going' so frequently, ordering her to use dried leaves instead. He grew very tired of having to release her from the tree to attend to her needs. In the end, he used a length of rope attached to her waist, tied with a dozen complex knots at her back, with the other end attached to the tree to allow her some freedom of movement that did not demand his involvement every time.

She didn't always reach her lavatory in time and the area reeked to high heaven. When her bowels finally settled and she had cleaned herself up, washed her clothes and buried her waste, the pair made a reluctant move.

Penelope could not quite comprehend the splendour of the sky at night in the outback. She asked Adam about a thousand questions each night, none of which were answered. He wasn't able to shut her up. At times he felt he could take no more and wanted to simply pop a bullet into her head. Fortunately, he hadn't any. Yet it would have made so much sense and saved him untold aggravation. He usually managed to shut his ears and pretend he was alone.

In truth, he felt better for a little company at times, even with all the useless talk and questions. She marvelled at everything, seeing most of it for the first time. Her inquisitive nature, her unbounded joy and sheer exuberance upon sighting her first dingo or goanna became humorously infectious, often making Adam laugh till his chest ached.

When they spied the homestead in the distance, the heat causing the structure to shimmer and undulate, they waited for nightfall to ensure there were no occupants.

Adam released Penelope from the tree to which she had been tethered during the evening. No amount of pleading or whining would prevent her nightly imprisonment. Though she desperately wanted Adam to know how ashamed she was of her behaviour toward him, he was resolute in his attitude. While he no longer spoke to her with pure venom dripping from every word, he was nonetheless rigid in his refusal to accept her sincerest apologies and wishes to make amends.

They made their way across the scorched land towards the homestead. It seemed intact from what Adam could see. Sand drifts had piled up high against one side of the structure, almost reaching the eaves. No one had actively cared for the desolate place in a very long time. Adam was somewhat reluctant to venture inside once they reached it, fearing all manner of creatures that may have taken it over. Snakes and spiders being at the top of that list of possible squatters that might object to their intrusion.

Wind chimes of bamboo and metal cylinders tinkled and clacked with the few breezes that sprung up periodically. Penelope looked like she was about to sprint at the slightest provocation or drop dead of a heart attack. Her eyes were wide as she stepped onto the raised wooden veranda at the front of the house. A swing chair and a couple of rocking chairs swayed to and fro with invisible hosts.

The atmosphere was worthy of a horror movie in Adam's opinion. Creepy, desolate and most likely, haunted. The creaking front door added to the illusion. Plain timber flooring with dusty rugs greeted them, leading to a long hallway that ran the length of the house, presumably to the kitchen.

With her heart in her mouth, Penelope inched forward at Adam's insistence. She baulked noticeably as he continually nudged her from behind. Her breathing had all but ceased as she made her way to the first opening on the left. Cobwebs, heavy with dust, adorned every corner and crevice. Adam looked at the living room where everything sat in perfect position, completely covered in layers of dust. Nothing had been disturbed in the room for years. The lounge setting, complete with lace antimacassars over the backs and arms of the chairs and couch, the TV and remotes, coffee tables and occasional tables, heavy timber bureau and ornate lampshades were all as they had been when the house was once cared for and lived in by the owners.

Nothing moved. Everything had a sombre stillness and silence about it. If a strong breeze were to enter the house the dust would probably choke them. There was a prevalent, musty, earthy aroma with a faint hint of something sour punctuating the air.

he next archway on the right revealed a formal dining room with a table for two perfectly set, only, layered in the timely sediments of nature. A large hutch stood against the left wall filled with fine bone china. The casement window, ornamented with dirty lace curtains, framed by heavy drapes, was too cloudy to allow any visibility through the pane.

Adam backed out of the room on tip-toes to allow Penelope to precede him to the next room on the left of the hallway which was the first one with a door. Penelope slowly creaked open the wooden door on its rusty hinges. All the noises from outside, like the wind chimes, were absorbed within the walls and heavy insulation of the house. It was as silent as a tomb.

When Penelope screamed, Adam clutched his heart thinking he was suffering an attack. The sound pierced his eardrums after the total silence, and Penelope careened into him when she turned to flee. They both landed heavily on the dusty floor in the hallway. It took all of Adam's strength to prevent her scrambling up and racing back outside. It was lucky for him that she was unable to move that fast while her ankles were shackled.

"Shit, Penelope. Calm the fuck down. What is it?"

"Can't...no, let me out. Let go..."

"Stop it. You can't run out of here. You'll end tits up on the floor again. Calm down. What is it? A snake? A spider?" He asked after restraining her arms from behind."

"P-p-people!"

"People?"

"Dead people! Old and...horrible, just...I can't go back in there."

"If they're dead they can't hurt you, girl. Just settle down a moment. You nearly gave me a bloody heart attack and my ears are still ringing from that high-pitched scream. Bloody Boris Karloff, eat your heart out."

"Who?"

"Never mind, just some old movies Donny used to bore me with in the beginning."

Adam edged his way around the door frame keeping a firm hold of Penelope. It was the main bedroom with an ornate brass bed and side tables. Under dirty mosquito netting, he saw two desiccated corpses looking like Egyptian mummies after they'd been unravelled. The smell he'd detected a moment ago was much stronger in the bedroom. No flies had made it to the corpses to lay their eggs because of the netting, ergo the corpses had dried up in the heat over a great length of time. Not that Adam was immediately aware of any of that. He would only work it out slowly, re-enacting the series of events in his mind that led to the circumstances in the bedroom.

He backed out of the room, closing the door to the grisly sight.

"This might be a good sign, Penelope."

"Are you fucking crazy? We have to get out of here," she screamed again as the panic rose again in her.

"Don't you see? Nothing has been touched since those two died in there a long, long time ago. There's hardly any of the smell left it's been that long. That means they are the owners, the farmers who lived here. They died of the superbug by the look of it. It happens quickly once it takes hold if they aren't in a hospital to have any help. There may be a treasure trove of stuff here to help us. There may be... Um, yeah. You're right. We should go back outside."

"What? I don't..."

"Come on move it. You were wanting to run out of here seconds ago."

When they reached the veranda, Adam spied the posts; square hardwood posts supporting the bullnose roofing. He pushed Penelope up hard against the post, swung her roughly around to arrange her arms around the posts once he'd released one of the handcuffs.

"What are you doing?"

"You wanted out, so you're out. I'm going back in and you can stay out here while I check the place out properly. Can't have you running off now, though, can we?"

"Eat shit and die," she spat.

"Charming. I'll get you a rocking chair to sit on. Just watch the red back spiders, hey?"

"What? Why do I have to watch out for them?"

"They're your sisters, part of the same family as the black widow spiders. Poisonous."

"Very funny."

"Not if you're bitten by one, no. Not funny at all."

"I'll stand in that case. Keep the bloody chair."

"They like tin rooves as well, so be careful they don't drop on you," said Adam pointing up and smiling.

"You're shitting me."

"I'm shitting you not. According to Donny, that is. I wouldn't know personally."

"What do they look like?"

"They have red backs, presumably," he said with a straight face. "I believe there's also a white tail spider you have to be wary of. Guessing it has a white...tail?"

He shrugged.

"Take me with you," she begged almost hysterically.

"Don't be such a drama queen. If you see any sort of creepy-crawly, squash it under your sandal. I shouldn't be too long."

With a singular purpose, Adam strode from the veranda, leaving Penelope to shake her head in wonder. The door opposite the owner's bedroom opened into the main bathroom. The deep claw-footed enamel bath was half-filled with putrid water. Adam wondered why anyone would want to take a bath while the world was turning upside-down. It was only later that he figured out the reason for it, that the farmers were preparing for the long haul with possible water contamination.

The next room on the right side of the hallway turned out to be a spare bedroom combined with a home office. Tucked into a corner was what Adam had been looking for. It was secured by a cheap padlock. He would have to find some tools with which to break in. Assuming that the couple in the master bedroom were farmers, Adam concluded that a shed full of tools and farming equipment would probably be found at the rear of the house.

Penelope was startled by the sudden reappearance of Adam as he rushed back out the door to race around the house.

"What's happening? Where are you going?" she yelled after him.

When he returned soon afterwards carrying a toolbox stuffed to overflowing with a wide selection of tools, she asked again what he was up to. Adam ignored her to return to the locked metal gun safe. He made short work of the flimsy padlock with his first swing of the rusted club hammer. The unsettled dust filled the room in seconds. Inside the gun safe was a high-powered rifle with sights for hunting large prey. Next to that was a small-bore rifle. A full box of ammunition for the smaller rifle sat on the top shelf of the safe. He couldn't find anything to suit the other one. He tried one of the shells in his pistol. Too small.

After briefly checking the rest of the house, he surmised that no other weapons other than knives and such were secreted around the house. He couldn't afford to allow his prisoner to get a hold of something to use against him, so he gathered what he could, securing it in the safe. He would still have to keep a very close eye on her while they occupied the house, which wouldn't be for very long. Adam spied a pantry full of canned and dried goods, as well as a lot of perishable stuff that had long ago ceased to be consumable.

As he suspected, there was no longer any running water. He imagined the couple would have used the hand pump he'd spied at the rear if it worked. The old windmill adjacent to the hand pump and trough, with missing vanes, had stopped spinning about a decade ago according to Adam's casual glance.

He walked back out to the front veranda where Penelope showed signs of panic. She eyed the rifle in his hands and watched as he opened the box of cartridges to feed the shells into the small magazine.

"Now we have bullets again for protection and game if we come across any."

Penelope gaped at the pistol tucked into the waistband of his shorts with incredulity, "You mean there weren't any of those things left in your gun?"

"Bullets? No. Lucky to find this and a box of ammunition."

"You mean I could have..."

She wasn't able to voice the end of the question. She realised how foolish she had been. She'd been suckered into believing he could kill her with the pistol.

"Okay, we need to get inside before we're seen," announced Adam.

"Seen? Seen by who?"

"By anyone still lurking in these parts just waiting to see signs of life out here. Donny said that Australia fell into lawlessness after the bombs dropped. Total anarchy. No one trusting anyone, shooting, looting, rape, murder and mayhem. Donny never left the bunker for the first couple of years. Even way out here there were still pockets of scruffy folks, gangs roaming the countryside stealing and killing indiscriminately until most of them fell victim to the superbug."

"You think they could still be around?"

"Hard to say for sure, but I'm not taking any chances. Better to be prepared than to be caught by surprise."

"What are we going to do then?"

"We'll stay here overnight, take what we can carry as far as food and other items that we think might come in handy, then head off again in the morning."

"I have to find something for me," she stated hesitantly.

"What?"

"Something for the blood."

"Blood?"

"Yeah, blood. My period?"

"What are you talking about?"

"Don't you know about that? Is there something the high and mighty Adam Harrow doesn't know for once? Something your precious Donny didn't explain?"

"I never said I knew everything. Pretty sure there are heaps of things I don't know. Now, are you going to explain or do I have to guess? If you're injured, you didn't tell me."

"A woman bleeds every month when she sheds the lining of her uterus if there is no fertilised egg."

"Bleeds where?"

"Where do you think?"

"How would I know? You get a bloody nose or something?"

"The uterus is below, idiot. I bleed from my vagina!"

Adam crinkled his nose and mouth in disgust while trying to digest the new information.

"Yeah, it's pretty gross and I usually get bad cramps with them as well."

"What will you look for?"

"Tampons, Mama called them, or pads. If I don't find any I can use old, clean rags like I used to in the compound."

"Every month?"

"Yeah, Adam. Every month like a clock."

"Like clockwork."

"Huh?"

"Like clockwork is the saying. Not 'like a clock'."

"Whatever," she replied in a bored manner.

"Yeah, you're right. I shouldn't be trying to teach you anything. Not my place and you wouldn't appreciate it anyway. Thank you for reminding me not to waste my breath on you."

"Lighten up old man. I'm in the middle of nowhere, hand-cuffed to the post of a house with dead people and I'm getting my period which hurts like fuck!"

"Whoa, now who's going all mental and serious?"

"Don't fuck with a woman during her time of the month, okay?"

"Whatever," he said mimicking her earlier response."

Adam chuckled as he released one of Penelope's wrists. As he made to grab the wrist once it was around the post, she pushed past him suddenly, hobbling off the veranda into the yard. She ambled as fast as her tired, shackled legs could take her before she glanced back to see what Adam was doing. When she saw him almost doubled up with laughter on the floorboards of the veranda she stopped dead.

Confused and angry, out of breath, she waited while her chest heaved. She saw Adam straighten up, still chuckling heartily.

"Why stop? Keep going, numbskull."

"What do you mean? Why are you letting me go?"

"You think I *want* you with me? You're a pain in the arse woman and I wish you would go take a flying leap. Only, I know you can't go far shackled like that. Without water or food, you'll end up crawling back here. You better think about that, though. If you leave, if you go past that yard rail, you leave for good. If I see you coming back here, or towards me today or in the days to come, I will shoot you. I have a rifle now. I can shoot more accurately and over a longer distance."

"I don't want to be locked up anymore."

"Then go. Have fun. Toodle-loo," he waved mockingly.

Penelope looked about doubtfully. She knew she couldn't make it very far in the ankle shackles. She also knew how hot it was in the open. Without water, she wouldn't last much more than a day. Her head drooped in recognition of her hopeless circumstances. Her stubbornness and wild nature would not enable her to escape or sway the man to change his mind about her captivity. He was adamant about his mistrust of her and she could do nothing to earn that trust back. She understood her predicament clearly, though it rankled her no end.

She returned to the veranda submissively, with her hands held before her, accepting his conditions. Tears of frustration and pity ran down her cheeks as Adam bade her walk inside ahead of him. When they reached the kitchen at the rear of the house he made her sit on one of the wooden chairs.

"Place the open cuff around the metal rail under the tabletop. You'll have one hand free for the time being to eat and drink something on your own."

Adam watched her carefully as she obeyed his instructions in pouting silence. He checked the cuff to ensure it was secure and unable to be removed from the table. If she wanted to go anywhere without his permission, she would have to take the heavy, laminated table with her, or find a way of destroying it. He pushed the table hard up against the kitchen wall where she had no way of reaching any of the drawers or kitchen cupboards. He placed her chair back under her.

"Just so you know, you're there for the next few hours. If you need to piss or shit, I'll give you a pot and you can go right where you are. You are not free to look around for whatever it is you want. You can tell me what it is, what it looks like and I'll search. You have no say about your conditions of captivity. I told you already when I'll release you and I'll keep my word about that. If you want to go before then, it's on the proviso that you take nothing with you and stay shackled. That's the only way I know I can get far enough ahead of you that you won't be able to follow. If you do, I'll hear you coming from quite a distance, rattling and jingling as you stumble about."

"You're an arsehole!"

"Yep, no doubt about that. An arsehole who is alive and intends to stay that way. If you want to keep breathing you'd better start following orders and watching your mouth. I've about had you up to my eyeballs. It won't take much to make me change my mind about keeping you alive."

Adam went to a set of drawers under the sink where he found a few folded tea cloths. He removed a bottle of water from his pack. He handed both to Penelope.

"Make yourself useful and clean that table off. Bloody dust is so thick it's dangerous. Clean this chair for me as well," he ordered while pushing a chair in front of her.

"I'm not your slave. Do it yourself."

"Fine. Guess you aren't hungry or thirsty then?" he asked simply.

When Penelope crossed her arms over her chest, he had his answer. He smiled at her recalcitrant and immature behaviour. Like any child, she would learn the hard way eventually. She would learn that Adam Harrow did not capitulate to temper tantrums, ultimatums, or any kind of emotional blackmail. She had nothing to barter with, nothing of value or interest to him. Nothing that could persuade him to be lenient or lax with her. She didn't even have any expertise or special knowledge she could bring to the table as bargaining chips.

Every time it seemed to Adam that she might begin displaying redeeming qualities, she proved herself to be false. There was nothing of the person he'd first met behind the window, the naked, black goddess who managed to turn him on like nothing else on earth, including Miss November. He sighed heavily as he withdrew the chair from her reach just as she was about to capitulate.

"I'll do it," she said sullenly.

"Too late. I'll enjoy a hot meal tonight and a cup of coffee while you go hungry. It's no use looking at me like that. You might act like a child and talk like a child sometimes, but you had better get it into your head that you aren't a child anymore and will not get your way by behaving like one. Grow up, Penelope Archer. You aren't a bloody princess, you aren't a champion of the game, you aren't anything so special that I have to kowtow to your stubborn moods. You want to eat and drink, then you'll have to earn it. You'll have to do as I say if you want to survive. It's about time you showed some gratitude for all that I've done for you."

"Maybe when you let me go..."

"NO! NO, NO, NO!" he screamed with spittle flying from the corners of his mouth as he rounded on her.

Penelope recoiled in horror, having never been yelled at or accosted in such a manner. Her face crumpled into tears.

"You stupid, spoilt little brat! You complete and utter imbecile. There is more to life than your selfish needs. Australia has suffered unimaginably and her people are dying still, I imagine. Whether by radiation or the superbug and you dare to think nothing about that? You self-centred twit! Life has more meaning than this, than you or me. The fate of the human species could be at stake here and all you care about is yourself. You make me sick. If you didn't serve a purpose I would shoot you right now.

"The only reason you are alive is so I can deliver Donny's notes through you and they can probably use your blood to begin producing a vaccine. Other than that, you are worthless. Less than worthless. You are possibly the worst example of a human being I am ever likely to come across. Woe betide us all if you turn out to be the norm rather than the exception. If that's the case then the human race isn't worth saving, it's already doomed."

Adam turned on his heel and stormed out of the kitchen, out of the back door into the rear yard, where he stood shaking with impotent rage, fighting off the inexorable march of grim depression. The mists of his gloomy darkness gathered about him, blocking out the harsh glare of the sunlight, forcing lightness and good humour into the nether regions of his mind where they were slowly strangled by despair.

Apparitions on dark wings exploded through his vision and in his mind. An enormous leaden shroud descended on him as the assault on his senses and emotions continued. Adam cried out in sheer misery and heartache as the foggy demons tore through him, shredding and tearing him asunder. He was being flayed alive. Stripped of his positivity and good nature as easy as peeling a banana.

He fell to his knees on the scorched earth with his hands to his head as bitter tears fell, the only moisture the baked gravel had seen in years. The overwhelming grief and utter uselessness he felt rendered him immobile, paralysing his will. He collapsed onto his side and lay dormant till the sun sank in the west.

CALAMITY

At three in the morning, the horizon was lit artificially as the house went up in flames. The parched timbers became the perfect fuel when set alight. The flames soared into the heavens, casting embers kilometres higher on the prevailing breezes.

"What, what's happening?" asked Penelope tiredly.

"They set the house on fire, of course."

"Who?"

"Whoever saw the lantern you turned on. It was a glaring beacon for anyone to see for hundreds of kilometres. Why do you think we waited for a night, observing the house before *we* went down the following day?"

"But if someone saw, then why didn't we..."

"Not the right kind of people. We're looking to find a semi-civilised, established group of individuals hoping to make a life for themselves. Not a rowdy bunch of anarchists looking to terrorise communities and cower the populace. They don't care enough to manufacture a vaccine, to help anyone. They are happy to live in gangs, to take anything they want without ever having earned it," explained Adam in a hushed tone.

"What happened to you? Why didn't you come when I called you?"

"I needed some time by myself. I needed to be anywhere but near you. You're lucky I came back at all. It was only the distant sound and then the moving lights that finally broke through."

"Won't they come looking for us?"

"Maybe. I hope I've obscured our tracks enough to throw them off."

"I still don't understand how you could have known."

"Nomadic marauders. Donny came across them a few times in his travels. He warned me. They aren't the types you want to associate with unless you want to engage in the baser forms of life including killing other humans? Might suit you. Want to go join them? No? We'd better keep moving then. They probably won't waste time searching at night for the owners of that candle we left lit for them. The way they seem to be racing around on their machines, they'll obliterate any signs we may have missed anyway. I'm not worried. They're doomed anyway. If just one of them touched anything in that house that I touched, they signed their death warrant. One infected person would spread it to the others like wildfire. Any survivors we'll see coming from way off and I have a rifle now...with ammunition."

Adam did not see the contemptuous look he was shot on the back of that comment.

Penelope had fallen asleep at the kitchen table. She had no idea what could have made the sounds outside after Adam woke her. Mechanical perhaps, but that was a guess. When Adam re-entered the kitchen looking washed out and drawn he nearly went berserk at her for turning his lantern on.

She'd managed to drag the table and herself to his backpack in the hope of finding the keys to her shackles. She was bitterly disappointed to find nothing. When she searched through a few of the kitchen draws in the hope of finding a weapon she might use against her captor, she soon realised he had already removed anything dangerous. Forks, butter knives and spatulas were the most threatening implements she could find. She gave up in the end. She wasn't able to free herself from the table and she wasn't able to get the table through the doorways. It didn't occur to her to tip the table over and simply slide it at an angle through the doorway, one set of opposing legs at a time.

It wouldn't have mattered if she had. Adam had placed everything in the safe and locked it with another padlock he'd found in a kitchen drawer. She didn't know where Adam had gone and couldn't see what was making him moan and groan for hours as night descended. In the gathering gloom, she placed the wind-up lantern on the table for the comfort of some light. Placing her head on her folded arms upon the laminate surface of the table, she fell asleep.

When Adam woke her with a fevered tirade about the light, she became aware of the noise. He grabbed a selection of food items and anything else he thought they might use or consume in a rush. When he was satisfied that they had what they could carry, he exchanged his precious lantern for a lit candle. He unshackled Penelope's ankles, then handcuffed himself to her. Then they ran out of the back door.

The sounds of engines and the bouncing lights became louder as they exited the house, though they were still some distance off. They had probably half to three-quarters of an hour head start on them. He tied a bundle of weighted farmer's overalls to his waist, allowing it to drag behind them to obscure their tracks as they ran. How successful they were, he would only find out in the morning. He thanked his father for that piece of strategy that came to him in a flash when he considered their flight from the old farmhouse.

After running flat out for as long as their tired bodies allowed, they slowed to a steady walk to get as far away from the dozen or more vehicles buzzing noisily around the house intimidating whoever the occupant was thought to be. The gang most likely had scouts going out most evenings searching for signs of human activity, just as they had been doing the previous night when they observed the house. The marauders could not have known about the existence of the farmhouse before or they would already have looted and destroyed it as they were intent on doing that evening.

By three in the morning, they could walk no further until they had rested. They watched the flickers of flame in the inky darkness of the moonless night. The whooping and cheering of the gang members circling the house on their machines carried to them on the slight breeze.

Adam was encouraged that others may have survived after witnessing signs of life on the surface for the first time since leaving the bunker. If the bad ones made it, then some good ones must have as well. At least, that was his assumption. He had to find a group of people who were worth saving, who would seek a qualified person to manufacture the vaccine. Though he detested the fact that he'd been born and raised as a lab experiment by an unfeeling, uncaring parent, he ultimately believed in the premise for it, the goal. He had to believe it.

If they could avoid falling into the clutches of the marauders and their kin to find that group of solid, civilised people who had not descended into the animalistic instincts of humanity, then he could bequeath them the notes. After that, it didn't matter what happened to him...or her. It only mattered that the human species was given a chance. Law and order would follow again once the population increased and families once more needed protection, schooling for the children, commerce and farming...life. Maybe a better life than the one that had been destroyed.

Maybe a newer, younger generation brought up in the wastelands of nuclear destruction might learn valuable lessons from the sins of the forefathers, to create something far better, more meaningful and longer-lasting. He hoped it would be so, otherwise, his life and his suffering would have been in vain.

Somewhere out there Adam knew that he would find that bunch of folks to set things right, to make it good and wholesome, without all the rubbish of the past intruding. Just like the new sprigs of green growth that sprung from the ashes of the Australian bushfires, so too would a new civilisation grow from the nuclear ashes of the past.

The End

DUMPED

A preview

Psychological drama

On the way to an island holiday with his fiancée, Mark Streeton undergoes profound psychological changes as a result of isolation, physical pain, and emotional distress when their plane is destroyed. Unfettered by the distractions of everyday life in the city, his mind is left to ferment the negative into more than was ever intended, capable of actions far beyond his perceptions. Ultimately, only a mirror of his brutality will bring his conscience to bear

DAY ONE

When Mark opened his eyes he was blinded by the remorseless sunlight, reducing his pupils to pinpoints. Then pain abruptly made its presence known. Peering downwards, he could see his right leg bent in a shape that was not normal for a leg. His breathing was laboured due to severely bruised or broken ribs.

When his eyes finally adjusted to the glare enough to squint, he discovered that he was in his seat, alone, outside the plane, on a beach! He saw no sign of the plane, or Louise, or anyone else. He remained securely fastened to the seat by the cinching seat belt, with his leg broken below the knee. Footprints led away from the seat into the distance.

He screamed in agony as he attempted to move. The screaming caused his chest to hurt and his brain felt like it was about to explode. The row of seats on which he sat, rested on the lower section of the beach, with waves lapping at the edge. He was soaked through, and despite the heat from the sun, felt a cold deep within his marrow.

Another minor pain reminded him that his seat belt (which probably saved his life), was biting painfully into his lower gut. Slowly, he straightened himself further to relieve the pressure. It only caused extreme, white-hot agony to course through his system from the broken leg that flopped uselessly beneath him. It took several minutes for the waves of pain to subside enough for him to resume thought. While keeping his body as still as possible, he released the seat belt.

One less discomfort to deal with; dozens of others to go it seemed. He surveyed his immediate surroundings without turning his head. He had possibly been in a slumped position for a long time before he sat upright. A colossal headache was gradually ebbing, though not quickly enough for Mark's liking. He allowed himself to become concerned at his solitude, with only the mysterious footprints to suggest another presence.

He could not see behind him and had no intention of turning his head any time soon. While he felt like shouting for help, he didn't believe it would gain assistance or be heard by more than the ocean or the sand. No other sounds of human life were heard by him. He thought only to rest for a time, to gather himself and his thoughts, to run through what he knew.

Louise! He could remember the heated argument he was having with his fiancée before waking up on the beach. He remembered a white flash the moment before the lights went out.

***

"Ladies and Gentlemen, this is the Captain speaking. I apologise for the bumpy ride. To avoid the worst of the bad weather, we are descending to a lower altitude and skirting the edges of the unexpected storm cell. Unfortunately, this will delay our arrival time. The good news is that the weather in the Hawaiian Islands is unaffected by the storm with clear sunny skies and balmy temperatures. Should you have concerns about connecting flights, please inform one of the flight attendants who will notify the appropriate airlines to make other arrangements. Please remain seated whilst the seatbelt sign remains on. Thank you for your patience. We apologise for any inconvenience. Enjoy the rest of your flight."

Ignoring the captain's interruption to their argument, twisting uncomfortably in his seat to face Louise once more, Mark wrestled with his seat belt which seemed too tight. "Are you out of your mind? I mean, you can't be serious?" he whispered.

Louise nodded her head solemnly.

"If this is a joke, it isn't funny, Louise", Mark added. "How can you do this to me? To us? We're about to go on the holiday of a lifetime. We have planned and saved for this pre-honeymoon holiday for years. Halfway there, WHAM, just like that you tell me you're pregnant with someone else's child? What the fuck is going on? Why are you doing this? What have I done to deserve this?"

"Glad you finally asked. Don't think I didn't see you at the train station six months ago."

"Are you insane? What the hell does that have to do with anything?"

"Don't play that game with me, Marky-boy, I saw you clear as day."

"I am trying as hard as I can to stay calm and keep my voice down here but I will lose it soon if you do not explain what that horseshit means. I have no idea what you're talking about, and you know I hate that name you always come up with when you're pissed off about something."

"It's over, Mark, I saw you at the train station when I went there to pick up, June."

"Wait a minute, June? That day when you went to the city for drinks with, June? You're saying you saw me at the same train station?"

"Catch on quick don't you?"

"Sarcasm does not become you, *dear*. I still don't understand what this is all about even if you did see me that day."

"Oh, come off it, I saw you. No need to deny it. When I saw you there, I knew it was over for us. How could you do it? I never cheated on you!"

"Didn't you just tell me you did? That you're carrying someone else's baby? That you will meet this person when we land, to have a holiday with *him* while leaving me stranded?"

"Well, sure. After what I saw that day, I started seeing Luke. At least I knew he wanted me and only me."

"Luke? What, no, Luke Harman? Now I know you're kidding around, but it's a shitty thing to do, Louise."

"I'm not kidding, I'm seeing your friend, Luke. You practically drove me into his arms."

"He is not, and never was, my friend. Are you going to tell me what you think you saw or do I go on guessing what it's all about until we land? When I finally give that slime ball his just desserts."

"Do that and we call the cops."

"You think I care? It would be worth going to jail to see him sprawled on the tarmac. How could you have hooked up with *him* of all people? Makes me ashamed to have ever been your partner if your taste in men is that bad! You two deserve each other and I hope he treats you like I know he will. Did you know he was into swinging? And both ways might I add."

"What does that mean?"

"Multiple partners, any gender, dear. I hope you were careful…oops, no you weren't. Gee, wonder what diseases you will catch? What will you give to the bastard you're carrying?"

"Jealous, Marky?"

"Confused, Louise, not to be mistaken with jealousy by any stretch of the imagination, and counting my lucky stars I find this out before our wedding. I, I… fuck! I can't believe how callous you are to do this. What did you think you saw?"

"You honestly can't remember? You do it that often that you can't even remember that incident?"

"I have done nothing at all, let alone often. Can you please just tell me straight? What is it I'm accused of?"

"I saw you with her; that…prostitute! Right there on the platform for all the world to see. Hugging and kissing and twirling around like long lost lovers. The familiarity you displayed was evidence of an on-going arrangement. I was so ashamed that you felt you had to pay for sex while you had me at home anytime you wanted. I felt dirty and used. You talk about diseases, what about the filth they sleep with, passing on to you and God knows who else? Didn't you think something was wrong when I refused to sleep with you after that day? No way was I going to catch anything from you, so I accepted an invitation from Luke to go out the following week. We've been seeing each other ever since and you don't understand what you are talking about when it comes to Luke. He isn't into other partners and certainly not male partners."

Mark sat there for a long moment absorbing the information as the plane droned on toward the island destination intended as their dream come true. He scoured his memory to find the day at the train station she mentioned, the day she went to pick up June. She told him in the morning at breakfast that she was going to the station at lunchtime to pick up her best friend. They would do lunch and shopping in Chapel Street afterwards. She asked him… what? Something about joining them at lunch? Prostitute? Mark had never…shit! Okay, okay. Shit, he supposed she was right to be shocked if she saw that.

"It wasn't at all what you thought. Why wouldn't you ask for an explanation?"

"I didn't need an explanation, I saw it with my own eyes, and, June saw it too."

"You don't understand…"

***

Mark remembered the bright flash. Lightning? Possible, he thought because they were trying to get around a storm system at the time. Bomb? Surely not with all the bullshit going on since

9/11. A surface-to-air missile like the one that shot down the plane over that Russian place? Hard to be sure as he didn't even know the plane route or what landmasses they would be flying over. His geography sucked big time, so he had no idea where he might be other than somewhere in the Pacific Ocean. They may not even be anywhere near the air route anyway, seeing as the captain said they were deviating from their normal path.

Who knew how long the plane remained in the air after he blacked out. Did the pilots get off a mayday call? Is the black box, which is really orange, nearby to lead rescuers to his location? Castaway? Impossible. Yet he was alone on an island. He was glad there were no volleyballs nearby for him to begin talking to.

There were no storm clouds. No clouds at all in a clear blue sky with a brilliant orb bestowing inhumane temperatures and light intensities upon the earth. Ahead of him, all he saw was an endless expanse of beach with waves rolling gently in perpetual motion.

Higher up the beach, he spied the ubiquitous coconut palms dotting the dunes. Under any other circumstances, an idyllic setting in paradise. The agony he endured reminded him that this particular paradise was tainted. Not only was he at the mercy of the elements and the unbelievable pain assaulting his body, but he was also entirely isolated.

After taking in as much detail as possible of his surroundings, Mark knew that his first order of business was going to have to be attending to his broken leg. He was certain he was in for a world of hurt if he moved but knew he could not remain in the seat for much longer. Sooner or later the tide would turn and he would be caught by the advancing waters. He knew he would have to face incredible pain to move beyond the high water line.

He had to find some way of splinting his leg before more damage or internal bleeding occurred. He checked his pocket for the paracetamol capsules that were there for the earaches flying caused him. He wished earaches were his only concern at present. The packet was still there with only two of twenty-four capsules missing. He punched out three which he swallowed with difficulty due to his dry throat. He realised he would need fresh water before too long as well.

Who knew how long he had been in the water and how much seawater he had swallowed before he woke. His watch was of little use as it was totally water-logged. The sun was high in the sky which meant it was around midday. The plane left Melbourne airport at around five in the morning. They had been at least seven hours into their eleven and a half hour flight across the Pacific, which meant it could no longer be the same day. Was that the name of the damn ocean? He wished he knew more, that he'd paid better attention in geography classes at school.

As far as Mark knew, there had to be quite a few islands along the flight path, though he could not be sure. He could not know how long the plane remained in the air or what direction it was flying at the time he blacked out.

He doubted that it was the same day of his flight, it had to be the following day. It would only be a matter of time before rescuers scoured the area along the flight path to find survivors, if they weren't already. He didn't panic about being found. He only worried about his condition, when he was eventually found.

To stay alive until then meant he had to prioritise. Leg first, thirst, hunger, and shelter later. He knew that the warmth of the sun would dry his clothes soon enough, so he scanned the upper beach area for anything that might help him set his leg. There was an overabundance of driftwood to choose from littering the high watermark.

He could make out some frayed hawser among the flotsam and jetsam scattered throughout the driftwood. He thought he may be able to unwind the hawser to retrieve manageable rope lengths with which to tie the splints to his leg. He could not plan anything beyond that task as he would most likely blackout from the pain a few times in between. The pain capsules would only take the edge off, nothing more. He gritted his teeth to prepare for the ordeal.

The first blackout occurred not long after he moved off the airline seat. The searing, relentless pain continued to plague him throughout his crawl to reach the driftwood. He screamed at the top of his lungs each time his foot caught on a lump of disturbed sand or seaweed. Mark could not imagine torture at the hands of an enemy during wartime being any worse. Thousands of POWs might argue that point, however. He was in no mood to debate the issue, though thinking of useless shit like that distracted him from the intensity of the pain.

He was unsure how often he blacked out during his crawl, it just felt like an eternity before he reached his goal. It didn't take him long to find suitably sized sticks with which to splint his leg. He began untwisting the large hawser into manageable strands of sufficient length. Once the rudiments of his first aid were gathered, he faced the next problem of aligning the two broken pieces.

He would have to stretch his lower leg to a point where the bones straightened. To accomplish that task would mean anchoring his foot somehow and stretching the leg.

Mark had no idea if he possessed the courage to achieve his goals involving pain on such a scale. He knew he had to try, otherwise, his leg would never knit and would probably require amputation. Amputation may well be necessary regardless of his efforts, but that didn't mean he shouldn't try. He steeled himself for the expected outcome. Placed his foot between two large driftwood trunks nearby, then pulled back suddenly and hard.

When he woke, the sun was well down on the horizon. He prayed fervently that he succeeded the first time around because he seriously doubted his ability to repeat the procedure. He peered down at his leg. It was as good as he believed he could manage without better equipment at his disposal. The pain of securing the splints to four sides of his leg didn't begin to compare to the previous manoeuvre.

He pushed another three capsules out of the packet. He would have to ration them to conserve them as long as possible. Eating and swallowing the capsules was getting harder the dryer his throat became. Water would become his next priority rapidly. He didn't know how long he could last without water. A couple of days tops? He didn't know how long the rescue would take, but he was determined to be alive when it arrived.

The night air would get cool, no doubt. It meant he needed to find somewhere to hole up for the night which was fast approaching. Exposed as he was on the top of the beach was not an option despite his recently dried clothes. From his low vantage point, he was unable to make out much beyond the dunes at the top of the beach, but he could see some low shrubs which he may be able to slither under for protection. He would need some crutches to get around with, but that would have to wait for the next day.

After the pain he had caused himself, he would need to convalesce, gather his strength for the days to follow. He hoped there would not be too many to endure before help arrived. He was strangely calm considering his predicament. Panic never helped him in the past, so he didn't think it would assist him in his present circumstances. He mustered his remaining strength for the task of moving himself beyond the dunes to find some shelter.

* * *

Mark gasped in awe at the panoply of stars visible that night. He lay just beyond the overhanging branches of shrubbery atop the crest of the dunes, staring up at the magnificent display, impossible to be seen through the ambient light of most cities. It had been a very long time since he had been camping. He moved from the country to the city of Melbourne to follow his career at the age of eighteen. After his younger brother Frank passed away from his final bout of cancer, leukaemia, Mark could not remain at home.

He and his brother would often go off together camping beside different creeks, rivers and lakes around central New South Wales when they were younger. Then cancer came, which ate away their time, their happiness and his well-being.

He had not been camping since. It would not have felt the

same without Franky there, so he didn't bother. He ran away to the city at the first opportunity to become a lawyer. He had visions of nobility like any other young student lawyer, which quickly disappeared. He was a public defender with Legal Aid and his clients were almost always guilty.

Mark represented the lowest of the low and he hated every moment. He was on the verge of changing jobs, trying to go it alone. He was waiting to talk Louise around after their holiday. He shook his head at the thought of his fiancée. Mark could not believe the stupidity of her actions. Had she just asked him about the meeting at the train station she would have understood.

He didn't even know if Louise had survived. Were they her footprints he saw? Surely she wouldn't have just abandoned him like that? Not that he really cared after what she revealed. For her to throw away everything they had worked towards over a misunderstanding, astonished Mark no end. He could definitely see how she might misconstrue what she had witnessed, but to assume so much without a word, then throw herself to that…thing, Luke, was unforgivable.

The premeditated revenge of dumping him on their way to Hawaii was the lowest act imaginable, only to be capped off by the revelation of a pregnancy to that lowlife prick! Mark seethed silently when he thought about them sneaking off. He started piecing together the snippets he recalled that didn't ring true at the time. The night she stayed over at a friend's place. A look of evasion when he asked about her evening. Her reluctance to make love of late and so many other moments that began to make sense in the light of the new knowledge.

How naïve he had been not to question her further when her answers didn't gel, when timelines didn't marry, when she was out more often than reasonable. He figured their jobs were causing them to drift apart slightly; he hoped that the vacation would remedy that. They were going to work out their wedding date on the trip, discuss arrangements, and make preparations.

Despite the problems they faced he never once imagined they were insurmountable. Mark believed she was the one for him, for better or worse. Luckily he found out the worst before they tied the knot. Not that he was such a traditionalist that he would not have considered divorce in the event of a revelation like an infidelity.

He was just glad that he didn't have to go through the orchestrations of divorce on top of the heartache. Mark had been involved in far too many divorce proceedings through his job without having to deal with his own.

He didn't feel an overwhelming sadness at having lost Louise as a partner, nor did he feel any grief at the possibility she may be dead. He was, if anything, angry. More than angry, he was furious. How dare she humiliate him like that? Louise obviously loved him very little, if at all, to be capable of such a premeditated act. To be having an affair with that creep for nearly six months!

That was the thing that made him more irate than anything else. To be sleeping with the man, possibly in their shared house, made him quake with pure fury and disgust. To think, that the mongrel had defiled the woman he loved, made him physically ill. Or maybe it was just the fact that he hadn't eaten anything all day, except pain killers.

He was bone-weary. He didn't think he would get much sleep because of the discomfort. He was wrong.

The following morning, Mark woke to the distant sound of engines overhead. He tried to scramble clear of his meagre cover as quickly as his leg would allow but knew all too well how futile the effort would be. He would be a small speck on a seemingly large landmass, with no way of attracting the attention of a passing plane. He needed a signal fire, or an SOS spelled out on the sand or something other than some feeble arm-wave from among the foliage.

No one would see him, but at least he knew they were searching. It was a good sign. He would have to gain some form of mobility in order to investigate his surroundings. Mark desperately wanted to find other survivors, to pool resources and ideas with them, to find a way to attract a rescue and survive. He risked increased pain attempting to walk around with improvised crutches but saw no alternative.

The island may be huge, at least, huge enough for someone on foot trying to circumnavigate it. Water was also on top of the list. Without water, despite the presence of coconuts, his chances of survival remained very slim. It may be days before the plane's return. He would have to be ready for them. He would have to have a plan, make fire…something!

He manoeuvred himself to the crest of the dune once more to survey the scene in the morning light. With the splint tightly in place, the struggle to move was made more bearable. It still hurt like a son-of-a-bitch, but bearable. He spied a few likely pieces of driftwood from his perch. Whether they would be the correct length he could not ascertain until he was down there. He slithered down the dune on his rump, careful to avoid his leg snagging anything on the way down. He managed to find a reasonable pair of sticks with Y sections on the top to cradle beneath his armpits and another protrusion lower down to act as a handle.

Mark opted to use the firmer sand near the water's edge to make the attempt rather than risk the soft sand of the dunes or the interior. The sand seemed to go for some distance beyond the dunes he noticed, after sheltering beneath the shrubs. The weight of the splints made hard work of keeping his leg off the ground, causing him to stop frequently.

Thankfully there were few obstacles to negotiate on his way. The heat made its presence known as the sun ascended. He would have to stop before too long as he was sweating profusely. Loss of bodily fluids would hasten his demise if he wasn't careful. He had to find water but thought it an impossible task if he was unable to go inland. He looked once more beyond the dunes to a seemingly impenetrable interior of dense foliage.

He could discern no hills or raised earth from which to survey the island. He had spotted many palms with coconuts on either the ground or the trees. Trouble was, a way to break into them, without any discernible means of doing so. Along the beach, in the distance, he saw some rocks protruding from the waves and up the shoreline, and...movement? It was too hazy to define any shapes accurately, so he staggered on as best he could, biting down hard on the pain the effort produced.

As he neared the shimmering rock formation he saw something bobbing on the gentle swell and more movement from the shore. He could not hasten his pace as his energy reserves were practically nil and the pain was excruciating. He had downed several more paracetamol to stave off the worst of it but felt it achieved little. The longer he struggled on, the more often his beleaguered leg dropped, allowing the foot to touch the sand. Spasms of intense agony resulted. He didn't think he could go much further. When he was close enough, he imagined he saw suitcases washed up on the shore and in the water among the rocks.

He realised it was not his imagination playing tricks on him at all. He recognised the floating objects and some of the scattered ones onshore as luggage and what he had thought were rock formations were actually more seats from the plane. Other debris had washed ashore as well, including a hostess trolley. The type of thing they wheel up the aisle with…

Could it possibly be? Could there still be drinks in there? Oh, Christ let there be a bottle or two left in there, he prayed. Anything, anything at all to drink, as long as there is something. He could not wait to get there, could taste the sweet water on his lips as he drew nearer. The movement turned into definable shapes. Animals. Pigs! Rooting around the seats and other objects.

They scattered reluctantly on his approach. The upturned stainless-steel trolley came into view. He nearly cried when he spied the vacant interior. Empty shelves, nothing! He cast about frantically trying to find a plastic bottle amid the suitcases, finally resting his eyes on a likely object.

It was almost buried in the sand, but it did turn out to be what he'd hoped. He unscrewed the bottle with great difficulty. With trembling hands, he lifted the bottle to his mouth.

Mark nearly spat out the contents in disgust when he recognised it as tonic water. He barely managed to keep it in despite the taste without the requisite tot of Gin. There was a smattering of other bottles washed up among the debris. Mark felt his stomach revolt as he spied the human remains on and near the seats. It was clear to him then what had attracted the pigs.

Partial corpses lounging on seats twisted out of shape. Large chunks removed from the seats and the cadavers from sharks and other sea creatures before the tide receded to be further destroyed by feral pigs. Traces of blood still draining away from the scene, diluted by the tide. Pink froth gathering at the shoreline amid clothing and body parts. Crabs and seagulls fighting over the spoils. Mark turned to the side and vomited. His stomach could not hold it in with so much gore about him.

As much as he wanted to escape the area, to avoid the horrible sight of human devastation, he knew he had to explore the luggage in an effort to find anything useful. He detested the thought of going through someone's personal belongings, especially with half of that someone still there, but he knew it was imperative to his survival.

An hour later, he stumbled off, leaving the carnage behind. He found several useful items which he had secured in a backpack he donned to continue his journey. Extra clothes of course, including a hat, sun lotion, and lots of it. Apparently, people did heed the cancer warnings because nearly every piece of luggage contained a bottle or tube of sun cream. Nail clippers which included a concealed folding knife would come in useful. How the little implement managed to get through the detectors he didn't know. It may have been packed in checked-in luggage rather than a carry-on. Either way, it was a boon not to be scoffed at.

He did find several more bottles of actual water. One tiny

bottle of Vodka, one can of beer and in someone's carry-on, a packet of potato chips. He had hoped to find more water and some more edibles but was not disappointed with his haul. It would assist greatly. He didn't find the one thing he desperately hoped to come across, something with which to start a fire.

He assumed there might be more luggage further along the beach, as well as more corpses which he didn't look forward to seeing. He could do nothing for the ones he left behind as he didn't have the wherewithal to bury them. He assumed too, that identification would be necessary, making burial a non-option. Mark was immensely relieved to have quenched his thirst for the time being. Hunger would be accommodated with some potato chips or whatever else he may find.

Late afternoon saw Mark struggling to go any further. His leg was too painful to continue and he was simply exhausted. His leg had swelled to twice its normal size. He had seen no tell-tale signs of infection other than swelling. Constantly monitoring the colour, temperature and smell of his broken limb, Mark made his way along the beach.

He also kept a wary eye out for signs of previous occupation by himself or others. He didn't wish to keep circling the island indefinitely. If he saw anything remotely resembling footprints or other signs of life, he intended to follow the suspect spoor. He had not managed to find anything that day. At the top of the high water mark, Mark surveyed the bushes once more for a likely place of refuge from the cool night breezes.

He was no longer overly concerned about the cold as he had more than enough clothing and a small blanket to keep him warm. He did worry about the rain, though and considering it was a tropical island, rainstorms were a given. It was not a matter of if, but when, the rain would come and whether he could find or construct some shelter before then, or more importantly, some way of capturing the precious liquid.

He still needed to determine the dimensions of the island and explore it fully in the hope of finding more supplies, or better still, survivors in better shape than he. All in all, he was pleased with his progress. He had administered to his badly broken leg, found a few potentially life-saving items after trekking along the shore despite the pain involved in keeping his leg raised.

He didn't look forward to what he may find on the windward side of the island. As best as he could tell, he was leeward, on the protected side. He remembered reading about that somewhere. Then again he could be thinking absolute bullshit and simply be kidding himself into believing his hyperbole.

He had visited Orpheus Island in Queensland with his family one time and the difference between the two sides of the island was like chalk and cheese. The side facing toward the mainland was an idyllic calm-water island setting, while opposite, facing the open ocean was a wild and woolly affair of harsh rocky outcrops lashed by monstrous waves. Part of this island had to face the prevailing winds at some point unless the entire area was beset by the doldrums.

The journey to the sand dunes at the top of the beach was a hazardous task on crutches. If he wasn't mindful of every step into the soft sands, he would overbalance easily, causing more pain than he cared to imagine. His body needed rest after the arduous endeavours of the day.

The image of the corpses bothered him more than he admitted, but there was something else about them that nagged at him. Something that he had seen and tried to forget hovered in the rear of his conscious thought. An elusive fragment of information, or something that he thought should have been seen and recognised, was not coming through.

ABOUT THE AUTHOR

Josef Peeters, born in Dusseldorf Germany, in 1961, immigrated with his parents and two brothers to Australia in 1964. Josef has followed artistic pursuits in performance, literary, and sculptural genres for most of his life. He now continues to write and self-publish for his satisfaction and pleasure while maintaining a Caravan Park business with his wife, Sandy, in Moulamein NSW, Australia.

If you would like to follow the author and keep up with his latest books, please visit his website; http://lakesidecaravanpark.wixsite.com/josef

If you enjoyed reading Josef's book please leave a review on either Amazon or Goodreads.